Readers love *Timing* by Mary Calmes

"*Timing* is a pure fun with an erotic and emotional, though not angsty, romance."
—The Book Vixen

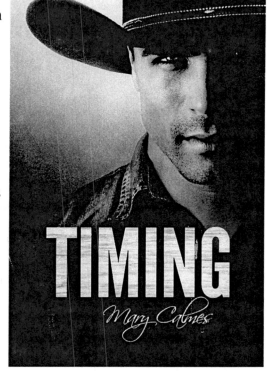

"…like all other Mary Calmes books, it is sweet and sexy and a lot of fun, too."
—The Blogger Girls

"I love Mary Calmes' alpha males and Rand is oh so Alpha! The sex between him and Stefan is super hot and then the love that gets declared super romantic."
—The Kimi-chan Experience

By Mary Calmes

Acrobat
Again
Any Closer
With Cardeno C.: Control
With Poppy Dennison: Creature
Feature
Floodgates
Frog
Grand Adventures
Dreamspinner Anthology)
The Guardian
Heart of the Race
Ice Around the Edges
Judgment
Just Desserts
Lay It Down
Mine
Romanus • Chevalier
Romanus & Chevalier
(Author Anthology,
Paperback Only)
The Servant
Steamroller
Still
Tales of the Curious Cookbook
(Multiple Author Anthology)
Three Fates
(Multiple Author Anthology)
What Can Be
Where You Lead
Wishing on a Blue Star
(Dreamspinner Anthology)

CHANGE OF HEART
Change of Heart • Trusted Bond
Honored Vow
Crucible of Fate
Forging the Future

L'ANGE
Old Loyalty, New Love
Fighting Instinct

MANGROVE STORIES
Blue Days • Quiet Nights
Sultry Sunset
Easy Evenings
Sleeping 'til Sunrise

MARSHALS
All Kinds of Tied Down
Fit to Be Tied • Tied Up in Knots

A MATTER OF TIME
A Matter of Time: Vol. 1
A Matter of Time: Vol. 2
Bulletproof • But For You
Parting Shot • Piece of Cake

TIMING
Timing • After the Sunset
When the Dust Settles
Perfect Timing
(Print Only Anthology)

THE WARDER SERIES
His Hearth • Tooth & Nail
Heart in Hand
Sinnerman • Nexus
Cherish Your Name
Warders Vol. 1 & 2

Published by Dreamspinner Press
www.dreamspinnerpress.com

PERFECT TIMING

Mary Calmes

Published by
DREAMSPINNER PRESS

5032 Capital Circle SW, Suite 2, PMB# 279, Tallahassee, FL 32305-7886 USA
www.dreamspinnerpress.com

This is a work of fiction. Names, characters, places, and incidents either are the product of author imagination or are used fictitiously, and any resemblance to actual persons, living or dead, business establishments, events, or locales is entirely coincidental.

Perfect Timing
© 2016 Mary Calmes.

Cover Art
© 2016 Reese Dante.
http://www.reesedante.com
Cover content is for illustrative purposes only and any person depicted on the cover is a model.

All rights reserved. This book is licensed to the original purchaser only. Duplication or distribution via any means is illegal and a violation of international copyright law, subject to criminal prosecution and upon conviction, fines, and/or imprisonment. Any eBook format cannot be legally loaned or given to others. No part of this book may be reproduced or transmitted in any form or by any means, electronic or mechanical, including photocopying, recording, or by any information storage and retrieval system, without the written permission of the Publisher, except where permitted by law. To request permission and all other inquiries, contact Dreamspinner Press, 5032 Capital Circle SW, Suite 2, PMB# 279, Tallahassee, FL 32305-7886, USA, or www.dreamspinnerpress.com.

ISBN: 978-1-63477-844-2
Library of Congress Control Number: 2016914707
Published November 2016
v. 1.0

Printed in the United States of America

This paper meets the requirements of
ANSI/NISO Z39.48-1992 (Permanence of Paper).

Table of Contents

AFTER THE SUNSET

Mary Calmes

CHAPTER 1

EVEN THOUGH it was late for it, just after seven, I had stopped at the local market to pick up groceries on the way back to the ranch. I wanted to surprise Rand when he got home, with me being there and with dinner. Originally I had told him that I would have to stay late for a department meeting, but it had been cancelled, and instead of going for drinks with the others, I bailed. Even after two years, I still got excited at the thought of going home and being there when the man I loved walked through the door at the end of the day.

So since I had decided to cook, I had to stop and pick up supplies, and I was standing in the checkout line when Mrs. Rawley, who owned the store, came out of the back to see me. It was nice of her to make the effort.

In the small community of Winston, where her store was, the people were divided between those who didn't give a damn that I was gay and lived with my boyfriend, rancher Rand Holloway, owner of the Red Diamond, and those who were vocally and adamantly opposed to the idea. And while those who whispered when I walked by, muttered under their breath, or tossed off slurs when my back was turned were in the minority, there were still enough sprinkled around town to make me conscious of where I chose to conduct my business and spend my money.

After so long, I knew where I would and would not be accepted, but now and then, people still surprised me. What was nice was that more often than not, someone who I thought was just waiting to do or say something hateful or snarky was actually just looking for the opportunity to offer a warm handshake or a smile.

"Can I have Parker carry that out to the car for you, Stef?" Mrs. Rawley offered.

"I was gonna ask," Donna said, clearly exasperated. "For crap's sake, Mama, I wasn't raised in a barn."

I enjoyed the mother-daughter interaction, which was mostly exasperated and sarcastic. "I'm good," I told Mrs. Rawley. "Be nice to your kid."

"Thank you," Donna snapped.

"Respect your mother," I said, grabbing my bags.

"What he said," she shot back at her eighteen-year-old as I left with the jingle of bells at the front door.

As I started toward my car, my snazzy red-and-black MINI Cooper, I saw the police cruiser parked beside me and the SUV that had me blocked in.

"Really," I called over to the two deputies in the car. They could not miss the irritation in my tone.

Both men got out, both smiling at me, and I noticed that one of the deputies, Owen Walker, had a cup in his hand. He moved fast around the front of the cruiser, and as I reached him, I could smell the chai as he offered it to me.

"C'mon, Stef, you know this ain't our call."

I took the warm cup, and he took the bag of groceries and looked inside.

"What're you makin'?" he asked me.

"Just some breaded pork chops and a salad, Deputy."

He looked up at me. "That sounds good, and it's just Owen, all right?"

"Sure." I nodded, smiling at him.

"There's wine in here too."

"And wine," I quipped with a chuckle. "Can't have good food without wine."

"I guess."

I smiled at him. "If it wasn't so late, I'd invite you and your family over."

"Maybe you'd like to have us another time," he said, his eyes suddenly on mine.

I wasn't sure if he was serious. He looked it, but I decided to test. "Maybe one Saturday we could barbecue if you want. The kids could see the horses."

"They would certainly love that, and my wife is dying to see how the house runs with the wind turbine system and the solar panels you all put in. She wants us to go green as well."

"Okay, then, I'll give you a call."

"You do that." He nodded as he lifted his hand, motioning with his fingers.

"What?"

"Gimme the damn keys so I can put this in the trunk for you."

"I can put my own—"

"Just give 'em to me," he growled, grabbing them from my hand.

"This is harassment," I told him.

He flipped me off.

"Stop yelling at him," the second deputy, James, *call me Jimmy*, McKenna ordered me.

I turned to look at him, and he pushed his hat back on his head. "Is it true?"

"Is what true?" I yawned, so glad it was Friday, so ready to just sit and veg and do nothing for my long three-day October weekend. Monday was Columbus Day, so I had it off. Not that my cowboy would be observing a federal holiday, but at least he would probably take off early to spend the evening with me.

"Is Rand really going to build a school in Hillman?"

My eyes watered as I rubbed them a minute before I turned and focused on Deputy McKenna. "Who told you that?"

"All your hands know, Stef, and most of 'em got wives and kids. How long did you think it would be 'til the whole town knew?"

I exhaled before I took a sip of the chai latte.

"Why does that smell weird?" Deputy Walker suddenly asked me, turning my attention back to him as he passed me my keys.

"It's chai," I told him. "You ordered it. How could you order it if you didn't know what it was?"

"I didn't order it. I went in and said gimme what Stefan drinks, and the girl, whatshername with the messy hair—"

"They're dreadlocks, Deputy."

"Owen."

"They're dreadlocks, Owen."

"Whatever. She gives me this smile like I made her day and gets to work, and five dollars and twenty cents later, I'm carrying around something that smells like cinnamon and cloves and somethin' else."

"How did you guys know I was stopping in town instead of going right home?"

"Lyle's out on the highway, camped behind the 'Welcome to Winston' sign, and he saw you drive on by and make the turn toward town."

I nodded. "How is Lyle?"

"He's good. He and Cindy are expecting again."

My eyebrows rose. "Really?"

He grunted. "Don't I know it? That's number five he and my kid sister are havin'. I told him they should take up bowlin' to give them somethin' else to do together."

I couldn't stifle the snickering.

"I thought my mama was gonna explode."

"I bet."

"I think the sheriff was hopin' to have a word with you," Jimmy chimed in. "It's why we're here interceptin' you."

"That's right," Owen agreed. "And back to the coffee," he began, and Jimmy rolled his eyes. "I really don't get why everyone loves that new place so much. My wife wants to live there, and my daughter stops in every afternoon now after school, and there's gettin' to be a line."

The new coffee/bakery/sandwich shop that had gone up four months ago between the bed and breakfast and the senior center had been, for me, a blessing. I made sure to stop in every morning on my way out of town to grab my chai latte and a homemade blueberry scone. They saw me coming and made my drink, the four people who worked there all knowing my face and name on sight. It was nice.

"They knew what you wanted when I said your name," Owen told me.

"Not a lot of chai drinkers in this town," I assured him.

"I expect not."

I tipped my head at the SUV blocking me in. "Where is the big man?"

"The sheriff is picking up his campaign posters from Sue Lynn's."

"Why?" I asked them. "No one is running against him. Why does he need campaign posters?"

"I suspect he likes to see his face really big," he said, gesturing, showing me how mammoth the sheriff's head would be on the banners. "I mean, shit, that's your tax dollars at work there, Stef."

I laughed and saw how at ease both of them were in my presence. "Listen, Deputy McKenna—"

"Jimmy," he corrected me like he always did.

"Jimmy," I sighed. "Why do you guys care if Rand is building a school? How does that affect you in any way?"

"I just think it's funny that he's building in Hillman instead of in his own town, is all."

I leveled my gaze on him. "He was kicked off every committee in this town as well as having his property lines rezoned so that the Red Diamond is no longer even in Winston but in Hillman instead."

"Yeah, I—"

"So your question makes no sense, as Rand is actually building in the town that the Red Diamond resides in."

His eyes narrowed. "Rand's been making a lot of donations and changes to Hillman lately. Do you know anything about that?"

"You know I do," I said, taking another sip of my latte.

He cleared his throat. "I heard the new school was gonna be a charter, but I ain't sure what that is."

"It means that they can pick and choose the curriculum and—"

"The what?"

"Curriculum is what you get taught, idiot," Owen snapped at him. "Go on, Stef."

I couldn't control my smile. "Rand wants things that the elementary school in Winston doesn't offer. He wants them to learn agriculture, which makes sense, and he feels that Spanish should be taught to the English-speaking kids and English taught to the Spanish-speaking kids. He wants them all to be bilingual."

"What for?" Jimmy asked.

"Because it will help them culturally and economically, and learning a second language improves your mind."

"Does it?"

"Yes," I assured him. "And little kids soak up language. It's easier to teach a little kid a new language than it is an adult."

"And so Rand's gonna build a school in Hillman just for that?"

"Right now all the kids on the ranch go to Winston Elementary, but there's no bus that comes all the way out to the Red Diamond, so they're all carpooling. But if Rand builds the school at the south end of Hillman and buys a couple of buses, then all the kids on the ranch as well as the ones who live on the north side of Winston can all go to school in Hillman. The bus can pick them all up every morning."

"When he builds the school, I want my kids to go there," Owen told us.

"You do?" Jimmy asked him, clearly surprised.

"Sure." He shrugged. "I think learning a second language is a great idea."

"There you go," I said, turning back to Jimmy. "It just makes sense."

"Rand sure has made a lot of changes since you got here, Stef," he told me.

"I think the sheriff wants to talk to Rand about that and about maybe taking his seat back on the community board of directors," Owen said softly.

But Rand had been voted off. When he had outed himself by moving me onto the ranch with him two years ago, the Winston community leaders had booted him from the seat that his father had held before him. They didn't even take the time to make it look good; instead they let it be known that the reason for revoking his seat was because of me, because Rand lived with me. The Red Diamond Ranch was the largest in Winston as well as in the outlying areas of Croton and Payson, as well as many others, but that had not stopped the mayor and the rest of the city fathers from finding a loophole to get rid of my then boyfriend and now partner. They were homophobic assholes, every last one of them, and when they had rezoned the county three months later, officially relocating the Red Diamond to Hillman, that had been the last straw. I had been surprised that Rand didn't fight it, but when he explained, I understood.

The day the rezoning had gone into effect, the mayor of Hillman, Marley Davis, along with her entire staff, had made a special trip out to the ranch to welcome Rand and the Red Diamond to her county. She had been the one to give her permission to have the county lines redrawn; she was thrilled to have Rand join her community and just knew he would be thrilled about it too. She was hoping that Rand would come to the next city council meeting, as they would be interested in hearing any thoughts he might have. He was also more than welcome to bring me.

I was stunned, and Rand's smile had been huge as he recounted the events that Friday when I got home.

"Everything happens for a reason, Stef," he told me, drawing me into his arms. "I never thought too much of Hillman before, but suddenly I can't think of them enough. I feel like we got us a home all of a sudden, and I think I wanna help those folks out. I got some money that I think will do us all some good if you help me. I mean, you got the background in acquisitions and finance and all. Will you take a look at some things and see what you can do?"

Of course I could, and would, and did.

And while it had been hard for Rand, severing all ties with the town he had grown up in, his warm welcome in Hillman twenty miles to the east had been overwhelming. Hillman had not been able to boast of having a large, thriving, three-hundred-thousand-acre ranch in their county, but since the home of the ranch was wherever the main house sat, now they could. I had thought at first that it was the money he represented that they were responding to, but it was also the man himself.

Hillman had become Rand's new hometown and, as a result, was reaping the benefit of both his philanthropy and his loyalty. He made a generous donation to the senior center, built a huge gas station/mini-mart with his friend AJ Myers that had already increased traffic in town, and donated five tricked-out computers complete with scanners and printers to the county library. He built a feed store, and put a new roof on the gymnasium of the high school when he found out it leaked during the last thunderstorm. In the next year, there were more city improvements in the works, and the proposed elementary school was at the top of the list. When Rand had been invited to attend school board meetings, he had been very touched. He was an important citizen in Hillman, his voice appreciated, his opinion courted, and his patronage eagerly anticipated.

"Stefan!"

Wrenched from my thoughts, I found myself standing in front of Sheriff Glenn Colter. "Oh, Sheriff, what can I do for you?"

"You bought the Silver Spring from Adam Weber last week."

I had to catch up with the conversation that we were apparently having.

"Didn't you?"

"I didn't," I told him, taking another sip of my latte. "Rand did."

"Adam said that you negotiated the deal."

"That's what I used to do, Sheriff," I said, watching the lines in his face tighten. "And even though I teach school now, at Westland Community College, apparently it's a skill I still possess. The whole background in acquisitions thing doesn't just go away."

"Well, Adam said that you were real fair with him so that's why he sold, but that he didn't mean to include the parcel of land down by the Dalton place."

"That's not what he told me."

"Well, he wants it back."

"Really?" I asked drolly. "You talked to him in Vegas, did you?"

"What I mean is," he said, then cleared his throat, "that's what he was fixin' to tell you before he left."

"Uh-huh."

"Stefan."

"You're talking about the parcel that butts up against the Coleman piece, right?"

He grunted loudly. "We both know that those folks from Trinity want that piece, because the way it's zoned now, if Rand sells them the Silver Spring and clear down to the highway, then they can make their own drive and not run through Winston at all."

"Yes, I know," I told him. "And with the gas station in Hillman and a resort between the Red Diamond and Hillman… why would anyone even go through Winston?"

"Rand bought up the land, and now he's fixin' to turn us into a ghost town."

I shook my head. "The people from Trinity—"

"That son of a bitch, Mitch Powell, wants to build a resort and a golf course and God knows what else out here, but only if he gets the land to the east where—"

"Rand sold it to him," I said, because it was no longer a secret and would actually create a whole slew of jobs for all the neighboring towns. Mitchell Powell, golf pro turned entrepreneur turned multimillionaire, was going to build *the* resort in the area. He was about to put Hillman on the map, thanks to Rand, who had basically collected a monopoly that no one had wanted or given a damn about, and sold it for buckets of money that he was poised to do great things with.

The Silver Spring, Twin Forks, and Bowman ranches, none of which had been working ranches in years, would all be converted into a huge, sprawling, 250-acre monolith of wealth and prosperity. It would be a very posh, very exclusive, very expensive resort, catering to the rich and famous, that would be far enough from the ranch as to not adversely affect it or change the lives of the people who lived there. The Red Diamond would remain the same, and the land that Rand had bought would finally be put to good use. And even though the town of Winston itself would not see the boon directly, as there were no civic projects planned, the people who lived there would benefit directly from the hundreds of new jobs about to be created.

If you didn't work on a ranch, there was nothing to do in Winston. You had to drive to Lubbock, just like I had to, to work. But now, thanks to Rand Holloway buying and selling and Mitchell Powell building, there was about to be a great influx of employment.

"Rand sold all three ranches to Powell?"

"Yessir, he did," I said, walking around him to the driver's side door. "Now move the cruiser. I wanna go home."

The muscles in his jaw tightened as he followed me. "How could he do that to the town he grew up in?"

"He just created thousands of jobs for the people of the town he grew up in," I told him. "Buildings will go up, and when that's done, there will be jobs at the resort to fill. This community just got saved."

"But where the resort would be.... Hillman will be the town the resort is located in, not Winston."

"Why does that matter? The people you serve will be better off for the influx of jobs."

"And Hillman becomes the point of interest between Midland and Lubbock while Winston is left as it is."

"What would you have Rand do about that, Sheriff?"

"You're a smart boy. You understand what I'm saying to you."

I squinted at him. "Papers have been signed, Sheriff. Mitchell Powell has come and gone with deeds and rights and more lawyers than Rand said he ever saw in his life. The people who sold their property to Rand did so under no duress. We both know that the Silver Spring and the Twin Forks have been dead for years, and the Bowman place... well, all Carrie wanted to do was sell and move to Oregon to be close to her son. Running a successful ranch in this day and age is hard work, and for some it's easier to simply get paid and get out. Rand found use for land that was going to waste, and because of that, his own ranch can be that much bigger and that much more lucrative and even more capable of supporting the men and their families, who live and work on it. Now I understand that you're concerned about Winston, but Rand had to do what was best for the Red Diamond, and in the process, he ended up doing right by the town."

"The mayor doesn't see it that way."

"I suspect Rand won't give a damn."

He scowled at me. "I suspect you'd be right."

I smiled back.

He visibly deflated.

"It's not your fault, you know. I know that you weren't one of those who wanted Rand off the board."

His eyes searched mine.

"I know your only reservations with Rand stem from the fact that sometimes he can be kind of an ass."

"Sometimes?"

I chuckled, smiling bigger, unable to stop myself. "It's late, Sheriff. Are you not eating at home tonight?"

"No. Mrs. Colter is visiting her sister in Abilene."

"Well, would you like to come by the house and have some dinner? I have more than enough for three."

"No thank you, Stefan, but I do appreciate the invite. I've got to go over to the Drake place and talk to them about Jeff."

It took me a minute because nothing at all ever happened in Winston. It was why Rand and I had been such big news. "Oh, the drag racing," I said snidely, baiting him.

"It ain't funny. They could get themselves killed doin' that."

"On the tractors," I said, trying really hard not to sound patronizing. "Yes, I'm sure they could."

He thrust his hand at me to shake. "Call me when you're makin' the lasagna again."

"Yessir, Sheriff, I sure will," I promised, taking the offered hand in mine.

He gave me a smile before I turned to get in my car.

"Stef."

I looked back at him over my shoulder, opening the door.

"Call me if you're makin' the pot roast too."

"Oh, okay," I teased him. "I didn't realize you had favorites."

"Damn right," he told me before he suddenly froze. "You ain't makin' any of those tonight, are ya?"

"No, sir, I'm not."

He grunted before he got in the mammoth car.

It was actually really nice that the man had favorites. Before I began my life with Rand, my culinary skills were basic at best. But the restaurants in Winston were both barbeque places, and while they were good, sometimes variety was nice, so one of us had to learn to cook, and of the two of us, I had more time. He really enjoyed it when I slaved away in the kitchen for him; why, I had no idea, but the look on his face when he came in the house and found me in the kitchen was enough to melt me through the floor. He really enjoyed the hell out of me being domestic.

I watched as the sheriff moved his SUV, honking as he drove away. The deputies both followed suit, and when I was headed for home, I had time to think about the transformation my life had gone through in just a short amount of time.

TWO YEARS ago, Rand Holloway and I had gone from enemies to lovers in sizzling style over the course of his sister Charlotte Holloway's four-day wedding blowout. The bride, my best friend in the world, had asked, ordered, commanded me to be her man of honor, and because she needed her brother there as well… Rand and I had been forced to share space. It was a recipe for disaster, as he and I could barely manage to be civil to each other.

Rand and I had never done anything but be a horror to each other, but that weekend the reasoning for ten years of guerilla warfare had become clear. Rand liked me, had always liked me, and in fact it was actually way more than that. He was sort of crazy about me. But putting an out and proud gay man together with a cattle rancher from Texas had been a tough idea for him to come to grips with. Once he had, though—once he had figured out the truth about himself, what he needed and what he wanted—he had been ready to let me know.

The path to true love had not been an easy one. While Rand and I were navigating the change from enemies to friends to lovers, my ex-boss, Knox Bishop, had been trying to kill me and frame me for fraud and embezzlement. It had been a very interesting week of my life and one that, in the end, had prompted my move across the country to live on a cattle ranch. And though I loved the man desperately, the transition was anything but easy.

Rand was a cowboy, and I was a city boy used to having access to all the things a metropolis had to offer twenty-four hours a day. Not that I didn't love the ranch or the man who owned it, but there had to be a happy medium, and I ended up making all the changes while Rand's life stayed pretty much the same. And while I understood that there was no other way for that to work—his ranch was the unchangeable, unmovable piece in the equation—even though logically I did get it, I ended up angry nonetheless.

I took my frustration out on Rand until I realized that the person I was really mad at was me. I was trying to live my old life and my new one all at the same time, and it wasn't working for anyone.

What was nice was that I even had the opportunity to try out such a lifestyle, even if it didn't end up working. I had been able to make the transition from Chicago to Lubbock because I was hired by Abraham Cantwell, my best friend's new father-in-law, to restructure his financial office. Unfortunately, with the changing economy, my new job was short-lived. Mr. Cantwell had to let all but two of his staff go and eventually closed his business, retiring later that year. In looking for new gainful employment, I had been faced with the decision to either look for a job in an even larger city than Lubbock or to stay there and take a position at a much lower salary than what I was used to. I could either commute, and keep an apartment in Dallas or Houston and visit on the weekends, or I could stay in Lubbock and go home every night to Rand. It was time to make a decision about my future, and since I had dived into the deep end two years earlier, I chose my cowboy and life on the ranch, even though the idea of losing myself there terrified me. When I fell back on my minor and took a position at the community college teaching Intro to World History, Rand had been beside himself.

"I have no idea why you're so happy," I had told him as I set up my small—tiny—cubicle of an office in late August in preparation for the fall semester.

"You chose us, Stef," he had said simply, his smile out of control as he looked around the broom closet that was posing as my new work space. "I don't think you know what you really did here."

But I did. I had trusted him and believed in him, put faith in the life we shared, and had chosen to lean on him instead of standing alone. I had been halfway in and halfway out for two years and had finally, completely, committed.

"Stef."

I looked over my shoulder at him and realized how big he seemed in the tiny office.

"You know I just signed that three-year agreement with Grillmaster to be the beef supplier for their entire restaurant chain."

He had spoken so casually, but I knew it was a big deal. I had helped him get ready and coached him on the contract. His lawyer had appreciated my help, and now, apparently, it was all signed, sealed, and delivered. I was thrilled for him and his ranch and so rushed across the five feet and launched myself into his arms.

I was surprised when he caught me and put me down on my new desk, wedged himself between my legs, his hands on my face, in my hair, as he looked down at me from his towering height.

"This is the biggest thing that's ever happened to the ranch, Stef."

It was a huge account, and one that I knew Rand and his lawyers—there were four now—had been working on for a while. "Why didn't you tell me before?" I asked excitedly. "We have to go out and celebrate and—"

"You know why I wanted that deal so bad?" He cut me off, stilling me.

"Yeah, so you could be that much closer to financial—"

"It was for you, Stef," he told me, pushing my hair back from my face, tracing my eyebrows with his thumbs, my cheekbones, to my chin. "That account is yours to take care of and grow and work. It was your idea to begin with. I wasn't even gonna bid on that contract, but you convinced me to try. Without you being my champion, I would have never thought that I could do something like that."

I smiled up at him, sliding forward on the desk, my hands on his hips, inhaling him, the smell of the summer sun on his clothes and sweat and the musky scent that was just Rand. "I'm happy to be the voice of reason in your head," I teased him.

His thumb stroked over my bottom lip, and as he looked at me, his eyes narrowed to slits of electric blue. My stomach flipped over.

Slowly, he bent toward me, and when I felt his fingers on my jaw, I tilted my head back as he wanted and received the claiming kiss. His mouth slanted down over mine possessively, his tongue parting my lips, rubbing over mine. I moaned deeply, and his hands were on my thighs, lifting, wanting my legs wrapped around his hips.

"Why are you wearing that shirt?" he asked me, the words spoken against my throat, his hot, wet breath on my skin.

"What?" It was a strange question.

"Why are you wearing *my* shirt?" he asked pointedly.

From the low, husky sound of his voice, I understood that my wearing his clothes had touched something very primal inside of him. He liked it a lot. "Because it was clean, and we need to do laundry," I said, shoving my groin against his abdomen, pressing into him.

"It's so fuckin' hot."

There was nothing remotely sexy about me dressed in an old practice T-shirt of Rand's that had his number on it, seven, from back when he played football in high school. I had noticed that there was a rip in it only when we were halfway to the college, but had no intention of driving all the way home just to change. It wasn't a huge hole, more a tear that you would only notice if you stared. And he had promised me a walk to the creek after we visited my new office and had lunch, having taken off the whole day like he never could or did, just to spend some time with me. So because my day would be filled with just us, I had seen no real reason to change. And now I was glad I hadn't.

"You know, between that there shirt and your hat, I bet none of these folks 'round here expect you to be faculty."

"No, probably not," I gasped because his hands had closed on my ass and squeezed tight.

"Fuck," he growled, and moved fast, taking off his hat, doing the Frisbee throw with it to the chair, and bending to shove the T-shirt up so he could kiss my bare stomach.

"Rand—"

"Sometimes I just wanna lick over every piece of you."

Oh God.

He pressed his lips to my abdomen and kissed and licked and suckled and nibbled until I was writhing under him on the edge of the desk. My belt was hastily unbuckled, the snap tugged on and the zipper roughly pulled. I felt his hands spreading the flaps, sliding over the elastic waistband of my briefs and then his fingers grazing the skin above my shaft.

I lifted up and he peeled everything down, jeans, underwear, and my cock bobbed free, hard and already leaking with just the promise of attention. I shivered when, without a word of warning, he bent and took me down the back of his throat.

"Rand," I called his name, hands in his hair, loving the feel of his hot mouth and the fierce, exquisite suction, the cold hard wood on my ass, the taboo of being in an office, and the knowledge that we were the only ones in the entire six-story building. School was out until the first week in September, and I was so very, very glad.

The man who had been a novice at blowjobs two years earlier was now well practiced, with a sense of his own power and an acute knowledge of all my hot buttons. He knew it had to start fast and end slow, knew I liked it best when he dripped saliva down my crease and pressed fingers inside me at the same time, and knew, finally, I would come loud and hard if I was manhandled and held down and fucked until I screamed.

"Let's try somethin' different," he growled, and I was bent in half, my knees, still trapped in my jeans, shoved against my chest, his hands on the back of my thighs as I felt his tongue slide over my entrance.

"Rand!"

He pressed his tongue inside me, and I had to grip the edge of the desk not to jolt under him. It felt so good, the stubble of his beard on my tender skin, the slow, sensual stroking, and his mouth against my fluttering hole. When he added a finger, my back bowed up off the desk.

I heard him spit, felt the second finger slide in with the first, coated in saliva, and scissor inside me.

"Oh Rand, please."

He fucked me with his fingers, as his other hand slid over the clenching muscles of my abdomen. "You are so beautiful, Stef," he got out, his voice gruff and low, as he reached for my jeans, yanking them off my left leg, not bothering with the right, just needing to be able to part my thighs, and spread me before him.

"You get off on looking at me like this, holding whatever position you put me in."

"Yeah," he almost snarled.

"You want to fuck me anywhere you want, mark me, and put me on my knees wherever you please."

There was only a growl from him.

"So fuck me," I begged him, pushing back on his thrusting fingers, wanting to be fuller, needing deeper, needing more.

"You're so tight."

"Fuck me!"

Slowly, he withdrew his slippery, talented digits and then grabbed hold of my ass, my cheeks, spreading them as I felt the engorged, leaking head of his cock press against my puckered hole.

I lifted up, ready for him. "I need you."

"And if we had lube, I would bury myself in you so hard you'd fuckin' scream my name, but we're gonna go slow until I feel your body take me in and then wrap around me all tight and hot."

The man had his own, aching, demanding need, but for him, always, I came first. He pressed forward into me, pushing gently but insistently, letting my inner muscles relax and remember the pleasure the intrusion would bring. They rippled with anticipation.

"Oh fuck, Stef, you feel so fuckin' good."

He eased back a fraction and then pushed forward, my channel clenching around the thick, hard silky length of him, precome and saliva mixing together, the slide not as smooth as usual, but the slight burn felt amazing, the pinch sending sizzling heat racing over my skin.

I lifted higher, forcing him to thrust inside to keep me still, and when I lifted a leg, resting my calf on his shoulder, he tugged me forward, and buried himself inside me, sheathing his enormous cock deep inside my ass.

"Rand!" I screamed his name.

His balls were against my ass as he began pumping into me, the smack of skin on skin like a hammer in the tiny room.

He felt too good. I was so full, stretched like I always was, as his shaft slid over my prostate, and he wrapped his fingers around my painfully hard, leaking cock.

I whimpered and moaned, lifting my other leg to his shoulder as he bent over me, driving inside, pistoning in and out of me, the desk shaking with the force of each driving thrust.

"Fuck, Stef, I gotta see!"

He moved me so gently, easing from my body, putting me on my feet before spinning me around, the angle changing so I was impaled, the sensation of him so deep that I caught my breath for a second before I was shoved face down on the desk.

"Oh fuck yeah," he groaned. "Look at your ass take my cock."

Rand loved to watch his massive dick slide in and out of my small, round, tight ass. Even more, he liked to fist his hand in my hair, yank my head back, and hold me there as he pounded into my body. His kink was to see the slope of my back and watch my pink hole as it swallowed the veined shaft of him inch by inch. I felt him tremble with lust.

"Fuck me so I feel it, Rand," I told him. "Fuck me hard."

The next plunge took my breath away.

"Jerk yourself off, baby." His voice cracked, lowered. "I can't do it. I gotta hold on."

I understood.

His part was to clench my hip so hard he'd leave bruises, tighten his grip in my hair so I was immobile, and give himself over to the orgasm roaring through him as he drove into me with brutal, savage intensity.

I didn't have to touch myself. When he nailed my prostate on the second thrust, I came on my desk, shooting my load over the cheap polished wood.

"Stefan!"

My name was howled as my channel was filled, thick and hot, and he fucked me through his orgasm and mine, pumping hard as my muscles clamped down, squeezing him, milking him dry, wringing every last bit of pleasure from our savage coupling in my new office.

"Great way to christen my desk, Rand." I laughed as he finally took a breath, wrapping his arms around me, straightening me up without pulling out, his chest plastered to my back.

He bit down into my shoulder, and I shuddered in his arms, reveling in the feel of him even through his clothes and of his now-softening cock still buried in me.

"I feel so good when I'm inside you, Stef, and not just because it's fuckin' heaven, but because I can feel your heart. You are all mine when I'm there, and I know it, and I just wanna brand you or something."

I grunted. "Do not get any ideas."

He laughed, and I felt his mouth open against the side of my neck. The man did like leaving his mark on me. I was lucky school didn't start for three more weeks; a hickey on the first day would not make a good impression.

"Thank you for staying," he said after another minute, turning me suddenly, spinning me around and giving me a full body hug, all of him pressed to all of me.

When we got back to the ranch after lunch, he walked me a different way to the creek than he normally did, along some railroad tracks. He made me wear my cowboy boots like he always did when we walked through grass or over dirt. It turned out that boots were not just decorative; they saved you from things like rocks and snake bites and a myriad of hidden dangers. The walk took longer than I thought it would, and after a while, because it was hot, I decided to go barefoot.

Rand was concerned.

"You're gonna get splinters."

What was funny was that of all the things in the world—spiders, snakes, acts of God—he was worried about splinters. It was stupid until I got one.

"Shit."

"Told you."

He bent and then flipped out the knife he carried all the time, and went down to one knee.

I moved back. "It's a splinter. You don't need to cut off my foot or something."

"Don't be a damn baby. I know what I'm doing."

I was amazed that the tip of the knife could be wielded so deftly. When he turned his back to me, offering, I climbed on. I had not had a piggyback ride since I was five, and it was kind of fun. I really enjoyed pressing my groin to the small of Rand's back.

"Stop," he ordered me. "Or you're gonna get put on your hands and knees right here, and once a day without lube is probably more than enough."

I was a little sore, but not enough to say no to Rand being back inside me. "Rand—"

"Wait," he interrupted me. "Just… I need to say something."

"What's that?"

"About earlier, I want you to know that between the deal with Powell and now this contract with Grillmaster, my ranch, our ranch, is good. I mean if I get caught in a stampede tomorrow, you and my mother and Char are all well provided for and—"

"For fuck's sake, Rand," I barked at him, pinching one of his nipples before I pushed off his back, dropping to the ground. "Why would you even say something like—"

"So you'll believe me when I say that all you were doin' when you were workin' that job was annoying the shit outta me." He growled as he turned around to face me. "I need you here, Stef. I need you to take care of my home and me and my life so I don't just become this goddamn ranch!"

"But you already are the ranch," I reminded him.

"No, Stefan," he said as he grabbed hold of the back of my neck and yanked me forward, forcing me to look him in the eye. "You are my life. Nothing else means anything if you're not here."

The way he was looking at me was almost scary. I had no right to be the man's everything when I was still so messed up, worrying about being able to support myself and save while working at a much-diminished salary. I needed to have a safety net, but Rand was telling me it was unnecessary. "I don't think you have any idea what you're saying."

"I'm speaking clear as anything. You're just bein' ornery."

"Ornery?" I laughed at him. "Who uses that word?"

"Listen to me," he began, ignoring my amusement. "We have us a joint checking account that you never touch. We have a savings account that you don't touch either. I'm telling you right here and now that I want you to close your account from Chicago and start using the one we share. If you end up not liking the teaching, you can open your own business, do whatever the hell you want, but I need to see your face every night."

I reached up and put my hand on his cheek. "You really didn't like it when I had to stay overnight in the city, huh?"

He turned his head, kissing my palm, before he stepped forward into me, face down in my shoulder as his hands slid up under my shirt and touched my skin. I trembled in his arms, the feel of his callused palms on my body making my pulse jump.

"Rand!" I was surprised when he bent and threw me over his shoulder, carried me to a nearby tree, dropped me on my feet, spun me around, and shoved me up against it.

"No, I didn't like it at all. You should be home when I'm home, period."

I didn't have time to speak, to argue with him, to tell him that his ideas about a mate were antiquated, before he reached down and dragged the T-shirt up over my head. I tried to turn, but he held me still, his mouth between my shoulder blades, kissing, licking, sucking on my skin. I got hard with the feel of his hands working open my buckle and belt, freeing my cock but nothing else, making no move to get me naked.

"Your skin makes me fuckin' crazy," he confessed, his voice low and husky, so sexy.

He kissed his way down to the small of my back and then turned me around in his arms, kneeling, hands fisted in my jeans as he licked the engorged head of my cock.

"Oh God, Rand," I whispered hoarsely, my hands clutching his shoulders as I pushed into his mouth, watching his lips slide over my swollen shaft, taking me in until his nose was buried in my groin.

I pulled back, and shoved back in hard, fucking his mouth, feeling his hands gripping my ass now through the denim, savoring his hot, wet mouth and his tongue swirling around my cock.

"Rand," I rasped out. "Gonna come."

He tightened his grip on my ass, forcing me down his throat harder, faster, and I came undone under his hands, in his mouth. He swallowed everything, sucked me clean, and then rose and kissed me ravenously.

Tasting myself on him was so hot, I moaned loudly, sucking on his lips, biting gently but firmly, letting him know he was not getting away.

He smiled as he deepened the kiss, making it slower, deeper, ravaging my mouth.

The moan became a whimper, and when I was breathless and shaking, he shoved me back, unbuckled and unfastened himself and shoved his jeans down to his ankles. I was about to drop to my knees in the cool grass in the shade of the tree, but he told me to take off my jeans and ride him.

I smiled when I saw the butter packet from the diner where we'd had lunch. "That is not lube," I said fondly, chuckling, watching as he squirted the imitation butter spread onto the palm of his hand and slathered it over his cock. "It's gonna get everywhere, and it won't come off after."

"Like I give a fuck about after," he told me, and I saw the heat and need in his steady gaze.

He watched me with hungry eyes as I peeled out of my jeans and stepped over him.

"You're gonna have grass plastered to your ass."

"I only care about your ass, Stef," he said, his voice a deep rumble in his chest. "Now ride your cowboy."

I shook my head. "That's so cheesy." I smiled, my breath shaky as I got down on my knees, straddling his thighs before taking hold of his throbbing cock and lining myself up to take him in.

"I'm gonna come just lookin' at ya," he croaked out, and I saw the desperation and his desire.

"Come inside me," I exhaled, lowering myself over him slowly, letting him feel my channel ripple around him, the muscles tightening and relaxing, swallowing him, until I was completely impaled.

His hands gripped my thighs tight, and when I lifted up only to plunge back down, he yelled my name.

"Tell me, Rand."

"Don't pull away. Just lemme feel you."

When I was on top, Rand liked it when I pressed down into him and pushed. He loved my inner walls holding him, liked to have me wrapped around him, squeezing. When he was on top, he liked driving into me, thrusting deep, but our present position was his favorite.

"You're mine."

And there could never be any doubt of the ownership he demanded and which I blissfully gave.

After we swam naked in the creek, we had climbed out, changed back into our jeans, shoved our underwear into my boots—they needed to be washed—and were lying there together on the end of the tiny dock, feet dangling in the water, baking under the late-August sun. I could hear the lazy buzz of insects, a splash now and then as a fish hit the surface of the water, and the sound of the leaves on the trees as the breeze blew through them.

"Best day ever," I told him, turning my head so I could look at him, his fingers laced behind his head, eyes closed.

His short, wavy, black hair was curling around his ears and sticking to the back of his neck, and his long eyelashes looked dark even against the tan of his face. The man spent his whole life outside in the sun, and only I had made him wear sunscreen and slather his face at night with moisturizer. He thought it was stupid. I didn't want him to get skin cancer and leave me. Leaving me was a big deal; he wasn't going to let any other man have me. He carried sunscreen in his truck now.

Looking at him, I couldn't help reaching out and running my hand over the wide, muscular chest and down the deep groove to the hard, flat stomach. Rand Holloway did not have gym muscles like I did. I was toned and defined, my own physique reminiscent of the guys in an Abercrombie & Fitch catalog, purposely acquired, whereas Rand actually used his body every single day. He lifted and pulled and dragged things heavier than him. He wrestled animals to the ground, carried fence posts, and swung a hammer. There was a great physicality to his everyday life, and it showed in every carved, hard inch of his massive frame.

"Come closer," he drawled out, ending with a yawn.

But I was engrossed with looking at him.

The glossy black hair that fell into his bright turquoise-blue eyes, the thick eyebrows that arched dangerously, and his sinful lips that twisted into half a smile whenever he saw me turned me inside out on a regular basis. The man was strength and heat and sex wrapped up in thick muscles and warm, sleek skin. I watched women, and a few men, respond to the raw physical presence of Rand Holloway and always understood their trembling reaction. He was powerful and sensual, and when he smiled, which he hardly did around anyone other than his family, his men, and me, it became suddenly hard to breathe.

Everyone who had ever seen Rand Holloway smile wanted to see it again. They enjoyed watching the Technicolor-blue eyes glint and witnessing the lines in the corner of those magnificent eyes crinkle in half. But if, by some miracle, he laughed with you, was comfortable enough to let down that barrier and just be himself, treated you like family, Christ, you were hooked for life. The deep rumbling laughter was a sound you never forgot, and he became a drug you had to have. Not that he ever noticed anyone's reaction to him, because he didn't care if people liked him or not. The only things he cared about were his family, his ranch, the people who lived on it and called it home, and me. There was no way not to love a man like that, heart and soul.

"Stef."

I lifted my eyes, and he caught me in his blue gaze.

"Put your head down."

I stretched out, laid my head on his bicep, and slid my denim-clad leg over his thigh.

He grunted. "You know, I know why you don't wanna use the joint checking account."

And just like that, we were back to our earlier discussion.

I was quiet because I didn't want to fight. I had worked all my life, depended on no one but myself for anything. My stepfather had thrown me out when I was fourteen. My mother had stood there and watched, slamming the door in my face. When I had pounded on the door to be let back in, it was thrown open and the beating had commenced. And while

I had no worry that Rand would ever physically hurt me, there was still the possibility that if he ever got tired of me, learned to hate me, that I could be put out of my home. I could never allow that to happen to me again. Money was my security net, money I made myself.

"Hello?"

"Rand, I don't wanna talk about—"

"I won't ever tell you to pack your things and go, Stef."

He knew me so well, knew all the fears that rode me.

"I swear it."

"Rand—"

"I won't."

"Just—"

"Believe me. Believe in me. Stefan… please."

God, the man knew I doubted him, doubted his love, the depth of it, the forever of it, and still he loved me.

"I know you love me, and I know you wanna be here, and I know you still worry."

Shit.

"Look at me."

I rolled my head sideways, and we were eye to eye, only inches separating us. It was very intimate; there was no hiding that close.

"If you want, I can take my name off the joint account, and it can just be yours, and that way you'll know it can never be taken from you. I'll still put money in it, but I won't touch it at all. Would that be better?"

"That's what's called being kept, Rand, and no… that would not be better in the least."

"Fuck," he grumbled. "I don't mean it like—"

"I know how you meant it," I assured him. "It's a very generous offer."

"Christ, now you're making it sound dirty," he groaned, and I sat up as he moved his hands, raking them through his thick hair.

"Very generous for a guy like me." I smiled, turning to look down at him, waggling my eyebrows. "A man with my background."

"Stefan." He warned me.

"A guy from the wrong side of the tracks."

"It ain't funny."

"It's a little funny." I chuckled.

"You don't… you ain't hearin' me," he said, and my laughter died in my throat when his voice cracked. He sat up beside me, crossing his legs so his left knee bumped me. "For a long time, all the guys would go home at night to their wives and their children and lit-up houses that smelled like food and got to hear all the good and all the bad that happened that day. I used to go home, and there weren't none of that."

"Rand," I began, putting my hand on his knee.

"Lemme finish," he said gently, taking my hand, sliding his fingers between mine, pressing my palm against him. "After you came, though, suddenly I'm just as excited to go home as everybody else. I open my front door and the music is on, and the lights are on, and the place smells amazing, and goddamn, Stef, even when I was married before, it wasn't like that. Even if you're runnin' late and I get in first, just you walkin' in the house makes it feel different. And I get it, ya know? You're it, you're my home."

I looked away because I was nothing. I was an orphan, and he had a home and a family and a ranch and everyone counting on him, and I was just…. *How can Rand want to build on me? How am I a foundation for anything?*

"Hey."

I turned back, slowly, taking a breath.

His hand went to my cheek, his thumb sliding over my bottom lip, and I saw the warmth infuse his eyes, saw them darken, soften, because he was looking at me.

"You don't really know what you did today, so I'm gonna tell you."

I nodded because my voice was gone.

"When you told me that you weren't gonna look for a job in Dallas, I knew for sure you wanted to stay with me and have a home."

My focus became breathing.

"I mean, before that, when you were runnin' back and forth, doin' all that driving, well, maybe you were tryin' to keep one foot in your old life and one in your new one, ya know?"

I did know and that was exactly what I had been doing.

"I saw you needin' air. Saw you gettin' all panicky 'cause your life was fallin' into place around you. The happier you got, the more you started fittin' in and gettin' comfortable, the more you started pacin' like an animal that was caged up. You were snappin' at everyone, ready to bite and scratch to get away, and sick that you had to. I ain't never seen a man who so wanted to belong and who was scared to, all at the same time. It makes me tired just watchin' you wrestle with yourself."

I cleared my throat. "So I'm a crazy person who—"

"Just… hush. You showed me how it was gonna be, 'cause when it was time to decide, you chose me and the ranch and your life here."

He narrowed his eyes, and as he squinted, I saw how red rimmed they were. I had no idea that anything I could ever do would touch him so deeply.

"It's why I can barely keep my hands off you. That's why I attacked you in your office today, 'cause it's *your* office. It's where you're fixin' to be because of me."

I finally understood. To Rand, until he physically saw the reality of my new job, he had not let himself believe it. To me, the space, my cubicle at the community college, was a dump. To Rand, it represented me putting down roots.

"You told me that you wanted to belong to me, and today I believe it."

I looked away from him because my eyes filled and my vision blurred with hot tears.

"Along with workin' there at the college, I still want you to oversee the Grillmaster account, you hear?"

I nodded.

"And if it don't work out for you at the school, you can just do that, all right?"

But how would that work?

"Are you afraid of how it will look to everyone if you work at the ranch?"

That was some of it; I would admit to that. "People will think I'm sponging off you," I said to the creek instead of Rand.

"But you'll know different."

"I just can't be a—"

"Soon no one will wonder why you're on the ranch, once we have kids."

Wait. Kids?

What? "What?" I asked breathlessly, my head swiveling around to look at him. God, when had I missed him planning his whole life with me in it?

"You'll have to stay home and take care of them."

Even though he had said kids before, in the past, all I had ever heard was child. But I processed the word that time. Kids. As in plural. As in more than one. As in *them.*

When had he decided that he wanted to have children with me? "I have no idea what you're even talking about right now. You—"

"I wanted you to practice takin' care of me so you'll be ready to take care of your children, and I was so scared that you wouldn't. I was thinkin' just maybe you were ready to leave me, but then you took this job so you could keep on seein' me and cookin' for me and—"

"I am not your wife!" I yelled at him. "And I won't be made to take on the role of—"

"I know that, but you have to get ready to take care of your children!"

My children?

"You're gonna be the one who picks 'em up from school every day. You'll be the one who helps 'em with their homework and watches them wash up and makes their dinner. I'll be the one who plays with 'em and watches TV and talks to 'em at the dinner table. I'll be their father, and you'll be—"

"Oh God." I couldn't breathe.

"I asked Charlotte if she would be inclined to help us start our family, and she said she'd help 'cause she always wanted to have babies with you anyhow."

Jesus Christ, the man was planning on putting me into a Norman Rockwell painting. "Rand—"

"No! I will not discuss this with you. The time to talk is over and done. When you asked me if I wanted you and I said yes, I started planning my whole life right then. When you lost your job, you decided to only look as far as Lubbock for a new one so you could come home every night to me. That tells me all I need to know, Stef."

Running was easy; staying was hard.

"I ain't tryin' to take anything from you, least of all your freedom."

"I know," I told him as he pulled me close. I ended up lying between his legs, my back curled into his chest, his arms draped across my collarbone.

"I drive you nuts, huh?"

"You make me fuckin' crazy."

"I'm sorry." I snickered because I wasn't at all. He had to deal with me, thorns and all.

"No, you ain't."

"Rand—"

"I love you."

I turned and looked at him over my shoulder.

"Don't ever leave me. I won't recover, okay?"

"Okay."

"Okay." He exhaled, like he had been holding his breath. "Christ, you're a giant pain in the ass."

There could be no argument.

CHAPTER 2

THERE WERE two new cars in the driveway when I pulled up to the house, so I was wondering who was there as I grabbed my groceries and went up to the porch. As I reached for the screen door, the front door opened. There was a man in my house I had never seen in my life, and he was talking to someone over his shoulder, so he didn't immediately see me.

"Knock it off, Gin," he laughed, shaking his head. "I don't care what anybody says. Rand Holloway being gay is a buncha shit. That man nailed more—"

"Glenn!"

He laughed at whoever Gin was as he pushed open the screen door making me back up.

"Excuse me."

His head swiveled to me and his eyes, brilliant and blue, widened. "Oh shit, man, I'm sorry. I didn't see.... Sorry." He winced, apologizing, easing the door closed so it didn't hit me.

I stepped sideways and plastered on a big smile as he cracked the screen door again.

"Let's try this again, huh?"

As soon as I was bracing the door open, he leaned back and extended his hand to me.

"I'm Glenn Holloway, Rand's cousin. I suppose he forgot to tell you that we were coming as well."

"Who else did he forget to tell," I asked, after clearing my throat.

"You and every other hand on this ranch." He smiled sheepishly, raking his fingers through the same glossy black hair that Rand had. His hair was shorter than Rand's, but just as thick. "We're all leavin' day after tomorrow for my brother Zach's ranch, but 'til then, we're stayin' here."

Uh-huh.

"Are you the cook?"

The cook?

"Do you have a room here or in the bunkhouse?"

"Unfortunately, I'm not the cook." I forced a smile. "Excuse me, can I…?"

"Oh yeah, sorry, where are my manners?"

I could venture a guess.

As I stepped into the great room, I saw another man and two women. The television was on, and it looked like they had made themselves comfortable with chips and salsa and margaritas. There was a pitcher on the coffee table as well as a bowl with salt on it and wedges of limes.

"Hi there." One of the women smiled wide, standing up as I moved across the room to her. "I'm Ginger Holloway, that guy's cousin," she said, tipping her head back toward the door where Glenn was. "And this here is my brother Brent and his girlfriend Emily."

"I'm Stefan," I told her, offering her my hand.

"Well, it's a pleasure," she told me, taking my hand and squeezing tight.

I turned to Brent, who rose, wiped his palms on his jeans, and then extended his hand to me. After we shook, it was Emily's turn.

"So Stefan," Ginger said, returning my attention to her. "How long have you worked on the ranch?"

I was saved from having to say anything by another woman coming in from the kitchen.

"Gin, there isn't anything else in there but wine and beer and coffee. Rand must—" She saw me. "Oh, hi there. Did you bring food?"

"I had planned to cook for two," I told the stranger.

Her smile was big, as were her baby blue eyes. Her short blonde bob made her look like a pixie. She rushed across the room to offer me her hand. "Hi, I'm the test, Lisa Whitten. Nice to meet you."

"Stefan," I said, taking her hand. "Test?"

Her laugh was nice, lilting. "Yeah, apparently I got invited along to what I thought would be a nice relaxing weekend on a dude ranch to check and see if their cousin, your boss, was really and truly gay." She put her hands on her hips and struck a pose for me. "Apparently my hotliness is to be put to the test."

The room erupted in laughter.

I nodded.

She was cute, no way around it. Her tan was golden, her legs long, all her curves were perfect, and she had sharp elfin features. She was the kind of woman who men would turn and watch and drool over, like Barbie with a short 'do.

"I hafta tell you." She gave me a wicked smile, leaning closer to me, her voice dropping. "After laying eyes on the man, I'm not really that upset about being tricked into this anymore."

"Because my cousin is hot!" Ginger whooped from where she was on the couch.

"You guys?"

One more woman stepped from the kitchen.

"Do you know if Rand has Wi-Fi out here? I have got to check my e-mail."

"No," I answered her. "Just a cable modem."

The woman looked up at me and smiled. "I don't suppose it's anywhere in the house I can go."

"His office is upstairs, three doors down."

"Would it be okay, you think, if I just hooked up my laptop?"

"Sure, just unplug his computer and hook yours up. He won't care as long as you put it back the way you found it."

"Thank you," she gushed, hand out for me. "Kim Palmer. Great to meet you."

"Stefan Joss," I said, taking the offered hand.

"You're saving my life, Stefan," she sighed. "Ginny and I own a catering business in Austin, and apparently we had some screw-ups today that I have to fix."

"I'll go with you," Ginger sighed, getting up off the couch, margarita glass in hand. "But I really hope Rand gets back soon, 'cause all tequila and no food is going to make me a little loopy."

"Going to?" Brent called over to her.

"Shut up." She giggled at him, following Kim up the stairs as I made my way to the kitchen.

Dumping the groceries on the counter, I was torn between being thrilled I was home and wishing to God his cousins were not.

There was a tap on the back door, and when I opened it, I was faced with Everett Hartline, one of Rand's men.

"Hey." I smiled at him, moving sideways out of his way. "You wanna come in?"

"No, I was just supposed to let the dogs in the house and stay there to make sure they didn't scare his kin."

I arched an eyebrow at him. “You’re making sure the pack doesn’t frighten his cousins?”

He grinned. “You know, before I worked on this ranch, I only ever worked with border collies or heelers, Australian cattle dogs and such. Rand Holloway’s the only man I know who keeps Rhodesian Ridgebacks on his ranch.”

They were beautiful dogs, Rand’s hounds from hell, but they were big, all between seventy-five to eighty pounds of muscle. So it made sense actually, because while they were not vicious or aggressive, tending to leave strangers alone instead of attacking at first sight, the people were on their home turf, and so they would be protective of Rand and the house and me.

I loved them all, which had amazed me. I was not the type who liked animals as a rule, but ever since I had been on the ranch, calves and dogs and horses had taken over my heart. I was perfectly content to sit in front of the fire on a cold winter day, watching television under a warm puppy pile of fur. There was one of the hell hounds in particular, Bella, who had staked her claim on me. She was more my dog than Rand’s, and he had said on a number of occasions that as soon as he could, he was going to visit his favorite breeder in Biloxi and get another puppy to raise on the ranch. Bella was apparently no good to him anymore as a working dog since she had decided that she wanted to be my pet. Supposedly I distracted her more than I did the others, and she would rather sit at my feet than run after cattle.

“Stef?”

“Sorry.” I grinned at him. “I think I’m tired. Where are the dogs now?”

I heard a yell at the same time from the living room.

“I’d say they were on the porch,” he grunted, turning away. “But you’re here, so you can deal with them.”

“You wanna stay and eat?”

“No.” He yawned, looking back at me. “Me, Jace, Chris, and Pierce are headed out to the Rooster to get laid.”

“Have a good time,” I called after him. The Rooster was a honky-tonk I had been in once. It had been more than enough. Between the sawdust on the floor and the music that resembled nothing I had ever heard, my plan was to never go again. “And good luck getting lucky.”

“Don’t need no luck, son, when you look like this.”

I rolled my eyes and shut the door before walking back out into the living room. It sounded like a bad horror movie, the snarling and growling going on outside the front door.

"Jesus Christ," Lisa moaned, looking terrified, as Glenn looked out the window.

Brent had a smile for me, as did Emily.

"Goddamn, Rand, who keeps dogs that big just to herd cattle?"

"What is that?" Ginger asked, having come halfway down the stairs.

"Just the dogs," I told her, slipping past Glenn and opening the door.

Everyone yelled behind me at once.

The second I opened the door, the barking stopped.

"Seriously," I told them, "the noise is out of control."

Six faces were looking up at me expectantly.

"Stefan, they don't come in the house, do they?" Lisa asked tentatively.

"Yeah, Rand doesn't like the dogs loose on the ranch at night unless he's with them. The dogs are hard to see in the dark, and he worries that anyone coming down the drive might accidentally hit them."

I stepped sideways, and they all came in and clustered around me, five tails in a blur of motion, five wet noses touching my hands. The sixth dog, Bella, was dancing around me, whimpering and whining, contorting her body into a half moon as she tried to shove her head under my palm.

"C'mon." I yawned, turning for the kitchen.

I heard their feet on the wooden floor, the jingle of their collars as they trotted after me. I held the swinging door open for them and then let it shut behind me.

"You're such an attention whore," I told my girl Bella, crouching down to pet her. I was instantly covered in dog. Her nose went into my eye as the others licked my face, my nose, my throat, and pranced in circles around me. "This is so gross," I laughed at them.

I petted each one, scratched ears, stroked backs, rubbed and finally hugged each one. When I finally rose, I went to the pantry to get their dishes down for water and food, and talked to them as I moved around. They were all sitting there, tails thumping, watching me. Rand used to have only four, but as the ranch grew, so did his pack. He had six now and would soon have seven once he went to pick up the new puppy.

When the door swung open, the dogs moved fast, forming a phalanx around me, which was funny for me, but not quite as amusing for Glenn and Ginger.

Beau was the undisputed leader. He was the biggest, and he had been with Rand the longest, five years. He looked pretty scary, hackles up, teeth bared, ears laid back, snarling. If we were outside, he would have ignored them, but he was penned in, and there was nothing between them and me except him. He went into defense mode that fast.

"Quit it," I told him, touching his head, petting him so he had no choice but to stop and look up at me. "It's okay, honey."

He talked to me, half howl, half bark, chiding me for keeping him from his duty, before he sat down with a huff of air and a disgusted expression.

"So what is it that you do on the ranch, Stefan?" Ginger asked me, squinting.

I didn't get to say because Lisa yelled from the other room that Rand was back.

The dogs went nuts because Rand was home, and all of them, except Bella, rushed from the kitchen to greet him.

It was funny. Ginger screamed, Glenn abandoned his cousin to get out of the way of the stampede of dogs, and I heard Lisa and then Kim yell from the living room. I finished measuring out the ratio of wet food to dry food in each dog's bowl, then filled the bowls of water before I washed my hands. I needed a shower, but I wanted to see Rand first.

"Jesus Christ, where the hell did he have to go for groceries?" Glenn groused, throwing open the screen door, shivering in the cold air. "We could have driven to Lubbock and back for how long you took."

I heard boots on the stairs, and then a bag of charcoal was shoved hard at Glenn's chest. "If you had given me any kind of warning about this at all, I might've been a little better prepared, asshole. As it is—Beau, get off me and get inside, you stupid—I'm missin' a dog. Where's Bella?"

"There's one standing with Stefan."

"Why the hell you guys couldn't have just called is bullshit, Glenn," Rand grumbled, not listening as he suddenly stepped into the room, dogs spilling in before him. "When Stef gets home, you guys are gonna hafta—"

"Hey," I called over to him softly.

"Stef." He said my name like he'd been hit in the stomach, as he stood there, frozen, staring at me.

"Surprise." I smiled at him.

Bella barked her hello, but didn't leave my side.

"Christ," he growled, walking by the couch, dumping the groceries there before he jogged across the room to me.

"Where are you off to, Mr. Holloway?" I arched an eyebrow at him.

"Shut up," he said before he grabbed my arm, fingers digging into my bicep, and yanked me after him into the kitchen.

I didn't think, couldn't think, and so when he swung me around and threw me up against the refrigerator, I scrambled to get close to him. My arms wrapped around his neck as I pulled him down, my lips parted the moment they sealed to his. I felt the shiver run through him as our tongues tangled, my body pressed tightly against his. I loved to kiss him, could taste him for hours, and feasted on his mouth.

His hands were on my face, holding me still, making sure I couldn't move, couldn't get away. He took full inventory of my teeth and my tonsils and everything else. I finally had to shove him off me to breathe, my head ready to explode. He rested his forehead against mine, both of us panting, heaving for oxygen.

"What are you doing here?"

"I live here." I gave him the same answer I always did.

"You were gonna be late."

"But I had to get here and stop you from falling in love with Lisa," I teased him.

"Stef—"

"Looks like I got here just in time."

"I'm gonna strangle you."

"Wait until I catch my breath." I chuckled.

He lifted his forehead, tipped my head back, and slammed his mouth back down over mine. The kiss was, for the second time, grinding, voracious, and rough. When I was whimpering, rubbing the hardening bulge in my dress pants against his thigh, he broke the kiss, lifting his lips from mine only to dip his head and press the first of many hot, wet kisses to the long column of my throat.

"Glad"—he said hoarsely as he sucked under my jaw—"you're home."

"Where are you going?" I asked him, even though my power to focus was deserting me quickly. My body was beginning to heat. His kisses had a drugging effect on me as well.

"My cousin Zach," he grumbled, and his voice dropped low as he nibbled my chin, "has an emergency. His ranch, once every three months, he turns it into a guest ranch for a week and—"

"What's a guest ranch?" I asked, opening my legs as he pressed his thigh to my groin.

He kissed me instead of answering, sucking my bottom lip into his mouth, biting it gently before easing back to look down at my face.

"Rand?"

"You know what's hot?"

I smiled up at him.

"This," he said, sliding a finger down the divot under my nose. "I don't know why, but it makes me wanna kiss you."

I laughed at him because he was adorable.

"And when your hair sticks up after we've been in bed—also, very hot."

What was hot was the man looking at me like I was the most alluring thing on the planet. He was making my stomach flutter. "What's a guest ranch?"

"Like a dude ranch," he answered, kissing me again, down the side of my throat, licking my skin, nuzzling, tasting.

"Really?"

There was a deep rumble from his chest before his lips sealed back over mine. My hands moved over his chest, feeling the hard pecs and rippling muscles as he tightened his hold on me.

It lasted too long; I couldn't breathe and had to pull back to drag in air. Instantly he bit gently down on my now-swollen lower lip, nibbling, sucking it back inside his hot mouth.

My moan was deep and full of aching, throbbing need.

His answering groan lifted my eyes to his.

"You make those noises, Stef, and I will put you over the table, company or not."

I coughed to try and get my overstimulated body under control. "So you'll go there, to Zach's ranch, and do what?"

His hands slid off my face, but he didn't move away. Instead he wrapped his strong arms around me, one hand on the small of my back, pressing me forward. "I'll put people on horses and take 'em off, I'll teach them to rope, and ride, and lead trail rides, all that sort of crap."

"But why? I mean, why do you have to go?"

"'Cause Zach, he always asks his family to help him out because if he pays his own men to be there, then there goes his profit."

"Your guys would do it for free."

He nodded. "They would, but I would never ask them."

"How come you didn't know about this before?"

"He doesn't normally ask me, but I guess he's got himself a bigger group this time than usual, and since he needs the money, he didn't wanna turn down the extra people."

"So you got drafted."

"I got drafted," he agreed.

"He's never called you before."

"Nope, normally he wouldn't, but he's backed into a corner right now, and he didn't have no other option."

"So you're leaving me," I teased him.

"Yessir." He grinned evilly. "For five whole days."

"I could die from that."

"Me too." The raw, needy sound of his voice made everything tighten down deep in my stomach as he leaned his head forward to kiss me again.

I lifted to meet him, and the kiss became a needy, whimpering, grinding, clothing-in-the-way, hands-everywhere connection in seconds. One day our chemistry would stop being raw and incendiary and would find a less passionate level. It just hadn't happened yet.

"Hey, Rand," Glenn called as he exploded into the room, "what the fuck is—oh."

When Rand's cousin opened the kitchen door, he found my boyfriend's mouth hovering over mine, his hand cupping my ass, the other in my hair, and my arms wrapped around his neck. Really, even if I'd drawn him a picture, or taken one, it couldn't be any clearer. So his next question seemed ridiculous.

"What are you doing in here?"

I tried to pull free, but Rand drew me closer.

"I'm mauling Stef. What's it look like?"

Even with the visual, it took Rand looking at him like he was dumb as dirt and me squinting at him for the scene in front of him to sink in.

"And you wasted your time invitin' that gal along, Glenn," Rand told his cousin. "I got all I need right here."

At which point Glenn Holloway finally got it.

I TOOK my time in the shower, and afterward I simply pulled all the water out of my hair, ran product through it, and messed it back up. I was home; I didn't need to be pretty. It felt good to be in a worn pair of jeans and big thick socks and a long-sleeved T-shirt. I wanted to eat and lie around and watch TV sprawled out in Rand's lap. I was hoping it wasn't going to be weird downstairs, but if it was, I would come lie in bed. And going to bed with Rand… just the idea sent a flash of heat over my skin. I wondered if I just stayed upstairs, how long it would take him to join me.

It was cute that the second I got out of the bathroom, Bella was there on the other side of the door waiting for me. Her huff of breath made me smile. She sounded like she was irritated.

"I take long showers," I said defensively. The head tip let me know that she had no earthly idea what I was talking about.

Minutes later I was at the top of the stairs ready to go down when Rand appeared at the bottom.

"I wanna talk to you," he said, smiling up at me.

"Talk," I told him, descending toward him, staring into his eyes. The heat that was returned made my stomach flutter.

"I'm leavin' in the morning."

"So you said."

"C'mere."

When I was a step above him so that we were eye to eye, I stopped. "Will you really be gone a week?"

"No, four days actually. I'll get to Zach's place tomorrow afternoon, and then bright and early Thursday morning, the guests will arrive. It's four days there at his ranch, it's done Sunday morning, and then I'll be home the same night."

I nodded. "So it's not like you'll actually be working his ranch like you do yours."

"Ours."

"Ours," I repeated, putting my hand on his cheek, liking the feel of the firm skin and stubble under my palm.

"I'm so glad you came home early."

"I would've been here in another hour anyway."

"Yeah, I know," he said as he leaned forward, kissing my cheek, the motion tender and sexy all at once. "But sooner is always better."

I sighed heavily as his nose brushed over the side of my neck.

"You smell good."

It was amazing how smoky and low Rand's voice got whenever he talked and kissed me at the same time. The gruff, low growl never failed to make me hard.

"I wish I didn't have to go."

I looked up into his face. "I could come."

He shook his head. "All the spots on the guest list are filled."

"No, Rand, I could help you."

His snort of laughter made me scowl.

"Rand." I lowered my voice, the warning there.

He cleared his throat, tightening his arms around me when I tried to shove free.

I growled at him.

"Love," he tried hard to stifle the chuckle. "Just because you live on a ranch doesn't mean you can ride a horse."

"Rand—"

"Stef." His smile was big and wicked and made his eyes glitter. "Baby—"

"Don't call me baby, and I can ride a horse, Rand."

"Correction: you can ride your horse because you basically raised her after her mama passed, but any other horse would not allow you to just sit there and do nothing."

"What're you—"

"That horse does everything, Stef. You just hold the reins. She runs when she wants, she walks when she wants, rides into streams when she wants," he chuckled, his hand sliding down my back, slipping up under the T-shirt to my skin. "She loves you, same as that damn fool dog, but any other horse and you're gonna break your neck."

"Rand—"

"I like your neck in one piece."

"I'm going," I told him matter-of-factly. "Case closed."

"No."

"Yes."

"Absolutely not," he said indulgently.

I arched an eyebrow for him.

"Baby, it's not how you think."

"I'm not thinking anything, and quit with the baby."

"Stef—"

"Excuse me."

We turned to find Rand's cousin Ginger descending the stairs behind us. He let me go as she took the final step to the floor, but one of his hands moved to the small of my back and stayed there. Her own was instantly offered.

"It's nice to meet you," I told her as we shook.

"I feel like such an ass," she said, biting her bottom lip, her hand squeezing mine. "What you must think of me."

I smiled at her.

"I just… I didn't know that you were living here, and when Glenn said that I should invite Lisa, I thought it would be funny." She breathed out.

I eased my hand from hers as Rand slid his up to the back of my neck, his fingers massaging gently, tenderly.

"I had no idea that you and Rand had been together for two years already. No one tells us anything."

"That's because when my mother got remarried, your father, along with Glenn's, stopped speaking to her," Rand reminded Ginger. "Maybe if your dad, good old Uncle Cyrus, wasn't such a prick, you would know more about my life."

"Rand," I scolded him.

"Whatever," he grumbled. "I'm going for Zach, not for you or Glenn or anybody else. And you better tell your girlfriend that she's shit outta luck about marrying this rancher, all right?"

She gasped as he leaned in, kissed my temple, and turned around, walking toward the kitchen, yelling.

"Oh my God, he's so mad," she said, her voice tiny.

"He's just upset because he doesn't like to leave his ranch or me," I said gently. "And tomorrow he has to do both."

She nodded as I saw tears fill her eyes.

"He's just loud."

"He's been scary as long as I've known him."

"Really?" I chuckled. "You think Rand's scary?"

"You don't?"

"No," I assured her. "Never."

She nodded.

"Tell me how you guys are related."

She wiped under her eyes. "Well, my father, and Brent's and Brandon's, is Cyrus Holloway, and he and Rand and Charlotte's daddy, James, are brothers along with Rayland, Glenn and Zach's father, and Tyler, who lives here with you all."

Rand's Uncle Tyler and I were very good friends, had been for longer than Rand and I had been together. I used to see him when his niece Charlotte, my best friend and Rand's sister, and I came to visit.

"Hey."

I looked over my shoulder, and Glenn was there with Brent.

"Stefan?"

"Yes?"

He shoved his hands down deep into the pockets of his jeans. "I'm real sorry I didn't put it together who you were. I should've asked."

"And I should have just told you," I said. "I'm sorry."

"Rand and his family and my dad and ours, we're having us a little problem with Rand's mama gettin' remarried as she still owns a portion of the grazing land in King, and my daddy thinks she should just sign it over to him since she ain't a Holloway no more."

"But Rand is."

"Yeah, but Rand has his ranch, and even though it don't do as well as mine or Zach's, it's still enough to take care of him and provide for his family."

I scowled at him. "How is the Red Diamond not doing well?"

He gave me a patronizing smile. "I know you don't know much about ranching, but there should be a lot of traffic around here if you're doing well."

"Rand sells his beef over the Internet mostly," I told him, trying not to look at him like he was stupid. "He has a company in Lubbock that deals with distribution and a PR company in Amarillo that does his marketing. Did he tell you about his contract with Grillmaster or did he fail to mention that?"

He looked like I'd hit him.

I waited.

"He—"

"Rand just bought and sold four nonworking ranches here in Winston to the developer Mitchell Powell, who plans to create a huge resort that will bring in millions of dollars in revenue to this county and the next. He's building a school in Hillman in the fall. How does any of that say that his ranch is not doing well?"

"I… my father said his ranch was failing."

"Twelve years ago." I was indignant. "But I assure you that the Red Diamond is much better off than yours or your brother Zach's."

We were all standing there silently as Rand yelled for everyone to come eat. As silent minutes ticked by, he suddenly appeared beside me.

"What are we doing?"

Glenn turned to look at him. "Stef tells us that you're the one who got the Grillmaster account, Rand. Is that true?"

He glared at his cousin. "So you're the guy who didn't have distribution rights before you bid on the contract?"

"Yes."

Rand nodded and then shrugged. "I ship my beef all over the US, Glenn. You should think about that side of the business. Only selling to local businesses will not keep you in the black and allows no room for growth. I diversified before I met Stef, but went further with it afterward so that no amount of stupid-ass redneck prejudice would keep me from providing for my family and the families of my men. Unlike your ranch, you won't see any people driving down the road to the house, but my server is clogged with orders."

Glenn was ashen, and I wondered why.

"I could buy you and your father's ranch and Zach's if I wanted. Tell that to your ignorant cracker father."

There was some really bad blood between the two families that I was only right that second hearing about.

Glenn was suddenly in Rand's face, finger poking into his collarbone. His face was red and he was close to snarling. "My father wants that land up in King, Rand, and so do I. Your mother has no right to—"

"You want the land?" Rand asked icily, stepping back, sideways, so that I was suddenly behind him, shielded. "Buy me out."

"I knew it!" he crowed. "Your mother signed it over to you!"

"The minute she remarried, the rights reverted to me, asshole. The land is mine now, Glenn, so you can tell your father that a Holloway owns it."

"You—"

"If he wants it, like I said, he can buy me out. I can graze my cattle other places."

"Got lots of other land, do you?"

"Yessir, I do."

"You know we don't have that kind of—"

"Then fuck you, Glenn," he snarled at him, trembling when I put my hands on his hips, willing him to calm down. "That land was my father's, and I have as much right to it as any of you."

"It's family land, and you've got no right to it!"

"I've got the same rights as you!"

"You're not welcome there"—his voice was cold as he leveled his gaze on Rand—"and neither is your boyfriend."

"The land is just as much mine as yours, Glenn, and there ain't shit you can do about it."

He balled up his fists, and Rand did the same, twisting into a defensive stance, prepared to fight.

"No!" I yelled, and both men turned to me. "Not in my house."

"Fuck you," Glenn barked at me.

"Don't speak to him," Rand warned his cousin. "Don't even look at him."

The world swirled around us. Profanity flew between the two men, Ginger was crying, her friends were clueless about what was going on, and in the middle of everything, Brent told Glenn to calm down because he was frightening Emily.

"Fuck you," Glenn yelled at him. "You're such a pussy-whipped piece of—"

At which point, Brent, who I'd thought was quiet and subdued and sort of dorky, ended up hurling himself at Glenn. It was chaos then until I heard Rand's Uncle Tyler, Glenn and Ginger's Uncle Tyler too, come in and yell.

"What in the blue blazes is goin' on in here?"

No one said blue blazes in real life, and that was funny. What was not, was the rifle he was holding in his hand.

Everyone froze because of it.

"I thought it was some kind of home invasion thing," he announced to us.

"You're watching too much TV," I told him.

He shrugged in agreement. "Now what in Sam Hill is goin' on?"

Really, the man's expressions were hysterical.

As Rand threw up his hands, I realized that no one was going anywhere now that Tyler was there to mediate.

"Here, honey." He gestured over to Lisa. "Come stand by me."

I rolled my eyes at the twinkle in his eye as she walked over to him.

"Oh for fuck's sake," Rand groaned.

I rounded on him and leaped, and he had to scramble to grab me. As I wrapped arms and legs around him, I heard the deep contented sigh that came up out of the man. He brushed the hair back from my face and looked into my eyes.

"Now you see there," Tyler mumbled. "If Stefan weren't home, you'd all be dead now."

And I smiled as Rand nodded.

CHAPTER 3

I HAD been really confused until Tyler explained it all to me. All the times I had been to the ranch before Rand and I had gotten together, other members of his extended family had been there and I had been warmly welcomed into the fold. That my being gay was suddenly a problem made no sense.

"You ain't never seen no Holloways," Tyler told me. "You seen Millers only."

"What?"

So Tyler told me that those men and women, the ones who had been kind and funny and everything else, were Rand's mother's family, the Millers. They all lived close by in Lubbock and Midland and Slaton and Paducah.

"Then I never met Rand's father's side of the family."

"That's right." He nodded. "'Cept for me."

I'd had no idea.

As I watched Glenn and the women leave a half an hour later, I apologized to Rand for causing the rift between him and his family.

"It's got nothing to do with you," he said, grabbing my hand and yanking me after him upstairs.

"Rand—"

"Stop," he cut me off, pulling me along.

I realized suddenly what was happening. "Rand, you still need to feed your cousin Brent and his girlfriend, and you have to pack and—"

"After," he told me, having reached the top of the stairs and dragging me down the hall with him. "And the food is there. They just need to eat it."

"But you need to be down there playing good host."

"Fuck it. They know I ain't one, and Tyler can entertain 'em just fine."

"But I should—Rand! You don't just fuck your boyfriend in the middle of dinner and make people wait to talk to you and—"

"You're not my boyfriend," he said flatly, shoving me through the doorway only to kick the bedroom door shut behind him. "You're my partner."

I was about to remind him that he was not raised in a barn when my eyes met his, and I forgot what I was going to say.

The man's gaze was all heat.

I licked my lips, and his eyes went right there before he lunged forward and grabbed me. His lips met mine in a frenzied kiss as his hands went everywhere else. When he pulled back, I gasped for air, knowing that my mouth would be taken again fast. I opened my eyes a second later when they weren't.

He was staring at me.

"What are you doing?" I smiled at him, my own hands on his hot skin, having burrowed up under the T-shirt and flannel one he was wearing over it.

The muscles in his jaw corded as he shivered slightly. "I'm lookin' at you. Christ, I could look at you every day for the rest of my life and never get tired of it."

His gaze never failed to make my stomach roll over because I could tell, anyone could, that I was cherished.

"You're so beautiful, Stef," he sighed, his hand on my cheek, "and your eyes, your gorgeous green eyes, just kill me."

I stepped back and pulled my T-shirt up over my head. I watched his hot eyes narrow as he gazed at me, and I was keenly aware of his desire. His breathing, the bulge in his jeans, his hands that reached for me—all of him wanted all of me.

I walked backward out of reach, unbuckling my belt, working fast to get out of my jeans and the briefs underneath. When I was naked, I let him reach me, and him being fully clothed and me without anything on brought a throaty moan up from his chest.

He pressed against me, his hand fondling my ass, and when I pushed back, he grabbed a handful and squeezed tight. My reaction was unrestrained, primitive, the rumbling groan torn out of me.

"Jesus, Stef," he murmured before he shoved me down hard onto the bed, and I watched as he frantically went to work on his own clothes.

He yanked off his boots and his flannel shirt, but his jeans were only opened, and the T-shirt was still on when he crawled up on the bed and grabbed my hips. I was rolled over onto my stomach and yanked up onto my hands and knees.

"You have the most beautiful backside I have ever seen in my life," he told me, his hand sliding down the slope of my back up over my bottom. "It is round and firm and just perfect. Do you know what you do to me? Just seeing the curve of your ass in your jeans makes me hard."

It was good to know, I thought, as I wiggled it for him.

"Stef," he groaned his husky tenor sounding like he was in pain.

"Rand, come—oh."

His mouth, his delicious, hot, wet mouth was on my ass. The bite on my right cheek made me moan, his hands spreading me stopped my breathing, and when his tongue slid over my entrance, I choked out his name.

"There you go," he said, before he swirled his tongue inside me, deeper and deeper, before I felt him add a finger.

I jolted under him, and I was aware of him moving, lifting his lips from me even as the finger remained. I pushed back, felt him shifting around, and heard the jostle of the nightstand and the snap of the flip-top cap.

"Oh God, Rand, please."

A second finger, slicked with lube, joined the first, and the burn felt incredible.

I shoved back, and he groaned deeply, scissoring his fingers apart, gently, slowly, but firmly, insistently.

"God, Stef, you're trying to suck my fingers down into you, and I want it to be my cock. I need it to be my cock."

"Then fuck me."

"Jesus, you're beautiful, the lines of you, your hair and your eyes and your warm skin and your ass… fuck."

He liked to look at me, loved to touch me, smooth his hands all over me before he had to get closer, had to be joined with me, sink his flesh inside of mine.

I levered back on his fingers, the burn, the pinch, having already been replaced with heart-pounding, blood-tingling anticipation.

"Stef, I can't—this is as ready as you're gonna be."

If he didn't do something, I was going to scream. "Rand… baby…."

His hands gripped my hips hard, and he shoved inside of me in one powerful forward thrust. I had no idea he could feel so good.

"Rand!"

And since he knew the sound of my voice, he didn't worry that he'd hurt me. He just eased out, only to plunge back in again, harder, faster, stretching me, filling me, as he held me tight, not letting me move.

I lifted up, taking him in deeper, and the strangled moan came out of him even as he ordered me to grab my dick because he couldn't. There was no way for him to stroke me off. He didn't have the concentration. His control was shattered by the adrenaline from earlier, and now he wanted only to be buried to his balls in my ass, hammer into me, and take me hard.

I begged him for it.

"Stef." He dragged my name up from his chest before he bit down into my shoulder. "Come for me."

Other men had tried to claim me, and I had laughed at them because I knew, in the end, that they were not stronger than me. And yes, most of them had been stronger physically, but no one could hold against my sneering contempt, my barbed tongue, and my scathing sarcasm. I was icy and mean and unfeeling, and they had slunk away with their tails between their legs, cowed and broken. I had never been anything but cold and indifferent, never giving my heart.

And then there was Rand.

Rand Holloway had always stood against the onslaught of my vindictive nature and given back everything I had dished out. And once I had found out he loved me and, even more amazing, that I loved him back, all that fierce, proud venom had alchemized into devouring heat. So for him, only for him, when he demanded my surrender, my submission, I gave it because I could deny the man nothing.

His name came from my throat in a gasp of breath as the orgasm crashed through me, all my muscles tightening at once, my climax triggering Rand's. His body gave out, and he collapsed on top of me, driving me down onto the bed. My laughter could not be stifled.

"Ass," he grumbled, unable to move, not wanting to move, content to ride out the aftershocks buried to the hilt inside me.

"Say it now," I demanded.

His lips were on my ear. "I love you so fucking much, Stef. You belong to me."

And even though I knew it, hearing it meant a lot. Who knew I would be just as addicted to the man's words as his actions?

RAND AND I had come downstairs after we cleaned up enough to be presentable, and his cousin Brent was dumbfounded. It was me looking debauched with swollen lips and hooded eyes and Rand sated and sweet, yawning with a smile that curled his mouth, that did it.

"I had no idea he could even look like that," Brent told me, tipping his head at Rand as he listened to something Emily was saying.

"Like what?"

"Not mean."

But even when Rand and I had been enemies, at first I thought he was a mean redneck. I later saw the man clearly, even when I was confused about everything else.

When the phone in the hall rang, I got up from the table where we were having dessert, the four of us plus Rand's Uncle Tyler, and excused myself to answer it.

"Hello?"

"Hello, may I speak to Rand Holloway please?"

"I'm sorry, he's busy right now. Can I take a message for him?"

"Oh yes, please, would you let him know that Katie Beal from the Truscott Rodeo called and that I called to confirm the participation of the Red Diamond at the rodeo on Friday."

I had no idea what she was talking about. "Rodeo?"

"Yes. And I know we normally don't call, everyone just shows up, but this is the fifth year, and, as Mr. Holloway knows, every five years the entire community of ranches that owns grazing land in King has to be represented, or by the stipulation put into the original deed, the party that does not attend forfeits their land ownership and their portion reverts to the other parties."

I instantly understood exactly what was going on. "The grazing lands—you're saying that if Rand doesn't show up this weekend to take part in a rodeo, then his grazing lands are forfeit and… what, redistributed?"

"Yes, it's parceled out equally, unless there is another owner in the same family."

It was all becoming clear. "So because Rand's uncle owns land in King as well, the rights that Rand has would revert to his uncle."

"To…," she was reading, "Rayland Holloway, yes, that's correct."

Everything fell into place, and I really had to give it to Glenn. Not only had he turned in an amazing performance, but he was probably on his way from our ranch to the rodeo even as I stood there speaking to the nice lady on the phone.

"And we received a tip from that same Mr. Rayland Holloway that the Red Diamond would not be participating this year due to a family emergency at another ranch, but I wasn't sure if Mr. Holloway, Mr. Rand Holloway that is, understood that this was the fifth year. He didn't attend last year, and I understand that his participation was missed, but it didn't affect his land rights."

So now I knew that Rand's cousin Glenn and his father had been scheming to make sure that Rand did not show up. I wondered if Zach knew what was going on, and if he did, I hoped he could live with himself for cheating Rand out of his birthright and for preying on his sense of honor. Because I knew that even if Rand were to find out what was going on, he would not change his plans. He would give up the grazing rights, relinquish his claim to the land, because he had given Zach his solemn word that he was coming to help him. For Rand Holloway, his word was his bond.

"Actually, Katie, my name is Stefan Joss, and I'm the co-owner of the Red Diamond, and I will be there representing our ranch."

"Oh." She sounded excited. "That's wonderful news—Joss, is it?"

"Yes, ma'am," I told her. "Can you tell me what day I have to check in?"

"Well, it's you and your men, Mr. Joss, and it's Friday morning at nine. I mean, it's just a small local rodeo, but the community counts on the revenue from the tourists."

"Of course."

"You'll need to give us all the names of everyone who will be participating on behalf of the Red Diamond in the individual events, and when you get here, there will be a camp site for your men and a small stable and a corral for your horses."

What in the world have I gotten myself into just because I didn't want Glenn Holloway to win? It seemed suddenly very stupid. I needed help.

"Shall I e-mail you all the information?"

"That would be great," I said, trying not to sound like I wanted to throw up.

"Would you like it sent to the e-mail for Rand Holloway that we have on file?"

"No, let me give you a new one."

We talked awhile longer, and she told me about the different events, about the trailers we would be staying in, about the dances, the bachelor auction, and the awards ceremony. I got overwhelmed just listening to her.

"I can't wait to meet you. Everyone says that having the Red Diamond attend is one of the high points. You have the only ranch that isn't located in our county, Mr. Joss."

"Yeah, I know."

"Rayland and his son Glenn will be so surprised."

"Oh, I have no doubt."

CHAPTER 4

THE ACADEMY owed me an award. The only time I wasn't acting in the following twenty-four hours was when I was in bed with Rand. There, with him, I was stripped naked both literally and emotionally, and all I could do was come apart under him. But from the time I got back to the table, before we hit the sheets, and then afterward, I was on stage. When I kissed Rand good-bye Thursday morning, waving from the porch at him and Brent and Emily—they had signed up to be guests at Zach's ranch—telling them all to be safe, smiling like an idiot until I couldn't see the car anymore, I felt like there should have been applause. It had been a truly amazing performance.

A half an hour after Rand left, Mac Gentry, Rand's foreman and the one guy on the ranch who had never warmed to me, stepped onto the porch.

"What?" he asked irritably.

I had called his cell phone, and he had ridden in from where he had been supervising some fence mending to speak to me.

"I need help," I said from where I was sitting on the rail.

He sneered at me, and I was suddenly just done. I could hire some men when I got there. Fuck it.

"Forget it." I shook my head, starting for the door. "Sorry to bother you."

He caught my arm, fingers tight around my bicep as he stopped me. "What is it?"

"Nothing, lemme go."

"Just tell me."

"You're a dick."

"That ain't news." He squinted at me. "Now what is it?"

"Rand's gonna lose the grazing rights in King if we don't show up at a rodeo."

"I'm sorry, what?"

I eased free of his grip and explained what was going on. He followed me into the house, and I passed him everything Katie Beal had sent me the previous evening, all the paperwork I had printed out.

"Does Rand know?" Mac asked me, his eyes flicking to mine.

"No."

He nodded. "Good. It would only eat at his gut all weekend."

"But I can go," I told him. "I own half of the Red."

"You do?"

I raised my eyebrows at him. "Yeah, asshole, I do, so maybe you should think about not being a total douche to me all the time."

The squint was back, and for the first time ever, I laughed at him.

I was stunned a second later when I got a very slight curl of his lip. I had no idea that Mac Gentry could smile. I had never seen him do it before. I had initially thought it was because I was gay, but it turned out that he thought I was going to leave Rand. He thought I would get bored with life on the ranch and that his boss, who was now happy and content and smiling, would go back to how he was before I took up residence in his home. No one wanted Rand breathing fire, impossible to please, and micromanaging them. They liked him how he was now. Mac, more than anyone, liked his boss as far away from him on a daily basis as possible. He liked that I wanted to help, and for the first time since I'd met the man, he talked to me like I wasn't absolutely stupid. It was a nice change.

"There are seven events at the rodeo. I'm sending six men with you and eight horses, two extra just in case you need them. You should take that fool dog of yours, too, as well as that mare Rand gave you since she's the only horse you know how to ride. I expect my stock returned in the same condition they left in. You hear me?"

"Yessir." I nodded, turning to leave.

"We're all gonna have hell to pay when he finds out about this, Stef."

"I know." I nodded. "Give me a better plan."

He just looked at my face.

"See?"

Two hours later—why we were leaving so early I had no idea—I was driving a huge pickup truck with double wheels off the ranch, Everett sitting beside me in the cab, Dusty stretched out behind me, and Bella lying on the seat next to him. Pierce, Tom, Chase, and Chris were in the pickup behind me.

"You look stupid."

I turned my head to look at Everett. "Pardon me?"

"I don't think I've ever seen anyone who looked less like he should be wearing a cowboy hat and boots than you."

The worn brown cowboy hat I had on my head had been a gift from Rand, as had the boots that were on my feet. While I wasn't entirely comfortable, fitting in was key. I did not want anyone to second-guess my right to be there.

"So what was your plan for this thing if Mac hadn't talked us all into it?"

"I dunno," I sighed. "I was thinking of calling Mitch Powell and seeing who he could maybe pay to go with me, and then I would have to pay him back."

My hat was pulled off fast, I got a quick slap across the top of my head, and then the hat was shoved back down hard. It took only seconds, but it stung like mad.

"Shit, Dusty," I groused at him, lifting my right hand to rub where it hurt.

The motion sent my hat down over my aviator sunglasses and my eyes. But Everett was there to slap my hand away and knock the hat back.

"Try an' keep your eyes on the damn road, all right?"

"I would if people weren't hit—"

"You never go off the ranch for help," Dusty scolded me. "Never."

"Never," Everett echoed him. "We take care of our own."

"But I'm not one of you guys," I told them. "You all respect and care for Rand, not me."

"You don't give yourself no credit," Dusty assured me. "Without you knowing about finances and such, Rand would not be making all the money he is."

"That's not true," I assured them. "Rand is a very smart business—"

"And if Rand didn't wanna make a home for you, then he wouldn't be fixin' to make all the changes in Hillman."

That part was probably true.

"Before you was here," Dusty chimed in, "Rand Holloway was a prick."

I wasn't touching that one with a ten-foot pole.

"Well said," Everett cackled.

"But since you been on the ranch, I can stand to talk to him for more than five minutes."

Everett was laughing.

I smiled, seating the hat on my head as Dusty yelled at Bella to quit moving. We all laughed as she muscled him out of the way, all seventy pounds of dog taking up position so she, instead of Dusty, was behind me. She put her head on the back of my seat to the left, and I felt her warm breath whuffing on my cheek before her tongue got my ear.

"Bell," I griped, wiping it off, reaching back to scratch under her chin.

"She's worried I'm gonna hit ya ag'in." Dusty chuckled. "I ain't never seen a dog more protective. It's sweet."

As she nuzzled the side of my neck, I had to agree.

We stopped for lunch and then again for dinner, and after we fed and watered the horses, took them out, walked them a bit, and then got them back in the trailers, we were back on our way. We reached Truscott just after midnight, and I was thrilled to see the area awash with lights. I left Chase in charge, and took Dusty and Everett with me to register.

The trailer for participants was clearly marked, and when we reached the front of the line, I gave the man sitting at the table the name of the ranch.

"Red Diamond," I said.

There were three people there, two women and the one man, and his head snapped up to look at me.

"We were told that the Red Diamond was not participating this year."

"Then you were misinformed, sir," I told him.

"Well, I'm so pleased." He smiled and fished through a stack of manila envelopes in front of him. "Oh, I see it here now. You spoke to Katie."

"Yessir."

"Are you…." He squinted at the printout he had pulled from the envelope. "Steven Joss?"

"It's Stefan, but yes."

"Wonderful." He smiled up at me and seemed genuinely pleased. "We were worried that the Red Diamond was going to give us a miss this year just like the two years prior."

"And we're sorry about that," Everett chimed in. "And I assure you, sir, that we will never miss another."

The man extended his hand to me. "I'm Hud Lawrence, and may I say that this is just about the best piece of news I've had all week," he told me as we shook. He grasped Everett's hand after mine, and then Dusty's. "Lots of folks come out just to see you all. This rodeo is mostly a small community one 'cept for you folks, and it's a treat to see your stock. I've got to give Gil Landry a call and tell him that you all showed up. I know he was lookin' forward to competing if you were fixin' to be here."

I nodded, accepted the registration packet from Hud, wrote the man a check for seven hundred dollars, a hundred per event, and stepped back so Everett could give him the names of who was participating and in what. Dusty chatted with the two women at the table—had them laughing with him in minutes, so charming were his big blue eyes and dimples—and was getting the gossip as Hud typed information into his laptop. Once everything was signed—release of liability forms, insurance forms—our numbers were given to us, as well as directions to our trailer, stable, and corral to work our horses. We thanked him and the two women and headed back to the others.

"Who is Gil whoever?" I asked Everett.

"He's a rancher here," he answered, irritable suddenly. "He and Rand have a kind of—I dunno, strange sort of rivalry goin' on. I don't really get it. They're friends, but they ain't. I'm not sure how to describe it."

"He hates Rand," Dusty told me. "That's how you describe it."

"But not all the time. He only hates Rand sometimes."

"Well, I'm sure he's gonna be disappointed that Rand's not here."

"Most likely," Everett agreed, but the look on his face was odd.

Everett Hartline was a strange man. He was absolutely dangerous and unpredictable, and his temper was horrible. He was also extremely loyal and very protective of his home, which was Rand's ranch. I liked it best when he wasn't armed. When he and Chris took their rifles at night to check on the borders of the ranch, I got nervous.

"Something you're not telling me?"

He shook his shaggy head, the light brown hair, streaked gold from the sun, falling into his dark blue eyes. No one would ever say that Everett was handsome, but once you saw his face, you never forgot it. He reminded me of the pictures of the cowboys from the Old West—rugged, hard, and tanned from living their lives outdoors. There was no trace of gentleness in the man, no softness, just mean edges that I never wanted to be on the wrong side of. He scared me just a little.

"So do you guys all know what events you're gonna do?" I asked him.

He smiled barely. "It's nice to hear you ask. Rand don't ever ask."

"'Cause he knows what all your strengths are," I sighed deeply, passing him the packet with all the numbers in it. "I'm just along for the ride."

"You're more than that," he said as we reached the others.

As they all started deciding who was going to do what, I yelled over that I was going to bed. No one heard me, but it didn't matter.

There were two trailers, and they each slept four so there was more than enough room. Once I was changed and under the covers, taking the bunk at the back, I took pity on the dog looking up at me like she was dying.

"Get in the bed," I told her.

She was up and tucked down on the other side of me, head on my hip with a happy whimper, seconds later. I didn't hear the others come in.

CHAPTER 5

BREAKFAST WAS amazing, good home cooking, and when Everett and I were on our way to watch the grand entry, where all the contestants entered the arena for the rodeo, a man stepped in front of us. He was immediately joined by three others. It was slightly intimidating, but the fact that he looked so familiar somehow kept it from being frightening. He had the same thick jet-black hair that all the Holloway men had, though his was dusted gray at his temples.

"You look like a Holloway," I told him.

"You know I am."

"Are you Rayland Holloway?"

He squinted at me. "Yessir. And you're Stefan Joss, my son tells me."

"Yeah. Where is old Glenn? I'd love to talk to him."

He grunted and the men behind him moved in closer. Everett bumped me with his shoulder when he stepped in beside me.

"What brings you to the rodeo, Mr. Joss?"

"It's the five-year mark for the grazing lands, sir," I answered.

His eyes narrowed.

"And as I own half of the Red Diamond, I had to be here to make sure we didn't lose our grazing rights."

It was fun because he looked like I'd hit him.

"So even though Rand's out at the Sarasota with your son Zach," Everett drawled out, laying it on thick, "the Red Diamond is here in the official capacity to compete and, therefore, retain the grazing rights in King."

Rayland stood there, absolutely white faced, mouth open like a fish, somehow looking slightly smaller than he had two minutes ago.

"'Cause as you know, there are no stipulations that anyone has to win or even place; just participation is required from all the ranches that graze their cattle on the land."

The hatred in his eyes was hard to face, but I had seen worse in my life, so it was par for the course.

I had to physically restrain Everett when the man took a step back and spat at my feet.

"Watch your back," he warned before he turned on his heel, shoved his way through his own men, and stalked away.

"Well," I said the second we were alone, "that went well."

"That man just threatened you," Everett barked at me, indignant and angry.

"Yeah, and it was crazy, over the top, very *Walking Tall* wasn't it?" I chuckled. "I mean, come on, 'watch your back'? Who says that? It's like a badly edited B movie."

He was looking at me like I was nuts.

"What?"

"I don't get you at all."

I shrugged, turning to walk toward the arena. "I wanna talk to him."

"Talk to who?" Everett said as he caught up to me.

"Mr. Holloway."

"You wanna talk to the man who just spit on you?"

"At me, not on me," I corrected. "And yeah."

"Are you serious?"

"Yeah. There's gotta be a way to fix all this."

"All what?"

"All this bad blood," I told him. "It's such a shame to have a family ripped apart."

"But as far as I can tell, it's been like this since Rand's father died, and that man back there wanted the ranch, and my boss said no."

I nodded because there was no way it was as easy as he was making it out to be.

"You're thinking that there's more to it."

"Yes." I smiled at him. "And that was very perceptive of you."

He rolled his eyes. "Sometimes it's just jealousy, Stef," he said, tugging on my arm. "C'mon, I gotta get to the arena and you need a seat."

He left me at the corral, bolting toward Chris, who was yelling at him to hurry the hell up, and I joined the crowd, blending in with everyone else in my jeans, boots, and hat. Reaching the main area, I climbed up through the crowd on the bleachers up toward the top until I found some space. The view was good, and I was surprised at the number of people who were there.

"So you own the Red Diamond?"

I turned and there was a man looking up at me from under the brim of his black Stetson. "I own half of the Red Diamond," I corrected him.

He nodded. "We heard you were here last night."

So this guy had to be Gil Landry, who Hud Lawrence had told me he was going to call. But to be sure, I asked. "And you are?"

"Gil Landry," he said, leaning forward, offering me his hand.

The man was even bigger than Rand. My cowboy was leaner, his muscles sleeker. Gil was bulkier, everything fitting tight from the shirt stretched across his wide chest and bulging biceps, to the denim encasing lean hips and long, thick legs. When my eyes met his, he smiled, which warmed the dark brown eyes and softened his face. Handsome man—not breathtaking like Rand Holloway, but few men were.

I took the offered hand, squeezed tight, and then let go. "Stefan Joss. Good to meet you."

"We were expecting Rand."

"He's helping his cousin with an emergency."

"I see." He nodded, indicating the woman seated beside him. "This is my sister Carly."

I leaned forward and took the hand she offered me. "Pleasure to meet you."

"And you." She nodded, tipping her head. "Though I have to tell you that I wish Rand had come with you. Seeing that man is one of the highlights of the rodeo for me."

I bet it was. "Well, I suspect he'll be here next year."

She tried to force a smile, but I realized how really sad she looked. "It's doubtful. Between his ranch and his new wife, we—"

"Wife?"

"Yes," she snapped irritably.

"Rand Holloway is—"

"I'm sorry." She softened her tone. "You own half the ranch, so I'm sure you must have met her. Stephanie, isn't it?"

I shook my head. "Rand Holloway is not married."

"How is it you own half the ranch, Stefan?"

"Because like I said, Rand Holloway is not married, and it's not Stephanie, it's Stefan," I said, rising, getting ready to find another place to sit.

"Wait." Gil stopped me, and my eyes were back on his brown ones.

I stood my ground.

He cleared his throat. "We're sorry, Mr.—Stefan. We had no idea that Rand Holloway was…." He turned and looked at his sister. "Did we?"

Her mouth was open, her eyes were huge, and she could not seem to stop staring at my face.

"So." Gil coughed, looking back up at me. "Have a seat here, and let me explain this all to you. We heard you moved here from Chicago. You probably don't have a lot of experience with this kind of thing, do you?"

I studied him, then his sister, and then went back to him. "I'm not up to bullshit today."

"You speak your mind."

"I have to deal with Rand's cousin Glenn at some point today, and his father, Rayland, just threatened me, so if you want to mess with me, so not in the mood, you know?"

He nodded. "Rayland Holloway is a dick."

"And Glenn's a pig," Carly seconded, finally finding her voice.

I sat down.

The rodeo was bigger than I thought it would be, but I had it on good authority, from Gil, that compared to some it was tiny. We had missed everyone riding in and circling while we were talking. All the competitors were already in a row at the center of the arena, and I saw Rand's men waving to the crowd.

"It's good that you came, Stefan," Carly assured me, reaching over her brother to pat my knee. "We get a much bigger crowd when the Red is here, and that helps the community so much. Thank you."

"You're very welcome."

I sat there with her and her brother and got an education on rodeo events during the course of the morning and afternoon. Watching the calf roping, or tie-down roping, was interesting, and Rand's stoic ranch hand Chris was the fastest and moved like a machine. The crowd certainly appreciated his technique and economy of movement, and when his time came in as the best, I was thrilled for him.

The team roping was next, or what Carly called heading and heeling.

"See, Stef, your man Chase just roped the steer's horns. He's the header, and now Everett, he's the heeler, he's going to lasso the back legs, and together they're going to put it in the dirt."

"Seems mean," I told her.

I got a few looks from some people around us, and Carly just shook her head.

"What?"

"Are you trying to get yourself killed?"

I smiled at her.

The lunch break pulled everyone from the bleachers to the different concession stands, and when I tried to leave them, Gil reached for me, put a hand on my shoulder, manhandling me like Rand always did, and steered me toward the food area. The three of us stood in line to get Indian fry bread with cheese and beans, and afterward decided to walk around.

Not only was it a rodeo, but a fair as well, with all the cotton candy and rides and the booths where you could win those huge stuffed animals that were only cool when you were walking on the midway. At home it was just crap that cluttered up your house.

"You know, that hat looks strange on you," Gil commented as we stopped so Carly could buy some gifts for her nieces.

"I get that a lot," I chuckled, remembering Everett dissing the same hat in the truck with me.

"I bet." He nodded, reaching out to touch the brim. "You don't really fit in here, do you?"

"I fit at the Red," I told him because, somehow, I got the strange feeling that he was trying, in a sort of backhanded way, to make a point. "I fit with Rand."

"Do you?"

His tone was icy, and I noticed that he was barely breathing. I looked past him at Carly and found her gazing at me as well. The second my eyes met hers, she smiled big and turned away.

"I would say that you want to fit with him, and so you think you do, but you don't."

My eyes returned to his.

"You're wrong."

"How can I be? I just spent the day talkin' to you, and you don't know shit about being a cowboy or life on a ranch. You don't know anything about what Rand really needs."

"And you do?"

"I do."

"And what is that?"

"The man needs the same thing I do: someone who can stand at his side, not someone he has to take care of."

I turned to go, but he grabbed my arm hard, wrenching me back around as he leaned in close to me, finger in my face. "You might have turned Rand's head with this—whatever the fuck this is—but when he comes to his senses, he'll want a woman who can love him and love his ranch and give him sons."

Sometimes I missed what was right in front of me. "Carly."

"That's right," he snarled quietly at me, digging his fingers into my bicep. He would leave bruises. "I've been pushin' him for forever to date her so he can see how good his life can be. It nearly broke her heart when we heard he had remarried. I didn't think I'd ever see her back to smiling, but then today when you showed up… hell. She's pleased as punch."

And I knew why she was happy. "She thinks it won't last."

"She knows, just like I do, that this is nothing. He will toss you out of his home in no time and finally look at what's been waitin' patiently for him this whole time. Carly will make Rand the best wife ever. If you were smart, you'd clear out before he throws you out."

"Get your hand off me."

It happened so fast. He let go of my arm, shoved me back, and hit me. I didn't realize until his fist was connecting with my jaw that he was that angry. Normally, I could defend myself better. I had been in enough fights in my life, but it was so unexpected. I didn't even have time to react before I was on the ground.

"What the fuck?"

I looked up, and Glenn Holloway was there beside me.

"Stay out of this, Glenn."

"Nice sucker punch," he said, offering me a hand without looking at me, keeping an eye on Gil. "Back the fuck off."

"Or what?"

"You really wanna do this?" Glenn asked him as he pulled me to my feet. "Or do you just wanna walk away?"

The two men stood there like rams ready to lock horns, and then Gil turned and left without a backward glance. All the Holloway men had crappy tempers apparently.

"Thanks," I said, touching my face, making sure my right eye was still in my head. "Shit, that hurts."

"Well, I expect so," he said matter-of-factly, picking my hat up from where it had fallen in the dirt. He didn't give it back to me, just held it. "Come on." He grabbed my arm.

I rolled my shoulder so he had to let me go. "Just—I'm done with being manhandled for one day, all right?"

"Sure," he agreed, pointing down the row of concession stands. "Walk that way."

I didn't realize that the White Ash had a food booth where they made steak plates. I was directed behind the counter, and since he couldn't hold himself back anymore, he had to manhandle me. He shoved me down into a chair and then walked away. I watched the flurry of activity going on around me. There was an enormous grill, and the man there was brushing steaks with sauce, checking the charcoal as well as the flame, and frying mushrooms over the open flame on the opposite side. Another man was slicing the cooked steaks into bite-sized pieces and dropping them into huge metal bowls. The next man in the production line was frying onions, sweet potato wedges, and russet potato wedges. At the final station, salad was being tossed and coleslaw mixed.

"God, it smells amazing in here," I told Glenn when he stepped back in front of me.

"Uh-huh," he grunted before he slapped a steak over my eye.

"Owww, shit!" I yelled. He had not been gentle at all.

"Sorry."

He wasn't sorry one little bit.

"Lemme see," he said, hand on my chin, tipping my head back to look at my nose. "What did you say to make him take a poke at you?"

"He wants his sister Carly to marry Rand."

"Still?" an incredulous voice asked.

I chuckled as a woman stepped in beside Glenn. She held out some Tylenol for me.

"That woman's been wanting Rand Holloway for years. I suspect if she was going to get him, it would've happened already."

"Thank you." I smiled, taking the pills and the water. "I'm Stefan Joss."

"I know who you are." She nodded. "And I'm Gladys, Gladys Showalter. I work for Mr. Holloway here."

"Pleasure to meet you," I said, shaking her hand after I took the Tylenol, and passing her back the empty water glass.

"Feel better," she said, patting Glenn's shoulder before she left to return to taking food orders at the front.

"What does Gladys do on your ranch?"

"She cooks and cleans, keeps my father and me from starving," he said, gesturing for me to replace the steak on my eye. "And she's right. Carly's been holdin' out for Rand for as long as I can remember."

"Oh, yeah? Did she and Rand ever get together?"

"Nope, 'cause Rand only screws girls at the rodeo who don't wanna keep him."

"Nothing serious."

"That's right."

"And Carly is not the kind of girl you fuck at the rodeo."

"No, sir. She's the kind you court at the rodeo, follow home, and marry."

"So Rand passed on Carly."

"Yep. All Rand wanted to do when he got here was drink and screw and ride the bull."

"Rand's a bull rider?"

"He does some saddle bronc as well, but yeah, Rand's the guy who normally rides the bull for the Red Diamond."

I could only imagine how hot the man looked doing that.

"Poor Carly, I used to watch her fawning all over him only to have him leave with some other woman, most times more than one a night."

"So Rand was a dog."

"He was more than that."

"And she still wants him."

"You always want what you can't have."

"I'm surprised Gil would want a man who treated his sister so badly to marry her."

"I think Gil's more interested in the Red Diamond than Rand."

"Gil could maybe use a loan?"

"I suspect so."

"Carly says you're a pig."

"She should know. At last year's rodeo, when Rand didn't show, she set her sights on me."

"And?"

"And nothin'. Do I look like I'm about to be a stand-in for Rand Holloway?"

"No."

"That's right. I ain't no consolation prize. I'm smarter than that."

"Oh, you're very smart." I smiled at him. "The way you made sure that Rand went to the Sarasota for the weekend—very nicely played."

But he didn't look happy or smug. "You won't believe me, so I ain't sayin' nothin'."

"Go ahead and say. I might even believe you."

He squinted at me. "I forgot the damn rodeo was this weekend. When I called my father to tell him I was on my way back and I wasn't goin' to Zach's since Rand was, he reminded me about this."

"But you didn't call Rand."

"Fuck no, not after that whole mess."

I nodded.

"How did you find out about the rodeo?"

"A very nice lady called me. I think I need to send her a card or something."

He crossed his arms as he looked at me. "None of us knew that Rand put you on the goddamn deed for his ranch."

"Why would you?"

"Seems like a lot to give."

"Aren't you going to give your wife half when you get married?"

"For one, I ain't never gettin' married, and for two, you ain't the man's wife."

"No, I'm not, but I'm as close as he's ever gonna get."

He grunted.

"You doubt me?"

"I don't think anything about it. All I do know is it seems that Carly's shit outta luck. Again." He cackled.

The man had a lot of wicked in him, and for better or worse, I was warming up to him.

"Yeah." I smiled wide, lifting the steak off my eye and offering it to him. "May I trade this one in for a cooked one, please?"

"God, you're a pain in the ass."

"Can I have mushrooms too?"

He made me leave the raw meat on my eye, but he brought me back a plate with steak and mushrooms and fries smothered in cheese and ranch dressing and bacon bits. I had coleslaw on the side.

"Thank you," I said sincerely as I sat up, unconcerned about my eye.

"Lemme see." He stilled me, checking it as I started shoveling food into my mouth.

The food was so good. "You guys should have a restaurant," I told him.

"Could you maybe chew and not talk with your mouth full so I can understand what the hell you just said?"

I swallowed hard and looked up at him. "You should have a restaurant. This is amazing."

He nodded and left me again, only to return seconds later with a huge cup of Pepsi and a Ziploc bag of ice.

"Why're you being so nice?"

"'Cause, you damn fool, you just got hit in the face."

"Thanks."

"Don't mention it."

"You should really sell this in a building where people can come all the time," I told him. "A restaurant would be a good investment."

"Oh yeah? Tell my father."

"He doesn't think so?"

"He thinks it's different at the rodeo and other events we sponsor because it's special, since folks can't get it all the time. He thinks if we had a restaurant, the appeal would be short-lived and we'd lose a ton of money."

"Oh, I disagree," I told him. "If you ever wanna try, call me, and I can put together a marketing plan for you and crunch numbers. I bet it would be easy to get investors. You wouldn't even need your dad."

He got very still, wary.

"Glenn?"

"Are you fuckin' with me?"

"Why would I do that?"

"Because I just got through fuckin' with Rand."

"Yeah, but that's your bullshit with him. This is different. This could be your life."

He was looking at me so intently.

"I could help you if you let me."

His eyes, which were really the most magnificent shade of peacock blue, did not leave mine. It was like he was checking for something.

"Glenn?"

"Eat your food."

After I finished everything, I let my head loll back, put the bag of ice on my eye, closed both, and relaxed. I didn't realize I had drifted off until I heard someone yell. When I opened my eyes, I found that my hat had fallen forward over my eyes and that the Ziploc bag of ice was gone. Tipping the brown straw hat back, I saw a woman holding on to Glenn's arm, her long red fingernails digging into his skin.

"Glenn Holloway, the bachelor auction begins right at six, so you best get all cleaned up and in your Sunday best before I call for you."

He looked like an animal caught in a trap.

I snorted out a laugh.

"Megan, I—"

"Oh, no." The cute bottle-blonde cut him off. "You swore to me and so did your daddy. I expect you to be there."

He looked very uncomfortable. Her eyes then slid over to me.

"And you are?"

"Stefan Joss," I said, standing up, massaging the back of my neck where it ached a little.

Her eyes were the colors of cornflowers. "From where?"

"The Red Diamond."

She tipped her head, narrowing the blue to mere slits. "Rand Holloway, did he come?"

Of course she knew who Rand was. "No, ma'am."

"You look married to me, Mr. Joss. Are you married?"

"I live with somebody, uhm?"

She thrust her hand at me. "Megan Reed."

"Pleasure." I smiled, taking her hand.

"I need someone to help with the bachelor auction, Mr. Joss."

"I've been to at least ten in my life."

Her face lit up as she clutched my hand. "Are you serious?"

"They do well as charity fundraisers as long as the guys are hot."

"Cowboys in Wranglers," she said like I was nuts. "What could be hotter?"

So help me God, I didn't say anything.

"Will you be my assistant?"

"Oh, honey, I would love to."

Her catch of breath made me smile.

"Oh, for fuck's sake," Glenn growled beside me.

Finally I was back in my element; charity events were something I knew how to do.

"Come with me," she said, taking my hand, tugging. "Oh my God, I'm so excited!" Her squeal of happiness was loud.

"You best watch yourself, Stefan Joss!" Glenn called after me. "Don't do nothin' stupid!"

I flipped him off as I walked away.

"Fuck!" I heard him croak back.

EVERETT WAS fit to be tied. Chase was spitting nails. Tom called me names, and Pierce growled. Not one of them wanted anything to do with a bachelor auction. They would absolutely never… ever… in a million… and then we reached the stage area, and they saw all the women. An ocean of women, hundreds of them were there just waiting for a chance to have a cowboy, if only for one night, one dream date. Suddenly I was brilliant, absolutely and without doubt fucking brilliant, and being bid on like a piece of meat was flattering instead of something sleazy.

I had not pressed Chris to participate because I had realized a year ago that he wasn't conceited or angry. He was shy. So when he leaned quietly next to me and said that he wouldn't mind being in the auction, I smiled wide.

"Holy shit." Megan was stunned when she turned and found me there in front of her.

I gave her a slow grin, watching her mouth fall open, her eyes go round.

"You… Stefan…."

The thing was, I cleaned up nice. I had ditched the whole cowboy vibe because it didn't matter anymore if I fit in or not. By the reaction of most people, I wasn't going to anyway. What did matter was that I had brought my men to the rodeo, and we had swept the events thus far.

Calf roping, team roping, barrel racing, and steer wrestling were behind us, and the next day we were facing saddle bronc, bareback bronc riding, and bull riding. Apparently by the number of people who had come up to congratulate me on the performance my men turned in, we were a shoo-in to sweep every category. I was trying not to smile like an idiot and strut around the place.

"I think I should auction you off, Stefan." Her breath fluttered. "I think I could make a lot of money."

My jeans were too tight, my hair was gelled to artistic perfection, and the bracelets I wore were back. The oversized watch with the thick biker band, all the details that had been hidden away so I could pass for serious rancher, were returned. The dress shirt clung to me, open lower than just the collar and unbuttoned at the bottom to show skin and how low the denim was riding on my hips. Anyone who was looking could not miss my display of sleek gold skin. I had been hiding, and now I wanted everyone to see me.

"Can I have the microphone?" I asked her.

She passed it to me, and I wandered out on stage as soon as the band wrapped up their song. I held out a hand for the lead singer, and he moved his guitar around to his back, held there by the strap, and took my hand in both of his. The only way I could tell they were a country band were the hats. Other than that—jeans, T-shirts, boots—they could have been a grunge band or alternative. But I had met them earlier, and they had been very happy to meet me. A master of ceremonies always kept things moving and on track, and they appreciated that.

"Let's hear it for Bootlegger, everybody," I called out, "and show them how much we appreciate them coming out tonight to entertain us!"

Thunderous applause as all eyes came to rest on me.

"I'm Stefan Joss from the Red Diamond, and I want to welcome you all to the Truscott Rodeo bachelor auction and dance."

Whistling, more applause, and catcalls greeted my introduction, and then I asked the ladies if they were ready to get them a cowboy.

The screaming started immediately, and my smile went neon. I was there to auction off hot men in skintight denim, worn boots, and Stetsons. Oh, I was so very popular.

I had twenty men to find homes for, and I did it four at a time, with the band playing three songs between each. I made a big deal out of every cowboy, giving kudos to Rand's men without running down anybody else. When Chris went up, and he was bid on fast and furious, the shy smile he gave me was very sweet. We had people line dancing on stage with me, women planting kisses on the band, and the event sponsors who visited the side of the stage when we were taking a break wanted to shake my hand. Megan nearly smothered me to death and told me over and over that already we had tripled the money from the year before and we still had men left to auction off. Hud Lawrence came by personally to thank me.

When I retook the stage after our intermission, the applause was deafening. The band launched into an improvised rendition of Queen's "Somebody to Love," and the place went nuts. I was laughing hard, Megan was bawling and clapping her hands, and the band was really into it. We got the lighters in the air, and everybody was singing along. When the song finally finished after what felt like a good hour, the applause went on and on and on.

Glenn took the stage after that, and I begged the women in the crowd to please take the man home and love him hard. It was crude and hot and even the man's scathing look could not stifle me. I was on an adrenaline high.

He pointed at me like he was going to beat the crap out of me. I waved.

The bids came loud and lewd, and the look on Glenn's face made me double over with laughter. Rand's cousin went for a thousand dollars, which made him the most expensive bachelor of the night. As I awarded him to Miss Rachel Webber from the Triple Star ranch, he shot me a look, which I couldn't read. I wasn't sure if it was surprise, anger, or fear, so I went with thinking he was flattered, put him out of my mind, and sang along with the band as they covered "Life Is a Highway" so the crowd could sing at the top of their lungs again.

All my bachelors were swept up, and when it was done, the band asked me what I wanted to hear. At which point, I caught sight of Glenn's father and had them sing some vintage ELO for me. "Don't Bring Me Down" came out as a driving rendition that was so loud, between the band and the crowd, that no one even noticed I was singing along in the microphone.

I hung up my master of ceremonies duties after that, and the appreciation was overwhelming. Megan hugged me so hard, and told me again that she thought I would be worth more than Glenn Holloway. I dragged her down into the crowd, and when I waved up at Blake onstage, he launched into "Crazy Little Thing Called Love" just to round out the set of oldies but goodies. Megan enjoyed dancing with me, and we moved well together. When another man came and cut in, I moved away even though she tried to hold on to me. But he was cute and I wasn't available, so I gave her a waggle of eyebrow, and she let me go.

I went to the side of the stage and reached a hand up for Blake. I got back a card with their contact information and a number scrawled on the back. When my eyes met his, he mouthed the words *cell number* and *call me*, and I put it in the back pocket of my jeans much to his very apparent delight.

Darting to the edge of the dancing area, I started back toward the trailer.

"Stefan!"

I looked over my shoulder and saw Glenn Holloway. I didn't stop walking.

"Will you fuckin' wait!"

But I kept my runway stride going, making him work to catch up. "Why aren't you dancing with Rachel Webber?"

"What?" He was indignant.

"The very pretty girl who could not keep her hands off of you."

"I—"

"The one who bought you," I teased him.

"That date ain't for tonight. I've got bull ridin' to do tomorrow."

He sounded so indignant. "I see. Well, you should still be dancing with her anyway."

"Why ain't you dancin' with the singer?"

I stopped suddenly, and he took two steps by before he rounded on me. "I'm sorry?"

"I saw how he was lookin' at you."

Why in the world was he trying to interpret any kind of look that he saw pass between me and the lead singer? "And how was that?"

"Like he was interested."

Why did he care?

"Rand ain't here. No one would know."

"I would know," I told him, crossing my arms. "And the lead singer isn't gay."

"He's not?"

"No, sir, he's not."

"Then what was with the card?"

"I think maybe he wants me to call him if I ever have need for a band."

He looked very disgruntled, and I had to smile at him.

"I can't believe you acted like that tonight. Rand would die of embarrassment."

"Embarrassed of what precisely?"

"Are you kidding? You made a total spectacle of yourself all night, made people think the Red Diamond is a joke, and dragged Rand's reputation through the dirt."

"Lemme understand this," I said, pinning him there with my gaze. "We raised more money for charity this year than they did in the last five and—"

"How the hell do you know that?" he yelled at me.

"Because Hud Lawrence told me," I cracked sarcastically. "How do you think?"

He looked like he was ready to punch me.

"The Red Diamond swept all the rodeo events, and people had a great time tonight, but somehow, in your mind, in your world, Rand's reputation got damaged. Why, because I was dancing? Was I dancing too gay? Do you think everyone knows?"

"Yessir, I think everyone of 'em knows you're gay!"

"And who gives a damn?"

"You could get yourself killed."

"Because they're all coming after me."

"They could be."

"Well, here I am."

There was only silence.

I made a big show of listening.

"You're really a wiseass, you know that?"

"Where's the angry mob? Are they late?"

He closed the distance between us and shoved me back hard.

"Is that all you got?"

"I should beat the shit outta you."

"Call Gil Landry; I'm sure he'd love to help you."

His snarl of outrage let me know how really drunk he was. The man was not all that solid on his own feet.

"Jesus," I laughed, grabbing his arms, steadying him. "You are wound so fuckin' tight, man, what the hell?"

His head snapped up and his eyes met mine. I was swallowed in inky blue a minute before he swept his heavy-lidded gaze over me, from head to toe. He missed nothing.

I had to think a second and process.

Did I see what I thought I saw or not? Was Rand Holloway's homophobic cousin actually checking me out?

“Glenn,” I gasped his name, watching the muscles in his jaw cord.

He yanked away from my hands, and we stood there, staring, silent.

“You,” he said, his voice hoarse, gruff. “How come you’re so….”

“What?” I asked when I was sure he wasn’t going to finish his sentence.

He didn’t answer, just took a step forward.

“Glenn?” I had to tilt my head back to hold his gaze.

“Are you gonna come watch me ride the bull?”

“Sure,” I said softly.

“Do me a favor and wear real clothes tomorrow.”

“Okay.”

“Not jeans like this,” he said, eyes trailing down my body, “and this shirt is bullshit.”

“Okay.”

“It’s barely on,” he said, his hand slowly fisting in the crushed silk.

I stood still, feeling the back of his knuckles against my chest, my skin. “Glenn.”

He turned suddenly and strode away. I had no idea what was going on in his mind, but I became aware of the whimpering behind me seconds later. When I looked toward the corral, I saw her there, head between the slats, looking at me, big brown eyes wet with happiness because she was looking at me. She was so well trained, as was my mare Ruby. The horse was standing in the corral chilling, and the dog had been keeping vigil, neither one of them a bother in any way.

But now the dog wanted to be allowed to see me up close.

“Come here,” I called Bella.

She was through the slats and bounding up to me, wiggling, whining, and dancing around my legs, in ecstasy now that I had returned. I bent to pet her, and she shoved her nose in my eye before she licked my nose and bumped my chin. And then she was suddenly rigid, hair standing up, stepping in front of me, pressed to my side.

“Stefan Joss!”

I rose as Rayland Holloway closed in on me, breathing fire, chewing brimstone. He looked more pissed off than usual.

“Is it true?”

I wanted to be mad at him, but frankly he looked too much like Rand, too much like Glenn, whom I was really warming to, and a lot like his brother, Rand and Charlotte's late father James, for me to dredge up any hate for him. And Tyler. He looked like Uncle Tyler too.

"Is what true, sir?" I called out to him as he charged toward me.

"Did you just—what the hell is wrong with your dog?"

Bella had put her head down, bared her teeth, and made a noise I had no idea she could make. It was obvious from the snarl of warning that she was ready to unleash teeth and claws.

"Just stop walking like that," I told him. "That's seventy, almost seventy-five pounds of angry, threatened dog there."

He stopped moving, and I saw something flicker across his face. Interest?

"She's a Rhodesian Ridgeback."

"A what?" he snapped at me.

I repeated the name. "You wanna see her?"

"No, I don't wanna see—"

"She's actually very sweet, but you're freaking her out with how you're moving."

"I ain't moving in no—"

"And I bet your dogs would protect you if I came at you the same way you just came at me."

He glared at me.

I pointed to the picnic table close by. He stalked over to it and sat down. After a minute, I followed him and took a seat at the other end of the bench.

We sat there in silence for several minutes, and Bella, having trailed after me, was there like my shadow, her head resting in my lap. As I sat there, my mind drifting, it occurred to me that all the time Glenn and I had been talking, Bella had watched, and not once did she growl or bark to alert me of her presence. As fiercely protective as she was, what was it about Glenn Holloway that didn't make her think he was going to hurt me?

"Dog's too big to work cattle."

The gruff comment brought me from my thoughts.

"No," I told him. "Even German Shepherds were originally bred to be herding dogs. You're just not used to seeing it."

We lapsed into another silence.

He finally lifted his hand, and I told Bella to go. She went to him and instead of sitting there and waiting, she put her head in his lap just as she had me.

His grunt before he petted her, scratched behind her ears, and rubbed under her chin made me understand that the wall was not as hard or as high as I thought.

"This can't just be about me," I started what I hoped would be a long conversation. "I just got here, only even been around for two years. There has to be more."

"I don't abide sodomites."

A word I had not heard directed at me, probably ever. Other words, lots of them, had been leveled at me at one time or another, but that one was new. "Yeah, but all this animosity because of that? I don't buy it."

"Yeah, well, believe what you want."

"So when Rand was married to Jenny, you all got along like peas and carrots?"

He turned and scowled at me.

The *Forrest Gump* reference was lost on him. "Well?"

He went back to looking out across the open range. Where our trailers were, and the stable and corral we had been assigned, was at the very edge of the grounds. Beyond us was just brush and grass and dirt and endless sky.

"So you weren't all singing 'Kumbayah' together, were you, sir?"

"I have no idea what you just said."

"Why the bad blood between you and Rand? I heard you wanted the ranch, and he said no."

Nothing, not even a nibble, but he had come to see me for some reason.

"Did you, too, come to yell at me about being master of ceremonies tonight?"

"Why? Who else yelled at you?"

"Glenn."

He grunted his approval. "Did he give you the eye?"

"No, Gil Landry did. And it's not that bad."

"Landry? Why?"

"He wants his sister to marry Rand."

"Or Glenn," he growled. "He just wants a Holloway, any one will do."

"I think Carly wants Rand."

"And maybe when he throws you out on your ass, she can have him."

"Maybe," I sighed.

He turned his brilliant eyes on me. "Don't flaunt yourself in front of people no more."

"Flaunt myself?"

"You showin' folks you're queer is gonna get you in trouble."

"When did I do that?"

"What?"

"Show people I was queer?"

"Just—wear somethin' else."

It was my choice in clothes again.

"You're dressed like a rock star."

Like the man had any idea how rock stars dressed. "I thought I looked gay."

He growled at me. "I don't want no one to hurt you is all."

"You don't give a crap if I get hurt."

"If you get hurt, then Rand—" He rubbed his forehead, having stopped himself. "There's enough. There don't need to be no more."

"So you want me to be careful because if I get hurt, Rand will blame you?"

"I'm here, ain't I?" he snapped at me. "If somethin' were to happen to you and he knows that I—just stay out of sight, all right?"

Be safe. "Why do you care? I thought you hated Rand."

"He—"

"You wanted to buy the ranch, and he told you to go to hell."

"He was too young to take on that goddamn ranch alone!" he yelled at me, which, for whatever reason, did not startle my dog. Perhaps it was because she had heard his voice crack just like I did. He sounded like he was in pain.

"You wanted to help?" I said thoughtfully.

He moved like he was going to turn toward me, but stopped at the last moment, forcing himself to remain still. "He was only a boy."

"He was in his midtwenties," I corrected him.

"It was a lot of responsibility to shoulder all alone."

The man had wanted to help. I saw it clearly. "What did you want?"

"I wanted to put the two ranches, the Red Diamond and the White Ash, together. I never wanted to buy the ranch and put him off it."

"The Red Diamond was, is, his father's legacy. How could he not keep it forever?"

He cleared his throat. "Rand…."

I waited, but he just shook his head.

"Sir?"

His head turned to me, and I saw the same electric turquoise-blue eyes that the man I loved had. They were similar to Charlotte's. I used to think hers and Rand's were the same, but hers were darker, like Glenn's, like their father's had been. Only Rand and Rayland had the same bright, distinctive, blue.

Electric blue.

Turquoise.

A blue you never forgot. A blue you noticed.

And only Rayland and Rand had them.

In the whole family.

But…. I squinted at him, and he looked away.

He cleared his throat. "I saw Rand at the Paulson auction in Sweetwater four months back. Did he tell you that?"

"No."

"He looked good," he said, and I realized he wasn't really listening to me, lost in thought, thinking about Rand, a wistful look on his face. It was obvious that Rand was important to him, but that made no sense.

I was so confused. *Does he hate Rand or not?* And I knew Rand looked good. Why tell me that he…. "I take good care of him," I told the older man, wanting him to know.

"Yeah, I done seen a change in him."

It was like being out in the middle of nowhere without a map. You had no idea which way to go. He had seen a change in Rand? He saw that the man was being taken care of? He accepted that fact, remarked on it, but still….

"Do you have a plan not to get killed?"

I was really so very lost. "I'm sorry?"

He turned to look at me. "For tomorrow, what's your plan?"

If he could start speaking English, it would be a bonus. "Could you tell me what you're talking about, please?"

"Well, I know you ain't fool enough to ride a bull 'cause it might just kill you when you're thrown off, so I was wondering which you were doin', the saddle bronc or bareback."

I had a very funny retort lined up for barebacking, but the question seeped into me and killed every trace of humor. "You're asking me seriously what rodeo event I'm participating in?"

"Yep."

“Why would I do anything but watch?”

“Well, because every rancher here has got to do an event. Glenn is riding the bull for the White Ash. Rand usually does the bull riding for the Red, but you can’t do that. You’ll get yourself killed. What event are you doin’?”

I had the urge to laugh, but I squelched it. Wait until I told Everett that I was planning to break my neck. “And if the rancher doesn’t participate in the event?”

“Then the grazing rights transfer custody, of course.”

Of course, of course, how stupid of me.

“I thought you would do one of the events today, something easier, but you’re fixin’ to get thrown in the arena. I will admit to looking forward to it.”

Shit.

“You get killed in the ring, that ain’t my fault.”

“Sir.” I cleared my throat, ready to change the subject. I wanted to talk to him, and continuing on about the next day’s events would make me crazy. One catastrophe at a time was all I could handle, and I had things I wanted answers to. Like why in the hell did Rand Holloway and this man have the same exact color eyes? Talking to Everett about which event I might be able to walk away from with my spine still in one piece would have to wait. “Would you tell me about your ranch?”

“What the hell for?” he growled at me.

“I’d just like to hear.”

“Why?”

“Why not?”

He was silent.

“What’s it like?”

“Whaddya mean?”

“How big is the main house?”

“It has twelve rooms.”

“Oh, shit.”

“My father, Henry Holloway, built the White Ash thinking all his sons would live on it and work it together, but Tyler and James and Cyrus all left.”

“So the White Ash belongs just to you or to the others as well?”

“Just to me. All the rest gave up their rights to it when they left to start their own ranches.”

Tyler had owned a ranch? I badly needed a history lesson on the Holloways. "So you have room for me, then."

"Where?"

"At your ranch. You have room, so I could visit."

"I suspect so."

"Okay, then, I wanna see it."

"Suit yourself," he told me.

Suit myself? So I could stay there if I wanted to even though he hated me. How did that make any sense at all? The man had spit at my feet, but now I could pop over to his place for a beer? "Mr. Holloway, sir, you are not making a lot of sense."

"Oh, no?"

"No," I said, looking him in the eyes.

"Rand," he said, clearing his throat. "He cares for you, does he?"

Why did that even matter? "Yes."

He nodded, gave Bella a final pat, and then got up and walked away without another word.

"What the fuck?" I said to my dog.

She tipped her head like I was the one who was confused.

Going into the trailer, I got out of my pseudo club clothes, took a quick shower, and was lying in bed trying to think of who to call when it hit me, and I dialed Rand's mother, May.

"Stefan honey," she greeted me, and I could hear her smiling into the phone. "What a nice surprise."

"Hi, May, I hope it's not too late to call."

"It's only eleven at night, sweetheart. I'm not that old."

"Yes, ma'am," I sighed.

"What's on your mind?"

"I'm confused."

"About what?"

"Rayland Holloway."

There was a loud bang and I realized that she'd dropped the phone on the floor.

"May?"

I heard her swear, which she never did, and then there was fumbling. She was good and flustered.

Quick cough before I got her back. "I'm sorry, I lost the—now what'd you say?"

"I need you to tell me about Rayland Holloway."

"Rayland?"

Her voice, the timbre of it, up so high, basically sealed the deal for me. I knew what I needed to already. I just wanted to hear the story from her.

"What about him?"

"Could you run over the story for me, please?"

"What story is that?" she asked, her voice dripping with sugar.

"Why he's fighting with Rand."

"Sweetheart, he—"

"Please," I begged her. "I want to understand."

"How would I—"

"They have the same eyes, May."

"Who does?"

"I'm not stupid. Please don't talk to me like I am."

There was a long sigh. "What would you like to know?"

"Who's oldest?"

"What?" She laughed, but it was forced, breathless.

"Of the Holloway brothers."

"Oh, well Tyler's the oldest, then James, then Cyrus, and then Rayland."

"Rayland said that Tyler had his own ranch too."

"He used to."

"What happened to it?"

"Well." Her voice evened out, and she sounded better because we were off Rayland and talking about something else. She was back on solid ground. "Sweetheart, Tyler used to drink quite a bit, and he went through a lot of women, and the last one, Dawn, well she wasn't like the others. She was smart. I think that's why she was the only one he really loved, but—and I really liked her, and what she did was wrong, but her reasons for doing it were sound."

"What'd she do?"

"Well, when she divorced Tyler, she took the ranch because by that time her name was on everything. And she did it for the people who lived on it and for the future of the ranch, but she put Tyler out of his home, and that nearly killed him."

"Does she still run the ranch?"

"Her son does."

"Tyler's son?"

"Mmmm-hmmm."

Jesus. "I thought Tyler didn't have any children."

"He has a son and a daughter."

"Christ, nobody tells me anything," I groused at her.

She laughed at me. "Well, sugar, it's not like they're close. I doubt Tyler's seen those kids in twenty years."

"Why?"

"You have to understand how broken he was after the divorce, Stef. He left with his tail between his legs and went to work as a roughneck in the oil fields."

"Then what?"

"Well, then James went to see him in Midland one summer. I don't remember when—I think right after Charlotte was born—and when he came home, Tyler was with him. James made him foreman, gave him the foreman's house, and he's been living on the Red Diamond ever since. He has been devoted to the ranch and first to James and then to Rand."

"That's so sad."

"Yes, it is, since his own son has a wonderful home and his daughter is a doctor in the same town. His kids are fine people. It's a shame he doesn't know them."

"You think he would ever want to?"

"At this point, that's not his call to make. It's theirs. If they want to see him, they know exactly where he is."

"Maybe he should extend them an invitation."

"He did maybe six years ago, and they both told him to go to hell."

I felt bad for Tyler, though his son and daughter's reaction made sense too. "Your family is a mess, May."

"The Holloways are a mess, Stef, not the Millers. My people actually talk to one another. They are not hard, stoic cowboys."

"Is Dawn still alive?"

"No, she passed about two years ago. She had breast cancer."

"That's too bad."

"Yes, it was. I still miss her."

"Did she remarry?"

"No. Holloway men are hard to get over."

It had taken May over twelve years to even think about loving another man after Rand's father had died. She had ended up marrying a very sweet man, Tate Langley, who was the complete opposite of the force of nature that her first husband was.

"Maybe if Tyler had passed, but he broke Dawn's heart. My cowboy never did that."

"Okay," I said, processing. "Now Rayland."

"Yes?" She was suddenly breathless again.

"Is he married?"

"He was. He's widowed now. Lily died five years ago come February."

"What did she look like?"

"Strange question." She hesitated.

"I'm just trying to figure something out, and I might have to draw out a Punnett square from high school biology class."

"Well, she was beautiful, part Comanche. Rayland's son Zach has her eyes, that lovely chocolate brown."

"I see. So Rayland has Glenn, who has dark blue eyes like James and Charlotte, and his son's Zach's are brown."

"Yes."

"And Rayland and Rand have the bright blue."

"Well, yes, they—"

"May?"

"Yes, Stefan?"

"Just because I'm blond doesn't mean I'm stupid. It's a myth, actually."

Silence on the other end.

"About blonds."

"Yes."

"May."

"Stefan, just—"

"I know why the man is so pissed, May, but he's hiding it behind homophobia and land rights and a whole mess of other stuff."

After a minute, I realized she was crying.

"Please tell me."

"You know already."

I took a breath. "Does Rand know that Rayland is his father?"

"No."

"Does Charlotte know?"

"Of course not!"

She was going to have a seizure when she found out. "That was brave of you, not telling her."

"Stefan, why are you even thinking about Rayland? How do you even know him?"

"Because we're spending quality time together here at the rodeo." I exhaled sharply.

"I'm sorry, where are you?"

"I'm at the Truscott Rodeo with the men, securing the grazing rights."

Several moments of silence ticked by.

"Oh my God, Stefan," she gasped. "How did you even know that—"

"A very nice lady called me."

"Stef, honey, you can't be there."

"Too late, I'm here."

"And Rand is where?"

"With Zach at his ranch."

"Whatever for?"

"He's helping run his dude ranch for the weekend."

"And he has no idea that the rodeo was the same weekend?"

"No."

"So you're there in Truscott taking care of things."

"Yes."

"No, no, no, Stef, honey, if you're there in Rand's place, you have to participate in an event."

I should have talked to her earlier. "Yeah, I just heard this."

"Sweetheart, what are you planning to do?"

"Saddle bronc, bareback, or—"

"No!"

"At least if I rode the bull, it would be over fast."

"Stefan!"

"Who cares, May. I'll get thrown off either a horse or a bull tomorrow. That's fine. The important issue here is not me but Rayland. You do know that it's killing him not to claim his son. You do know that."

"I do," she whimpered, and I could hear the tears ready to pour out of her.

"Tell me what happened, May, please."

It had been, she told me, a love affair.

The first time May Miller saw Rayland Holloway, she was smitten at first glance. He loved her back, but he was young and had still been the roaming kind, not the settling-down kind. She was ready to be a wife, to get married and start a family. Just the thought sent him running to the rodeo circuit. A month after he left, May discovered she was pregnant. Alone and afraid, she turned to her parents, fearing for the worst. They had surprised the hell out of her. They were both looking forward to seeing their grandchild.

"You have no idea about some people, Stef, until you test them."

So there was May, prepared to be a single parent, working at her father's feed store when, three months later, James Holloway returned from Vietnam, just stopping to see his father on his way through town, excited to start his own ranch and begin a life in Winston away from his family. He was ready to be his own man, removed from his father's shadow. Henry Holloway had been thrilled at the change in his son, in the fire he saw in him, and gave him his blessing as well as the down payment for the land that he would build the Red Diamond on. James was excited to commit to his life, to the building of his dreams, and to finding a woman to share it all with. When he stopped at the store to pay his respects to her father, he saw May. She had grown up while he was away fighting on the other side of the world, and when he looked at her with his eyes on the future, ready to build his life from the ground up, he saw the woman whom he wanted to live his dream with him.

She had been flattered by the attention James lavished on her, but in the end it was only fair that she confessed the truth, that she was carrying his brother's child. She was surprised for the second time in a short amount of time when James told her that he didn't give a damn. He loved May—had, she found out, always loved her—and he would adore and shelter the child she was carrying. She wasn't convinced. So he went first to ask her father for her hand, and then he brought her a ring. When she told him no, she went home to fall apart in her bedroom. Her father sat with her while she sobbed, and told her the choice was hers. She could stay with him and her mother forever, but he thought maybe she should take a chance on a Holloway. The first had been too young, just a boy, but this one, James, was a man.

They were married and moved to Winston the following month. Rand was born five months later, and they waited to call and tell people until another four months had passed. No one could make the trip right away, and that was fine with James and May. With the timetable covered, they were free to go on with their lives without anyone knowing the truth, that Rand was not James Holloway's biological son.

Three years later, Rayland Holloway, finally ready to settle down, finished with the rodeo and, having married a woman he met in Tulsa, was on his way through Winston headed for home. He was bringing his new wife with him to his father's ranch, a ranch he would take over when Henry Holloway passed, and decided to stop to visit his brother. He was planning to tease May about how one Holloway was, it seemed, just as good as the other. It was a surprise visit, but it turned out that James and May were not the ones in for the shock of their lives.

He had driven down the long drive that led to the main house, and when he and Lily got out, they saw a little boy hanging on the fence. When he turned to them, Rayland almost passed out. May came out on the porch, saw his face, made one of her own, and he knew everything that she had wanted to hide. But James was there too, and he invited Lily inside for some lemonade. It took Rayland two days to finally get May alone and drag the truth from her. She had told him that James knew and that none of them would ever speak of it.

Rayland wanted his son.

May told him that Rand was James's son and not his.

"You even named him after me." Rayland's voice had cracked wide open.

And she had, to be fair, but that was all in the past.

Rayland said he would divorce Lily and she could divorce James, and they could be married. But May would not do that to a man who was faithful and loving and whom she had come to love more than she even thought possible. As she placed her hand on her abdomen, she told him that she was pregnant with James's child and he should make peace with his life. He and Lily, she was certain, would have beautiful children of their own.

"Can I ask," I sighed deeply, "what James thought about Rand?"

"No father was ever prouder or loved their son more, Stef," she told me. "You have to understand, Rand loved James, and James loved both his children fiercely and protectively. He knew Charlotte was the only one who was truly his, but Rand and he were exactly the same. All the values, the love of their family, of the land, their way of life, all of it… they were the same person. James passed on everything to Rand. I look at my son and don't see Rayland: I see James."

I swallowed hard. "So what happened between you and Rayland?"

"He went home to his father's ranch, the White Ash, and nine months after he married Lily, Glenn was born."

"And after James died?"

"Rayland came to buy the ranch, and Rand told him to go to hell. It was hard, watching them, because Rand was grieving for his father, and Rayland was there, right in front of him, wanting to tell him everything. It was horrible."

"Rayland says he didn't want to buy the ranch, just put the two together."

"When did he tell you this?"

"Tonight."

"You asked him?" she choked out.

"May, you know me. Of course I asked him."

"Jesus."

"But like I said, he says he didn't want to buy it."

"Well, all I know is what Rand told me, and Rand said the man wanted to buy it and then sell it, and Rand was not about to ever let that happen."

"Sounds like they maybe weren't actually listening to each other."

"Could be."

"May?"

"Yes?"

"I know you loved James. I saw you at his funeral. When did you fall in love with him?"

"I loved him for a long time, but after Charlotte was born…." She sighed. "I saw how much he really loved Rand."

"I don't understand."

"Well, for three years, I figured that James was doing the best he could to love Rand, but that when a child of his own came along, that I would see the difference, and I might have to leave him. Rand deserved to be loved completely by a father or not at all."

"What happened after Charlotte was born?"

"Nothing."

"You lost me."

"I mean he didn't change one bit toward Rand and treated Charlotte the exact way he had when Rand was a baby. James loved his children the same, exactly the same, and loved me like crazy," she sighed. "And when I realized that James was a man who could love my child from another man as much as his own, I fell hard."

I smiled into the phone. "You finally let yourself fall in love with your own husband."

"Oh, yes."

There was no way I couldn't ask, I had to know. "Was he happy?"

"James used to say that the blessing of his life was being loved by a good woman and his children. The man loved his family more than anything."

I knew that. I had seen him with Rand and with Charlotte. He was gruff and hard, a man of very few words, but he never failed to hug them hello and good-bye, and at the end, he had even warmed to me.

"Can I ask why you think that Rayland just doesn't tell Rand the truth himself if he wants him to know so badly?"

"Because he knows as well as I do that there is no way in hell that Rand would ever believe him. It has to come from me."

"He's never tried to blackmail you into it?"

"He has no proof of anything. What's he going to tell Rand, that they have the same color eyes?" She sighed heavily. "And the only other person Rand would have believed died a long time ago."

"Rand is his son."

"Rand is James Holloway's son. It's not who creates you, Stef, it's who raises you. You'll know what I mean once you and Rand have children. They might be half of you and half of Charlotte, but they will belong to you and Rand."

My head hurt and so did my heart. *Wouldn't Rand want his own children once this came out?*

"Stefan, honey, you're going to be a wonderful father and so will Rand. Don't let any of this put you off your plan. I know you. I know what you're thinking."

"I—"

"He wants you, Stefan, and if you think about it, Rand loves his father, and his father's genes are carried in Charlotte, not him. So really, a child out of you and Charlotte is what he wants. Does that make sense?"

It did, sort of. "God, May, this is a heavy burden to carry all these years."

"You have no idea."

"Rayland wants Rand to know."

"I know he does."

"I think it's tearing him up, and he's striking out, trying to get Rand to see him, to stay in his life, and unfortunately, right now all he's created is anger and animosity."

"Yes."

"Jesus, May—Tyler's kids, Rayland's kids, who isn't messed up?"

"Tyler's kids are doing fine, and Rand and Charlotte are both fine, thank you."

"Rand is not going to be fine and neither will Charlotte."

"Only if you tell my secrets, Stefan, and I would remind you that you have no right to. How people look at Rayland and Rand when they're together and not see that the son is almost a carbon copy of the father, I do not know. It used to twist my stomach into knots, so I was glad that we only saw them once a year at Christmas. I would see Rand with James and watch Rayland lookin' at them, and it would make me bawl like a baby."

"I gotta go," I said as my eyes filled. Christ.

"Stefan, no, I want to talk to you about the rodeo."

"It's fine, May. I'll be fine."

"Not if you die being thrown off a horse."

"Hopefully that won't happen."

"Stefan Joss!"

"Sorry."

"You need to forget about the grazing rights and get on home. Rand cares more for you, love, than he does about some land."

"No, I know." I didn't tell her that my plan was to go home with Rayland and Glenn. "Thank you for trusting me with the story, May. I love you."

"Oh honey, I love you too."

I hung up because she was crying and I was starting, and God, what a mess!

Chapter 6

I HAD gone down to where the bucking chute was, dressed, as requested, more conservatively. But I was no longer blending. The black jeans and Prada boots, the charcoal gray sweater and sunglasses looked more Hollywood than Dallas.

"Hey." I smiled at Glenn when I found him.

His eyes ran over me. "What're you doing here?"

"You asked me to come see you ride."

"From the stands, asshole."

"Oh." I nodded. "Okay."

But he caught my shoulder when I turned to go, and eased me forward toward the side of the ring.

"You can sit up here, but don't fall off."

"I'm actually pretty coordinated," I assured him.

His eyes were locked on mine.

"Did your father tell you that he's letting me come home with you guys tomorrow?"

If he was surprised, I never saw it. "No, he didn't."

"I can't wait to see the ranch, Glenn."

He cleared his throat. "So you should bring your horse around to our trailer tonight after the dance, 'cause we're leavin' around four in the morning."

"Okay."

"You can ride with me."

"Sounds good. Do you have room for Bella in your truck?"

"Who's Bella?"

"My dog."

"You're bringing your dog too?"

"If that's okay."

"Sure," he said softly, hand on the fence, leaning closer to me. "Bring your dog."

I noticed the flecks of green in his dark blue eyes. Really, all the Holloway men were just gorgeous creatures. "When we get to your ranch, I'll show you how well I can ride."

"I look forward to that," he said, reaching for me, his fingers sliding across my cheek. "Let me look at your eye."

I tilted my head so he could see, and he pressed gently at my skin.

"I am gonna kick the shit out of Gil Landry."

The man had no idea how possessive he sounded. "It's fine."

"It's not," he said as his fingertips slid down along the edge of my jaw and off me. "All right, get up there and don't move."

"Got it."

He left me then.

"What the fuck was that?"

I turned and found Everett. "Wow." I smiled wide. "Look at you. The chaps are hot."

He glared at me. "You cannot consort with the enemy."

"Take a pill," I laughed at him. "Oh hey, I need your advice. Should I ride the saddle bronc or ride the horse without a saddle?"

He turned his head to Chris, who had joined us. "Am I still drunk?"

"No, why?"

He looked back at me. "Tell Chris what you just said."

I put the same question to him that I had asked Everett. He grabbed for the fence.

"Okay." Everett pressed his lips together, turning to me. "Are you drunk?"

I had to explain fast, over Everett yelling and Chris looking like he was going to be sick, about the provision in the rights agreement.

"You can't ride saddle bronc or bareback!" Everett yelled at me. "You can't, Stef, you just can't. You'll get thrown off, and you'll die."

"I can't die. I have to go to the White Ash after."

"I'm sorry, I really am drunk," Everett deadpanned. "Did you say you were goin' to the White Ash after the rodeo?"

"Yeah."

"No."

"Yeah."

"Absolutely not," he laughed at me. "If I have to tie you up and throw you in the back of the trailer with your damn horse, that ain't happenin'. It's bad enough we did this without Rand knowing. If we go home and you ain't with us… might as well dig our graves ourselves."

"It's not like that. Rand will be fine."

"The hell you say! Rand Holloway is gonna string us all up by our balls!"

But I had bigger plans. "He won't. I'm just going for a visit with his family."

"Wait, look at me."

I rolled my eyes.

"What the fuck happened to your eye?"

"Gil Landry punched me."

His face drained of color.

"Everett," I coaxed gently. "Breathe."

"Are you kidding? Rand will—oh holy shit."

"I'll just wear these," I said, pulling the oversized sunglasses from the top of my head and putting them on. "See, no harm, no foul."

"He's gonna fuckin' kill us," Chris gagged.

"He can't actually do that."

"But he can make me want to kill myself by working me close to death."

"You're overreacting."

"If I was Gil Landry, I would be shitting bricks right about now."

"Why?"

"'Cause just 'cause you're a guy, don't mean that Rand don't see you as any less than any man here sees his wife. Gil forgot that and took a swing at you. You don't hit a man's spouse and walk away. The man should hide."

"Rand's not like that."

His eyebrows lifted. "You ain't never seen Rand Holloway really, truly angry, but I suspect you will soon."

"I've seen him mad plenty of times."

"You ain't never seen him in a fight."

"No, I haven't."

"I have. It's scary as hell. By the time he's that mad, somebody's fixin' to die."

"Well, let's not tell him, then."

"He'll see the damage, Stef."

"Not if I'm out at the White Ash."

He growled at me.

"All of you guys need to learn to use words," I teased him.

Hands were thrown up in defeat. I loved to win.

Bull riding looks cool on TV and in movies, and if there is anything as romantic as a bull rider, I don't know what that is, but really, it's scary as hell to watch. An hour later when Everett was thrown from the back of the bull and then nearly trampled, my heart stopped for just a second. But once the man was standing behind the fence, I could breathe again.

Glenn was up after him, and he was thrown off as well, but he had stayed on the longest, so the announcer called out that he had probably won. That was the good part. The bad part came seconds later when the bull charged him.

I yelled a warning, lots of people did, but it was too late for him to do anything but turn. The bull caught him, and he was thrown into the fence. I heard the sickening snap of bone from where I was.

I ran for him, falling to my knees beside him. I saw the bull and curled over him, shielding his chest and head, I waved my arm and the bull stopped, whirling, before charging again. I yelled and was relieved to see the rodeo clowns. Three of them were there, circling, keeping the bull off me and Glenn.

"Stef."

I looked down at him. "Just lie there. We don't know what's broken."

"Get," he gasped and his voice broke, "out of here before you get yourself killed."

"Me. Who gives a damn about me," I grumbled, reaching for him. "Lay still."

The ambulance was there fast, and as they were loading Glenn in the back, I darted over and shook each man's hand who had saved my life. I guessed that the guys dressed as clowns didn't normally get thanked, from their bemused expressions. They seemed genuinely pleased that I had taken the time to express my appreciation. I ran back and got into the ambulance, and we whipped out of the arena.

"What are you doing?" Glenn barked at me as the paramedic checked him over.

"Going with you, of course."

"You don't have to—"

"Shut up, Glenn," I ordered.

"I—"

"Let's shut up, Glenn," the paramedic told him.

He shut up.

The ride to the hospital took a half an hour, and when we got there, they rolled him into the back with me following, after I explained that I was his brother.

"You don't have to stay here," he groused as the nurse took his temperature.

"Yes, I know."

"Don't fuss at your brother," the nurse cautioned him.

He rolled his eyes, but stopped talking when I smirked at him.

"Do you ever listen?"

I waggled my eyebrows. "You should ask Rand."

EMERGENCY ROOM time is like basketball time; it's endless. After the preliminary exam, he had to get X-rays and then back to the room, and as I sat and filled out paperwork, I had to wonder where his father was or any of the men from the ranch. Why was I the only person there?

They gave him a shot, and he fell asleep after that, but he woke up when the doctor was setting his arm. It wasn't nearly as bad as they had first thought. It was a clean break above his wrist, so he was expected to make a full recovery.

"He'll be in this probably eight weeks, considering he's a rancher and he's gonna want to use it," the doctor was telling me when Glenn's eyes fluttered open.

"So your brother here chose dark blue for the cast," Doctor Charles Patel told him. "And as I was just telling him, eight weeks in this easy."

Glenn groaned.

"How ya feel?"

"Like I got trampled by a bull," he said snidely.

"You're right." The doctor grinned at me. "He is funny. I'll be right back."

He left and I was alone with Glenn.

"Why are you still here?"

"Because you're still here, idiot." I smiled at him. I was sitting beside him on the bed, but apparently he hadn't noticed that yet.

He closed his eyes, resting his broken arm on his chest. "Why dark blue?"

"So the cast will set off your eyes." I cackled.

"I really hate you."

"Yeah, I know."

"I gotta fill out the insurance forms."

"I did that already."

"You did?"

"Yes, I did."

"How'd you do that? You go through my wallet?"

"Yep."

"Christ."

"At least they let you keep your underwear."

"You checked, did you?"

"Of course," I teased him, patting his chest, shifting to move.

He put his hand over mine, pressing my palm down into his chest. "Thank you for staying."

"You're welcome."

His eyes drifted open, and I saw how bright and shiny they were, how glassy. The man was really out of it.

"Glenn," I sighed. "Close your eyes, rest for a little bit."

He was just staring up at me.

"Glenn?"

He made a noise in the back of his throat.

"What's wrong?"

"Rand's a lucky man." His eyes drooped, then snapped back open.

"That's very nice of you to say."

"You hate me, huh?"

"No, I don't."

"You don't?"

"No," I assured him as his fingers slid between mine.

"Good," he said, losing the battle to keep his eyes open.

IT TURNED out that I didn't need to call a cab, because Rayland Holloway showed up an hour later to collect his son. He was not that excited to find me there with Glenn, but he appreciated it. Glenn sat between us on the ride back to the fairgrounds, and promptly passed out, his head bumping my shoulder when he fell asleep.

"He seems comfortable with ya."

"He's not the homophobic asshole I thought he was."

"And I am, is that it?"

"I didn't say that, but you're awfully defensive."

He grunted at me.

"You know, it's funny, but did you ever think about what's going to happen to your ranch when you die?"

"Well that's a fine thing to say."

"I just mean, you can't abide sodomites," I said softly, using his word. "But you have no way of knowing who any of your sons will end up loving."

His knuckles were white on the steering wheel.

"Love is a funny thing, Mr. Holloway."

He was silent.

When I got back, I found out that the bareback riding had begun in my absence. I went quickly to the registration tent and made sure they had me down for the saddle bronc. It turned out that Hud Lawrence already had me riding in that event, and had my number ready and everything. As it had been the only category that none of my hands had signed up for, it was the one he had put me into.

"Thank you, Mr. Lawrence." I smiled at him.

"You're very welcome," he said, like it made all the sense in the world to him. "You know, Rand normally rides the bull, but you're built more for saddle bronc."

I wasn't built for anything, but I smiled and nodded instead of arguing.

"The event starts in an hour. You best go get ready, grab your rope and chaps."

I ran back to my trailer to try and find something else to wear. I was out of cowboy clothes, and so I was rooting around in Pierce's clothes, since he was the closest to my size, when the door opened and Everett and Dusty walked in.

"Hey." I smiled big at them. "Mr. Lawrence says I need a rope and chaps. Can one of you guys explain the mechanics of this to me?"

Dusty went white as a sheet, and I made him sit down, put his head between his knees, and breathe while I got him some water. Everett was yelling again.

"Goddamn it, Stef, you don't run into a ring with a bull!" He was yelling about earlier when I had tried to save Glenn from being turned into guacamole.

I shrugged as I fanned Dusty with my *People* magazine.

"Where is he?" I heard someone yell from outside the trailer.

"Seriously," I told Everett as Chris and Tom pushed their way into the small space.

"Who's riding bareback?" I asked.

"Pierce," everyone said at once.

"And Chase is watchin' out for him," Chris told me.

"Okay," I said, "who's got chaps I can borrow?"

You would have thought I was asking to borrow a jock. The looks on their faces were just outright horror.

NEVER, EVER, in a million years would I have thought that I would be up on a horse in a bucking chute. It was just so far out of the realm of possibility. But so was the fact that when I was up there, looking out across the arena and to the side, I saw Rayland Holloway walking toward me. When he reached me, Dusty moved so the owner of the White Ash could take his place.

"I'll give you a pass on this, Stefan," he told me, and I was surprised that we were on a first-name basis. "I never thought you'd have the balls to be up on this animal."

"You mean Widow Maker here?" I tried to chuckle, but my mouth was too dry. The horse was antsy and stamping its feet and not helping me get my nerves under control even a little bit.

"The horse's name is Argent," he told me, "and he belongs to my neighbor Waylon Taylor who owns the Triple Sage."

"I thought broncos were wild."

He scowled at me. "That horse is worth ten grand, and it's no more wild than your dog. All ranchers have some rough stock. Rand does, too, I'm sure."

"What's rough stock?"

"Like horses that don't get rode 'cept at the rodeo," Everett translated for me. "Just mind what you're fixin' to do here and don't worry 'bout nothin' else."

He did not want my mind wandering, didn't want me distracted.

"Okay." I nodded, trying to remember everything he and Dusty and Chris had been barking at me.

"So get on down," Rayland suddenly ordered. "I'll let you keep the grazing rights."

"But that's not just your call," I argued. "It's you and all the other ranchers, and if they don't agree, then we've come this far to fail, and I can't have that."

"It's me. I own more of the land than anyone, and if I say you're fine, then you're fine, you pigheaded piece of crap!"

Unfortunately, it was the last thing he got to say to me, because the chute opened then and the horse, with me on it, charged forward.

Eight seconds. You can count it on your fingers. It seems like nothing. Anything can happen in eight seconds. It's over in a heartbeat. Eight seconds is a completely forgettable amount of time, unless you're on top of an animal.

I had seen Everett on the bull that morning, Glenn as well. It didn't look that hard from the ground. When I flew into San Francisco from Hawaii four years ago, the plane hit a serious patch of turbulence. Off-roading in a jeep had been bumpy, and I had even been in a car accident once, with Charlotte, where the car had flipped over. But nothing at all in my life prepared me for riding a psychotic horse with no other desire than to have me off of him.

I understood why there was no horn on the saddle; my balls would have been smashed into goo if there was. The free-swinging stirrups made my legs feel like a marionette. I felt like I was doing the splits. I had tried to remember what Dusty said about making sure that my feet, my boots, were close to the horse's shoulders before his front legs hit the dirt. I tried to do everything my men had told me. I tried to hold on to the rein that was attached to the halter on the horse. God, I really tried. And eight tiny little seconds seemed like cake in my head. How long could eight seconds possibly be?

Eight seconds is the magic number because the animal, bull or horse, gets tired after that. So they say. For me, the horse went up, I went up, the horse came down, I did too, and then once more up and then I was free, and I felt like a balloon sailing through the sky. If only I were as light as a helium-filled piece of plastic and didn't have the whole gravity thing to worry about.

I hit so hard, dust came up, and I couldn't breathe because my lungs imploded on impact and my back was broken. And my last conscious thought was that people did it for a living on purpose and for the love of God why? And then there was thunder and nothing else.

CHAPTER 7

IF I was dead, everything would not smell like manure. This was my logic, so I figured I was still breathing. When I opened one eye, I heard a gasp.

"Oh God, thank you, thank you, thank you, thank you."

My other eye opened, and I saw Everett. "Hey," I said, but my voice sounded bad, scratchy and rough.

"Just lay there and don't move and try not to scare the shit out of me anymore for one day."

I nodded.

"Don't move!" he barked at me. "The ambulance is coming."

"No, I don't wanna go to the hospital."

"We'll see," he said, hovering over me.

But I knew my body better than anyone else, so when he turned to look for the paramedics or the ambulance or whoever he was expecting, I rolled sideways and got to my feet.

"What the fuck?" he yelled at me as a cheer went up from the stands and Dusty and Chris and Tom and Pierce and Chase joined us in the ring.

Dusty was all over me, and I put one arm across his shoulders and the other on Chase and let them help me from the middle of the arena. They walked me to a gate, lifted me off my feet, and carried me through. On the other side, the paramedics were there on standby, and I was put on the back of their truck so they could check me over.

I told them my name and the name of my ranch, Dusty explained what had happened since apparently they had not seen my spectacular ride for themselves, and Chase told them how I had fallen and how hard and how fast. He was worried about my head.

Dusty was worried about my neck.

Chris was concerned about my ankle because I couldn't put any weight on it.

Everett was with Chase and worried about my head. He felt that my pupils were way too big.

“Did I win?” I asked Glenn Holloway as he reached us.

“Fuck no,” he growled at me. “You were only on the horse like two seconds.”

“Really? It felt like so much longer.”

“I expect so,” he said, reaching out and curling a stray lock of hair around my ear. “Jesus Christ, Stefan, my father said you didn’t have to ride.”

“He was late.” I smiled at him as the nice lady paramedic shone a light in my eyes.

“Okay, Mr. Joss,” she said softly.

“Stef,” I corrected her.

“Stef.” She smiled, gesturing behind me. “We’re gonna have you lie down, all right?”

“Why?”

“Because I think you have a concussion.”

“Really?”

“Oh yes, really.”

“A bad one?”

“I’m not sure, so we’re going to take a trip to the hospital.”

“I’m coming with you,” Glenn told me.

My smile was wide. “Two trips in one day. How bright are we?”

“Oh, yeah,” the nice lady paramedic said sarcastically. “This whole rodeo thing is brilliant.”

“We’ll follow,” Everett told me.

“No, no, no.” I grabbed his hand as I saw spots. “Stay here and pick up any trophies and make sure that the ranch participation and mine is recorded.”

“One of us needs to go with you,” he argued with me, and I noticed that his expression, usually twisted into a scowl, was really very concerned.

“Don’t worry. Rand really isn’t going to hurt you.”

“It’s you I’m worried about, Stef, not Rand.”

And I would have said something comforting, but I suddenly needed to throw up.

THE CONCUSSION was mild; my reaction to it, for whatever reason, was not. I was sensitive to light, I was nauseated, and my head was throbbing so hard that they gave me a shot of pain medication. After that, I was just fine. They wanted me to stay overnight, but I didn't want to. I had to be in a truck at four in the morning.

"I'll watch him," Glenn promised the doctor, and I waved.

My ankle, as it turned out, was not the problem. I had broken my right fibula, which was better than breaking my tibia or my ankle, but which still hurt like crazy. I was given a second dose of pain medication after they put my leg, from knee to foot, in a cast.

"I'm surprised you didn't break your neck the way you landed," Glenn told me, and from the look in his eyes and the sound of his voice I was guessing that I had scared the crap out of him. "What the fuck were you thinking?"

I tipped my head at his cast. "Grazing rights, asshole, just like you."

"But I've ridden a bull before."

"Which makes the fact that you got hurt just like I did that much funnier," I laughed at him. "What time is it anyway?"

"It's a little after six," he told me.

"Well, are you driving me back to the rodeo, or are we walking?"

"I have a date," he told me. "We're catching a cab."

I agreed and asked for pain medication to go. The doctor, Norman Aust, did not want me to leave, but after I lied and said that Glenn would watch me like a hawk, he agreed to let me go.

"Sorry," I told him as I hobbled out on my crutches, "I think Doc thinks that you're my boyfriend."

"That's alright," Glenn grumbled, walking behind me.

"Oh yeah? It's okay my doc thinks you're a homo? Thinks you're queer?"

"God, you are fucked up. Get in the cab."

I got in and kept up a steady, rambling dialogue for Glenn all the way back to the campgrounds. Once we were there, he was going to walk me back to my trailer, but I had called ahead, and Everett and Dusty were there to meet me.

"Hey!" I greeted them, and the looks I got of absolute horror were funny.

They talked while I hobbled, and halfway there I stopped and explained to them that the whole walking with crutches thing was exhausting.

"This really sucks." I smiled at them. "And don't look at me like I'm crazy. I'm not crazy."

Everett just shook his head as he took my crutches away, put my arm over his shoulder, and waited while Dusty positioned himself under my other one. I moved a lot faster with them on either side of me.

My shower was an experience, and I wanted a nap when I was done. Wrapping my cast in garbage bags was a pain in the ass, but since I couldn't get it wet, I had no choice. And I was dirty and gritty and there was sand in my hair, so I had to get clean. Bella put her head in my lap when I was done and didn't even try and wrestle my socks from me like she normally did. I stretched one of my black socks over the outside of the bottom of the cast because otherwise my toes would freeze off. I had no idea how I was going to drive or ride Ruby or do anything at Rayland's ranch. I was thrilled the rodeo was officially over.

Dusty and Everett and the others came to collect me, and you would have thought that all of them had broken their legs instead of me. I had to take some Vicodin, and because I hadn't eaten all day, it made me kind of loopy and a little queasy. I needed food.

They all stuck close to me through dinner, and then I was escorted to the bleachers. I sat there and clapped and cheered, whistled and yelled when every category was called. The only two events that another ranch won were the bull riding that Glenn Holloway had taken and the saddle bronc, which the Twin Oaks took. But my ride was not the worst, only second to the worst, which filled me with a small amount of pride. I was pleased to see Glenn walk up onto the stage and receive the appreciation of the crowd. Rachel Webber, his date for the evening, was glowing.

A different band took center stage the second night; this one was tame, all covers, no original music at all. But they were decent, and the dancing was in full swing as I was looking for Rayland Holloway. I wanted to find out where to meet him at four in the morning. I didn't see the man anywhere, but I saw Glenn, and even though I didn't want to interrupt his date with Rachel, I crossed to the table where they were.

"Stef," Glenn greeted me with a warm smile, standing up to take my hand. "I never did thank you for earlier. Apparently that bull was gonna stomp all over me if you hadn't gotten there when you did. I guess a lot of people got it on their phones, and between last night and today, I think you're a hit on YouTube."

And that was funny for like a second and a half.

Rand.

I was so dead if he saw it.

I forced a smile. "Well, you returned the favor when you went with me to the hospital, so thank you back."

"You all right on those?" He gestured at the crutches.

"Sure."

"Maybe you should rest, huh?"

"Maybe," I agreed, looking at Rachel. "You look beautiful tonight."

She flushed beet red, and I bent and kissed her cheek.

"And you are very good for my ego, Mr. Joss." She beamed up at me. "I'm so glad you're all right. You gave us all quite a scare earlier."

"Thank you, ma'am."

My eyes were back on Glenn and his on me. "Are you still coming home with us tomorrow?"

"I am if you tell me where to meet you."

"I'll come by in the morning and get you and your horse and your damn dog," he told me, his eyes glowing.

"She's a cute dog. You'll like her."

"My dad says she's scary as hell."

"She won't be scary to you."

"Good." He nodded.

"I'll see you in the morning, then."

"In the morning."

I left them and found a seat to watch the line dancing. It was a much smaller crowd than the previous night, and people were leaving, as it was Sunday night a little after nine and most had to work the following day. I was enjoying watching Rand's men dancing and didn't even notice when Carly Landry took a seat beside me until she cleared her throat, and I turned my head.

"Hi," I greeted her.

"I'm so sorry about my brother, Stefan."

"It's okay." I went back to watching the dancers, using my crutch to move a chair over next to me so I could elevate my leg. "He loves you. I get it."

"But it doesn't excuse him hitting you."

"I'll live," I told her, adjusting my ankle on the chair to take the weight of the cast.

"I think that…."

I waited a second before I looked back at her. "You think what?"

Her face was pinched with pain. "I'm sorry, but I think just like my brother does, that this is a phase for Rand. He's going to come out of this, and when he does, he's going to come looking for me."

She was holding on to that hope so hard, so tight. I was going to say something when my phone rang. Seeing the number, his number, on my display, my heart fluttered.

"Excuse me," I said, slowly getting to my feet, the crutches hard to maneuver while I was trying to answer my phone.

"Oh no, Stef, please stay."

"I have to take this. My…." I hesitated. I didn't want to hurt her feelings. "Best friend wants to talk to me."

"Oh, of course." She smiled at me. "But please do come back."

"Do me a favor?"

"Of course."

I left one crutch leaning on the table. "Will you ask my friend Everett to bring this back to the trailer for me? You remember him from the awards, right?"

"Sure." She smiled at me.

I nodded, and started walking away with one crutch as I hit the answer button on my phone. "Hi, I missed you."

"Did you? I don't know how. You've been so busy saving people from fuckin' bulls!"

"Wait—"

"Jesus Christ, Stef, you must've taken ten years off my life with that shit!"

Oh, he was mad, and he didn't even know the best part yet. "See—"

"Your ass better be in the truck headed for home right fucking now!"

I laughed at him. "That's actually not possible."

"Why the fuck not?"

"Well, I promised—"

"And what the fuck were you doing parading around in those jeans and that shirt last—"

"Parading?"

"You are not allowed to put on your fuck-me clothes if I ain't there to do the fucking!"

And for whatever reason, I could not stop smiling. "Is that right?"

The growl of frustration made my smile nuclear.

"Did you think I was hot?"

"Stefan, so help me God, I am going to beat the living—"

"Who sent it to you?"

"Stef—"

"Who?" I laughed, wondering if it was Everett or Chris or Dusty.

"Pierce."

"That little narc," I said, laughing. "It's always the quiet ones."

"You are in so much trouble."

"Why? I came to save the grazing rights, Rand. How can I be in the wrong?"

"Did it ever occur to you that I own a very successful business and that one of the marks of a good businessman is being organized? What makes you think I didn't know the damn rodeo was this weekend?"

"You had no idea," I told him, "until someone told you—I'm thinking Zach."

He grunted.

"Don't get all self-righteous on me. That's bullshit."

"Fine, I didn't know, but I wouldn't have wanted you there alone."

"I'm not alone. I have half the ranch with me!"

"But I'm not there!"

"So what? You're where you needed to be, and I'm where I needed to be. It all worked out for the best."

"Why didn't you tell me where you were going?"

"Why didn't you tell me you missed this rodeo for the last two years?"

"Because it had nothing to do with you or us, so why would I mention it?"

"Rand, I don't just wanna know about stuff that affects you and me. I wanna know about everything. And I definitely want to know everything about your family."

There was a long silence, and I had to stop and lean on the fence. I really needed to lie down.

"Rand?"

"Why?"

"Why what?"

"Why do you need to know everything?"

"Because if I'm really your partner and you want me to stick around, then your family is my family."

"You know I want you to stick around."

"Then?"

He took a breath. "Okay."

"Okay what?"

"Okay my family is your family, asshole."

I laughed at him. "I appreciate it."

"I want you to come home."

"I will."

"When?"

"Soon."

"God, what a mess."

I was about to give the man heart palpitations, so I decided to change the subject while I still could. "You know, all the guys have been worried about what you were gonna do to them when you found out they came with me."

"They're your men as much as mine. That all made sense to me."

God, I loved him.

"And I understand since I didn't tell you, why you raced off to protect my rights, your rights to—"

"I did it for you, Rand. I mean, I know that the ranch is half mine, and I used that this weekend to my benefit, but when I think of it, I think of you."

He was quiet.

"Rand?"

"I used to think of the ranch and think of my father." He took a breath. "You saying that you think of me—that might be the best thing you've ever said, after you love me and you were gonna stay."

My throat hurt.

"But you should have told me what you were doing, where you were going."

"Yes, I should have."

"I'm sorry, did you say I was right?"

"Don't be an ass."

"According to you, I already am one."

I laughed at him. "Hey, I know this is gonna sound stupid since I came here and everything, but I was thinking that maybe you should give Rayland the grazing rights?"

It took him a minute to respond. "What are you talking about?"

"You don't really need to graze the cattle there, do you?"

Nothing.

"Rand?"

"No, I don't."

"You have other land, but Rayland only has this and his ranch."

"What's your point?"

"I just think that there's a lot of bad blood between you and him, and I think it would go a long way to making peace."

"And why do I care about that?"

"Because we're talking about your family."

"Lemme understand. You want me to just give the man my share of thousands of acres of land just because you think it would be a nice gesture?"

"I think it would be an olive branch."

"Uh-huh."

"Rand—"

"After what he just did to me? Are you kidding?"

"I just want you to think about it."

"I'm thinking about a lot of things, Stef, but I'm not ready to do anything with that land right this second, all right?"

That was fair. "All right."

"Okay, so my cousin Zach is gonna sell his ranch." He exhaled deeply.

"Really."

"Yeah, he's done. He's not sure what he wants to do, but he's tired of ranching, and from seeing his men this weekend, they're tired of being there with him. I offered a few of them jobs, and two of them are taking me up on it."

"And the others?"

"The others don't wanna work for a gay man."

"I'm sorry, Rand."

He grunted. "It's their loss, Stef. It's a privilege to work on the Red Diamond. I won't ever beg anyone to take my hand."

His pride made me smile. I loved the confidence in the man's voice.

"Except for you, that is," he laughed softly. "You, I will beg."

"It's not necessary."

"No?"

"No."

"Okay, then, Stef, please come home."

"Not yet."

"See, it ain't workin' not to beg."

"I have things to do first."

"Like what?"

"Like getting you to give the grazing rights to Rayland."

"We just put that conversation to bed."

"Let's wake it up."

"So you're saying if I agree to give the grazing rights to my uncle right now, you would come home?"

It was my one card to play.

"Yes."

"Done," he said without pause.

"Great," I sighed. "So I'll meet you on the White Ash, and you can give Rayland the grazing rights."

"Oh fuck no!"

"Oh fuck no, what?"

"Oh fuck no, you are not going out to the White Ash!"

I smiled into the phone. "Why don't you meet me there?"

"Stef." His voice lowered in warning.

"Or wait for me at home."

"Stef."

"I need you to see Rayland."

"Why?"

It was not my place to say. "I just do, and Glenn needs our help."

"Glenn? Since when do you care about Glenn?"

"Because your family should be together, Rand, not apart," I told him. "The grazing rights will smooth the way with Rayland, and Glenn likes me, so—"

"Likes you?"

"Yeah, we're friends."

"You and my cousin are friends?"

"Yeah."

"Since when?"

Since the hospital two times, but I didn't want to say that, so I went with the other. "He saved me from Gil Landry."

Beats of time passed. "I'm sorry?"

"You know, Glenn really wants to start a restaurant, and I want to help him with that, and I really think he needs a friend, and he held my hand so tight today at the hospital that I think—"

"Held your hand?"

"Glenn is on the verge of either taking a left turn to greatness or making a right into mediocrity and loneliness."

"That's very dramatic."

I was still hopped up on pain medication. "He could be just like you if we help him."

"Like me?"

"Yeah. Happy. You're happy, aren't you?"

Silence.

"Aren't you?"

"Not right this second," he groused at me.

Just thinking about him scowling on the other end made me smile.

"Yes, Stef, I'm happy," he admitted grudgingly.

"Well, then, come pick me up at the White Ash, okay?"

He was silent and so was I.

"You talked to my mother, didn't you?"

It was lucky that I was still holding on to the corral fence. "Yes."

He made a noise of understanding, and suddenly the light came on for me as well.

"Your dad," I sighed.

"Of course," he said irritably. "James Holloway never backed down from anything, least of all the truth. He told me a long time ago that Rayland was my biological father."

I coughed. "Your mother doesn't know, you know."

"Yeah, I know. Rayland doesn't know I know either."

Longest damn weekend of my life.

"Who told you?"

"I figured it out and then made your mother tell me."

"How did you figure it out when no one else can?"

"Because I really look at you, and I will notice anyone else who looks like you," I told him. "I always thought of you and Charlotte as having the exact same color eyes, but even Charlotte's are darker than yours. She's got that violet color, and Glenn's are cobalt, but yours are all your own except for—"

"Rayland."

"Yeah."

"And so, were you gonna say something to me?"

"You know I was. How could I not?"

"Even though it wasn't your secret to tell?"

"There can't be anything between us, Rand, or we won't make it."

"I agree, and so you know, that means something to me. The fact that you would take my side before anyone else, that you would tell me even if you thought I wouldn't believe you—that's a big deal, Stef."

"But I had no doubt that you would believe me."

"What? You think I would take your word over anyone else's, even my mother's?"

"Of course," I said matter-of-factly. I had been worried about how hurt Rand would be. It never even crossed my mind to think that I would need to convince him that I was telling the truth. "I know you trust me."

He took a long breath. "I wanna see you real bad."

The ache in his voice twisted me up inside. "Rand, let's just get everything out in the open, all right? Come to the ranch, talk to Rayland, talk to Glenn. Let's have a good old-fashioned knock-down, drag-out fight. Bring Tyler, bring Zach. I'll call Charlotte. It's time. Secrets have a way of festering. Aren't you sick of it?"

"I don't think on it much, but I would like my mother to know that I know. It might let her sleep better, and Charlotte should know that I'm only half her brother."

"I doubt it will change anything."

"We'll see."

He sounded sad, and it hurt to hear, but I knew that Charlotte loved him, and I knew too that nothing would ever change that.

"Call your mother, will you?"

"Yessir, I will."

"And then come to the ranch and talk to Rayland."

"All right."

"And pick me up while you're at it."

"Anything else while you're barking out orders?"

"No, that's it," I sighed happily.

"So," he said softly, "why did Glenn have to save you from Gil Landry?"

Amazing. After everything, all the talking we'd done, all the revelations of the past few minutes, the man had still retained that tiny piece of information.

"Who cares?"

"Oh, I fuckin' care." His voice lowered ominously. "What happened?"

"It's no big deal. Gil Landry took a swing at me, and Glenn stopped him from doing anything more than put me on the ground."

There was no sound at all, like he wasn't even breathing.

"Rand?"

He coughed. "I'm sorry, what?"

"You heard me," I chuckled. "My buddy Gil really wants you to marry his sister."

"I see."

"So, when are you coming to Rayland's ranch?"

"When are you leaving?"

"At some horrible hour of the morning," I groaned. "Jesus, Rand, four is not a time decent people wake up."

"It's the time ranchers get up," he assured me, and he was trying to sound playful, but his tone was stilted and cold.

"Rand?"

"Just let it be, all right? I'll see you at the ranch tomorrow."

"I can't wait to see you."

"Me too, baby," his voice rumbled, and my heart leaped in my chest.

"I really enjoyed the rodeo, you know."

"Next time we'll go together."

"It's a deal," I sighed, but my leg throbbed, and so I winced without even meaning to.

"What hurts?" he asked gently.

"Nothing."

He chuckled. "Has anyone ever told you that you're a really shitty liar."

"Really? I think it's more the opposite actually."

"Then maybe it's just me."

"Could be." I smiled into my phone.

"Tell me what's wrong."

I cleared my throat. "I'm fine. Just got a little banged up today."

"When? I watched the video with the bull on the website, and it didn't look like you got hurt."

This was news. "The rodeo has a website?"

"Yeah, it's what Pierce sent me the link for. They put highlights from the rodeo up to get people to come next year, you know?"

"That makes sense."

"I'm on the website right now."

The warning buzzer went off in my head. "Well, shouldn't you—"

"Stef."

"Yes?"

"There seems to be a…. How did you get hurt, Stef?"

I coughed. "What are you looking at?"

"I'm waiting for something with your name on it to load."

"It's probably more of me auctioning off bachelors."

"I don't think so."

"You should watch Everett and Chris doing the team roping. It was really some—"

"What is this?" he asked, talking to himself.

"Rand."

"Man, this is taking forever."

There was no getting around it. "Rand, you know that every rancher has to compete in the rodeo, right? I mean actually compete himself or herself to secure the grazing rights?"

"Sure," he told me.

I waited because my beautiful, sexy cowboy would work it out in a minute.

"What're you… wait."

I braced for an explosion.

"Oh, fuck," he breathed out.

"I'm fine."

"Whah… Stef—what'd you do?"

I took a breath. "I can't ride a bull like you, and after I got back from the hospital with Glenn, the only event left was the saddle bronc."

There was a catch of breath but nothing else.

"Rand?" I said after a minute because a slow feeling of dread was starting to sink into me.

"No." He sounded like he was going to throw up. "What is—no."

"Don't watch anything."

"Why not?"

"Because it'll just upset you, and I'm fine," I told him. "I just broke my leg."

He sucked in his breath.

"And just the lower part of my leg. It's no big deal."

The phone was muffled, and I was pretty sure that the man I loved was coughing up a lung. When he hung up, I was confident that it was to spare me the sounds of him retching. I took the opportunity to continue my limp toward the trailer. I sighed deeply when it was in sight. My phone went off, and I saw Rand's number pop back up on the display.

"You all right?"

"No." He sounded sick and mad at the same time.

"I'm all in one piece."

"Looks like a lot of people took video of you."

"Because I'm pretty," I teased him.

"Stef—"

"Did you watch one yet?"

"Not yet… it's still loading."

Which meant the file was huge either because it was really long or in really high definition. Either way, I did not want him seeing it. "Don't watch it."

"Why not?"

"Because you got sick just think—"

"Here it is," he said.

"Are you home? Where are you?"

"I'm at Zach's. The guests are gone, and I'm in his study. I'm gonna leave in the morn…. I'm… I'm… oh my God." He exhaled.

"But you should see me. I'm fine. You're talking to me. You can tell from my voice that I'm fine."

He was quiet. I couldn't even hear him breathing, or not breathing.

"Rand?"

"Wait."

"Rand, just—"

"I said wait!"

He sounded really bad, and it was heart-wrenching to hear him so worried about me. I was quiet for long minutes.

Finally, he cleared his throat. "Do you have a concussion?"

"I—"

"It's a simple question, Stef. Do you or do you not have a concussion?"

"What even makes you ask that question?"

"Because of how hard you hit the dirt."

"Oh."

"Stef."

"Yeah, I have a slight concussion."

"And you broke your leg?"

"Just my fibula, the small bone, not the big one," I told him.

"I know what a fibula is."

"Okay," I said because he was scaring me with how calm he sounded.

"You know, concussions are tricky. Somebody's supposed to either keep you awake or watch you all night long. You got someone there to do that?"

"No, Rand, I—"

"Is there someone there I don't know about who's fixin' to take care of you like I could take care of you?"

His voice was rising.

"No, Rand, you—"

"And you're planning to go to the White Ash tomorrow?"

"Yes," I said, not even sounding like me.

"So since you and Glenn are so close now, may—"

"There's no way you're jealous of your cousin," I told him.

"No?"

"Knock it off," I told him. "My head hurts, and you're screwing with me. It's not nice."

He sucked in his breath. "Okay, here's what's gonna happen. I'm gonna leave for the airport right now, and you are gonna stay right there and wait for me. Do you understand?"

"I can't. The rodeo's over, Rand. I can't stay here. The guys need to get back to the ranch, and I made a promise to Rayland and Glenn to get out to White Ash. I won't break my promise after I spent the weekend getting both of them to trust me. I—"

"You can wait for me. No one will throw you out of that trailer. No one's expected to leave until noon tomorrow."

"People are leaving already."

"Not the people who brought stock and horses, Stef. None of the ranchers or their men are leaving until tomorrow."

"Glenn and Rayland are leaving at like—"

"You're not. You're staying right there and waiting for me."

"Rand—"

"Stefan Joss! Do you understand?" he shouted.

"I want to see the White—"

"You don't, Stef, not really. I know you. You wanna come home. What you want is for me to sign over the grazing rights. What you want is for me to clear things up with Rayland and my mother, and you want me to find out from Glenn how serious he is about the damn restaurant."

And I did. I wanted all of that.

"I'll talk to everyone, I swear I will, but I will do it on my terms on my ranch. If they wanna talk to me, they come see me, not the other way around. Do you understand?"

Rand had his pride, and it was not my place to try and strip that from him. "Yes."

"I am coming there to fetch you home, and that's all. Maybe before you got hurt, I would have followed you out to my uncle's ranch, but not now."

I really wanted to go home.

"Now you come home, Stef, end of discussion."

There was no fight left in me. I needed him, needed to see him. "Okay."

"You're supposed to teach class on Tuesday, or have you forgotten?"

Crap. I had, actually.

"You're lucky tomorrow's Columbus Day, or you'd really be screwed."

He was right. "Come get me."

"Do not fuckin' move. Where's the goddamn trailer?"

"I have the last one before the open range."

"Fuck!"

He was still very upset. "But, Rand, I'm—"

"If you say you're fine one more goddamn time, I will fuckin' lose it. Do you understand me? Are you fuckin' kidding me?"

"What was I supposed to do?"

"Not put your life on the line for a piece of land I don't give a fuck about!"

"I didn't know that!"

"But you want me to give the land to Rayland!"

"Because he's your family!"

"You're my family, not him! Jesus Christ, Stef, you could've been killed, and what the fuck does that do for me, huh? That fucks me for the rest of my life 'cause I get to be without you, you selfish son of a bitch!"

"I was thinking of you!"

"If you were thinkin' about me, you would have never gotten on the horse!"

"Rand—"

"And Everett and Dusty and Chase and—"

"Rand—"

"They're all fired, Stef. Do you understand how fired they are?"

No. "Rand, you can't do that!"

"Oh no? Fuckin' watch me! How dare they let you get up on that—"

"Stop yelling!" I yelled at him, which was funny, but not at the moment because I was livid. "You don't get to fire men from my ranch because you're pissed. They all came with me, they've been here for me, and yeah they didn't want me to ride the crazy horse, but I did it for you and for the ranch, and yeah I got hurt, but so the fuck what? And Rayland should have the land because he didn't take it. We give it on our terms because we want to, not because he's a conniving piece of crap who got one over on us. The guys and me, we did this, Rand. We told him and all the rest of the homophobic assholes around here to go fuck themselves. And Gil Landry and his sister, who thinks that you'll get over me, can go screw themselves too, 'cause you will never be over me."

It was quiet on the other end.

"Are you done?"

"Yeah, I'm done."

"Stay there and wait for me. Do you understand?"

"Yes, I understand." I sucked in my breath suddenly, shivering with a cramp in my leg, the pain of it and from being outside in the cold.

"You should get off your leg."

"Yes, I should," I agreed.

"Did you even for a second think about the worst thing that would happen when you got up on the horse?"

"No, I only wanted to protect you."

"Where are you now?"

"Now I'm looking at my trailer and Bella in the window."

"You took your dog?"

"Why does everybody keep saying that like it's weird? Yeah, I like my dog. So what?"

His laughter sounded so good.

"Rand—"

"You're right."

"About what?"

"That I won't be gettin' over you."

"Oh yeah?" I sighed.

"Yeah. I do better when you're around."

It was suddenly hard to breathe.

"So I can stay in this trailer until tomorrow? They're not going to come throw me out of it after the guys go?"

"The guys ain't goin' nowhere neither. Everyone waits there for me. You tell them."

"You're sure?"

"I'm sure."

"Okay. If Rayland and Glenn stay here, will you talk to them about the grazing rights?"

"I will invite them to the Red, Stef, that's it."

Which was better than nothing. "Thank you, Rand."

"Don't fall asleep."

"I won't."

"Did the doctor give you something for the pain?"

"Yes."

"I don't want you to take something that's gonna knock you out."

"I'll be all right."

"You keep saying that, and you keep getting hurt."

"Hurry up," I grumbled at him playfully.

"I am!"

I really couldn't wait to see him.

CHAPTER 8

I WENT to the trailer, let Bella out, and decided to walk back to where the dancing was and explain things to Glenn. Everett was there before I got far, bringing me my crutch.

"The beauty queen asked me to bring this to you."

"Who?"

"Carly Landry."

"Oh, that's right." I forced a smile.

"You look like you been rode hard and put up wet."

"That sounds disgusting," I told him. "I'm heading back to the grounds; do me a favor and find Glenn Holloway and ask him to come see me."

He nodded and I watched his eyes fall as he shoved his hands down into his pockets. I knew I was looking at guilt.

"You told Rand where I was, asshole."

"I told Pierce to let him know. Yessir, I did."

"And when he was on the site watching me keep the bull off of Glenn, he watched me get thrown off the bronco."

His eyes met mine. "So I suspect that he's on his way."

I nodded.

"Am I fired?"

"No, don't be an idiot."

He looked surprised. "Really? He ain't mad?"

"Oh, he's furious, but not at any of you guys, just at me."

"Really?"

"Yeah, don't sound so happy about it."

"I ain't happy. I'm just surprised is all. I expected him to be plenty mad."

"He'll be here tomorrow."

"Well, then, I expect we'll be here to see him. We weren't planning to leave until about noon tomorrow anyhow."

"Rayland and Glenn are leaving earlier than that, so that's why I need to talk to Glenn," I said, getting both crutches under me, ready to trudge back to the main grounds. "You really think Carly's a beauty queen?"

"I think she's a stuck-up bitch who won't give me the time of day now when she knows I'm just a cowboy, but if I won the lottery tomorrow, I might just look a bit better."

I smiled at him. "If you would just talk to Regina Kincaid instead of walking by her every time you see her, then your life might actually get around to starting, Everett."

He looked like I'd slapped him. "Her brother and her father hate me."

"They don't hate you. They think you only wanna get laid, and that's not the man they're looking for to be the husband of the angel of their family."

He cleared his throat. "Her father said, and I quote, that he didn't want a white man in his family."

I grunted. "I was there when he said it, and his exact quote was that he didn't want a white man that didn't attend church regular in his family. That's what he said."

Everett's eyes were on me.

"You're not a bad man. In fact you're a very good one, but you have ways that need to be changed if you want a woman like that. She teaches school, she goes to church, and she is stunning. I have never seen such big brown eyes, and that beautiful smile, and her skin is just—"

He made a noise so I'd stop.

"But you're a dog, and she's better than that, like way better."

"She's out of my league."

"Not if you really wanted her," I told him. "But you would have to want her more than the life you have now, and only you can say if you do or not."

He nodded.

"So, are we ready to go?"

"No," he sighed, and I could tell his brain was spinning before his eyes were suddenly back on mine with a look I had never seen before.

"God, what?"

"On the best ranches I've ever been on, the men were more like family. Most times those ranches don't last. They get bought up by large cattle companies, or they go under for some other reason, but the Red Diamond is a big ranch that acts like a small one, and I understand after this weekend that the reason it stays that way is 'cause of you."

I squinted at him.

He took off his hat, fiddled with it in his hands.

"I don't mean to sound ignorant, and I ain't sayin' you're a woman, but with us, with the men, your regard is softer than Rand Holloway's, and I suspect that's why you balance him out."

It was the nicest thing he'd ever said to me. "I appreciate that, but it was how it was before I came along. You gotta know the ranch is Rand and vice versa."

"No, sir." He shook his head. "Before you came, it was a fine place to work, but we weren't no family."

The feeling hit me, surged over and through me; my jaw clenched, and my eyes burned as I shivered to keep from falling apart. His words meant more than he could have known, because it meant that maybe, just maybe, I was as good for Rand Holloway as he was for me.

"Things have changed since you came."

For everyone, it seemed, not just me.

"Rand seems settled now that you're on the ranch, and I might want to know things about that."

He looked uncomfortable, his hat doing circles now in his restless hands. I would give him his out. "You mean you wanna try being settled, right, not sleeping with a man?"

I braced for it, and he smacked my arm really hard.

"Shit, Everett!"

"Well I can't hit your head or I might kill ya, and I can't kick ya in the leg neither. Man, you are an annoying piece of crap!"

Like I had never been told that before. "Do me a favor and go get Glenn Holloway for me, willya? There's no way I can make that walk back. I'm ready to pass out now."

"Well, then, go to bed."

"Rand said I couldn't, something about the concuss—"

"Oh shit, that's right," he said, turning to leave. "I'll go fetch Glenn and be back to watch ya. Just stay here."

"You don't have to tell me twice," I teased him. "Hey, who fed Bella today?"

"I did."

"Thank you for remembering."

"Remember?" He looked at me oddly. "Who can forget? Your dog's just as annoying as you are."

I smiled at him as he started walking away, and I noticed how he turned and called Bella to him to take the walk.

She looked up at me.

"Go get him, Bell, get him," I said playfully.

Her head tilted to the side like I was an idiot as she sat down beside me.

"It ain't no use, Stef." I heard him laugh. "That dog loves you best."

As I ran my hand over her muzzle and she bumped my fingers, her tail beating hard in the dirt, I had to smile. She certainly did.

I went inside and got my parka and my beanie because it was colder outside than the two nights before. I was sitting on the bottom step of the trailer, throwing a tennis ball for my dog when she stopped suddenly, froze, her dirty, fuzzy, green quarry between her paws.

"Stef?"

I waved at Glenn. "Sorry to call you out here, but I'm done walking for one night."

He hesitated, stopping where he was, eyeing my dog.

"She won't hurt you."

"She's fuckin' scary, Stef."

I called her, and she moved fast, stopping in front of me so that I could touch one of her silky ears.

Glenn walked slowly, carefully, his eyes never leaving her.

"You rode a bull today," I reminded him. "Cowboy up."

"Yeah, well, the bull won't go for my jugular."

"She's harmless."

"Says you."

"Throw the ball for her."

He picked it up, showed it to her, and threw it.

"I think she squinted at me," he told me when she didn't move a muscle.

I started laughing, and she moved and shoved her nose in my eye before she nuzzled my hair and smelled me.

Glenn chuckled. "She thinks you're her pup."

"Possibly." I smiled, petting my dog. "Get the ball, Bell, go get it."

She eyed Glenn instead.

He knelt down and she moved slowly, checking him out. After she allowed him to pet her, she was suddenly off like a shot to get the ball.

"Damn, that is one careful dog."

"Hey, listen, it turns out I can't go home with you guys tomorrow, but if you could wait until Rand shows up tomorrow, I—"

"Rand's gonna be here tomorrow?"

"Yeah, and if you could, Glenn, I'd love it if you actually came home with us. I'd like you to talk to Rand about your restaurant idea."

His mouth was open, but no words came out. When Bella dropped the disgusting slobber- and dirt-covered tennis ball at his feet, he picked it up without thinking and threw it for her.

"Did you hear me?"

"I did."

"And?"

"Rand hates me."

I shook my head. "No."

"No?"

"You should come back out to the Red. Ask your father if he will too."

"My father?" He was stunned.

"Please."

"God, Stef, are you sure?"

"Positive."

"You want us to wait for Rand?"

"If you can."

"I can. I don't know if my father will."

Oh, he will, I thought. "Just ask him, okay?"

He cleared his throat. "Sure."

"I need to sleep," I told him, realizing that I didn't even think I could crawl to bed. "I'll see you tomorrow."

He was really looking at me. "You know, you're kind of pale. Do you need help inside?"

"No."

"Stef, you should let—"

"I'm good," I lied. "You go enjoy what's left of your night."

He nodded. "Okay, then, we'll look for Rand in the morning."

"Great."

"They're gonna serve breakfast tomorrow before everyone goes. You should come up there and sit with us if you can."

"If I can even move in the morning, I'll be there."

His brows furrowed. "You sure you don't need me to stay?"

"No, and besides, you gotta get back to Rachel." I smiled at him. "You know, it feels like it's three in the morning, but it's probably like ten."

"Ten thirty," he corrected me.

"See?" I shrugged. "Getting thrown off a horse really screws up your sense of time."

"It's going to the hospital that does it."

I shrugged and we laughed like we were war buddies before he left me tossing the ball for my dog. It was all the movement I could manage.

CHAPTER 9

IN MY sunglasses and cowboy hat, I was sure that I must have looked hung over instead of in the pain that I was in. But I arrived—more sore that morning than I had been the previous day, but decidedly more clearheaded. I was going to try and stick to Tylenol and nothing stronger if I could manage it. Everything else made me loopy and way too chatty.

I was surprised to see Carly Landry there at one of the tables sitting with her brother. I took a seat while Everett went to get me a plate.

"Stefan."

I looked up and she was there, hovering over me.

"It's good to see you this morning."

I waited for whatever it was she wanted.

"May I sit?"

"Sure."

"Glenn was looking for you earlier."

Which was good, and I was going to say something to that effect when I turned to her, only to find that she was not looking at me at all. She was completely absorbed with something else. Her lips were parted, her eyes were wide, and her hands fisted on the table. I scanned the crowd, trying to find what had her so transfixed.

Rand.

I was stunned. There, cutting his way through people, was Rand Holloway. He just walked in a straight line, and everyone moved out of his way. He was wearing his gray Stetson, flannel shirt, jeans, and boots, and somehow, on him, it was breathtaking. From Carly's reaction, I was not the only one who thought so.

Rand's stride was all his own. There was fluidity to it, a rise and fall, and he walked with a confidence that no one else I knew had, an absolute knowledge of his place in the world. The effortless display of his strength, power, and masculinity brought my heart up into my throat.

"Rand is here," Carly announced unnecessarily, and as she rose and waved, he noticed her, and when he saw her, he saw me.

I smiled as his eyes narrowed as he reached me.

"Rand," Carly said breathlessly, "I'm so glad to—"

"Stef." His voice cracked as his hands went to my face and he bent toward me.

"Don't," I cautioned him, turning fast, kissing his palm before I leaned back. "How are you?"

The muscles in his jaw corded, but he swallowed everything down. I saw the effort it took, and watched as he picked up the chair beside me and turned it before he sat down. He was facing me, his knees on both sides of mine, and his hands went to my thighs, holding them. I took a deep breath as a surge of feeling tore through me. I was hurt, and I had held myself together because I had to. But he was there and I could lean on him, and I had never, ever, been so happy to see him. His warm hand found its way back to my cheek.

"You shouldn't touch me."

"I don't give a damn what anyone thinks, Stef. I love you and that's all there is."

Looking at him, into the electric blue eyes I loved, I felt better. "Thank you for coming."

"I came as fast as I could," he told me, his voice low and deep, very husky, very sexy.

I nodded as he leaned back and lifted my broken leg up into his lap.

"You're supposed to keep this elevated," he told me as Everett joined us.

"Hey, boss," he greeted Rand warily.

"That looks good," Rand told him, eyeing the eggs and biscuits and gravy that Everett had brought for me. "Bring me one, Ev, and tell Chris and Pierce that Stef and I need coffee and orange juice."

Everett didn't move, just stared at Rand, waiting.

"Did I stutter?"

"No, sir." His smile came suddenly, and it was bright. "Thank you."

"No, thank you," Rand told him, and touched the brim of his hat.

Everett let out a deep breath and then left.

I watched him go, and in the process of turning back to Rand, I found Carly. I had completely forgotten that she was there. She did not look like the same person. There was so much that she was showing me: pain, humiliation, hatred, and longing. Most of all there was that, the longing.

"Rand."

He turned slowly from his examination of my leg and his eyes flicked to hers.

"It's nice to see you."

He nodded. "And you. You look good."

"Thank you."

"How are your folks?" he asked, making conversation as his fingers dug into my thigh, massaging the knotted muscles there, cramped from walking oddly yesterday.

"They're well."

"Good, please give them my best."

"I will."

His eyes flicked back to my face. "Could you take those off for me?"

I really didn't want to.

"Stef," his voice rumbled, my name sounding decadent.

I took the oversized sunglasses off and put them on the top of my head, pushing my hair out of my face.

He studied me for long minutes, and I saw the muscles clenching in his jaw.

"Rand," I said softly, coaxing, trying to soothe the hurt and anger I found in his eyes.

"I need to have a word with Gil."

"No," Carly and I said together.

"Have you looked at your eye?" Rand asked me through gritted teeth before he tenderly lifted my leg off his thigh, stood, and gently lowered it onto the chair.

"But Rand," Carly began. "Gil was only—"

"He hit Stef and Stef belongs to me," he said, so calmly that for a second I missed that the man was furious as he started away from the table.

"Rand!" she called after him.

He increased his stride to reach her brother. Nothing anyone said, even me, was going to stop him. And I understood. No one was allowed to hurt the people who Rand Holloway loved.

"Gil!" he barked out.

I saw the man in question rise up out of the chair he was in. He looked terrified, which prompted my next yell for Everett. I was actually much relieved to see Glenn and Rayland walking toward us with some others.

"Glenn!"

He heard me, saw Rand, and bolted toward him. Unfortunately, he wasn't quite fast enough. As my boyfriend reached the table, Gil threw a roundhouse punch at him that missed him by a mile. What did that say about my fighting prowess that he had landed a punch on me so easily? And it wasn't like I didn't know how to defend myself, but the blow Rand returned was leagues beyond anything I had in my arsenal. It was dead on, full of power, catching Gil squarely in the face. I heard the pop even from where I was, saw the gush of blood, and realized that it had taken only seconds for Rand to break the man's nose.

"Goddammit, Holloway!" Gil yelled as Glenn and Everett grabbed Rand, pulling him back.

"Fuck you. It should've been your jaw, you stupid piece of shit!"

Gil put his head back as several of his men shoved napkins at him to stem the flow of blood.

"This is all your fault."

I looked over at Carly and saw how angry and hurt she was.

"Do you think he's going to thank you for this a year from now, five years from now, when he has no children and no friends? He'll have no one to have over to his home, no other parents to spend weekends with, no friends to go to the movies with or double-date with, because he won't have a wife—he'll just have you."

The venom and hatred in her voice was scathing.

"That man was made to be a father, made to be a friend, and you're robbing him of all of it, all he could be, you selfish piece of shit!"

It was, as usual, about more than me. I was a catalyst lately, and that was okay. Instead of making her own life, she had been banking on a man to give it to her. Unlike most of the women I knew, who made their happily ever after themselves and then found someone to share their dream with them, Carly was waiting for the guy on a white horse. I wish she had asked me; I would have told her that if she built her castle, someone would want to live in it with her. But she had to put it up first.

"You're taking away the home he could have! You're taking away everything!"

"Carly," I said quietly.

"I—"

"Just stop," I cut her off, "because what you don't know about Rand Holloway is a lot."

She sucked in her breath as she glared at me with wet, red-rimmed eyes.

"I don't know what kind of ranch you live on, Carly, but on the Red Diamond, Rand doesn't have time to see a movie or spend time with friends," I soothed her. "The man takes Sunday off mostly, and on that day everyone who lives on our ranch makes a trip up to the house, and we all have dinner, all the families, all the wives and kids. Everyone brings something, and in the summer we barbeque, and in the winter it's more stew and pot roast and things like that. Rand's friends normally see him on Saturday night after he's worked all day. He's been known to meet them to play cards or visit a bar to watch a game."

The tears were flowing, but she was listening.

"Yes, he's lost some friends because he chose me, but he's also got some new ones."

She took the napkin I passed her.

"And his family is the same because they all love me, and the ranch is thriving like crazy." I smiled at her, reaching for her hand. "Rand Holloway doesn't need a wife. He just needs to love and be loved in return."

The trembling she was doing turned fast to shaking. "It's filthy and you're sick, and if you think he really loves you, you're dead wrong. How could he?"

There would be no breakthrough, no epiphany, and I was so sad for her that I squinted so I wouldn't cry. I really was a bit more exhausted than I was giving myself credit for being.

"Okay," I breathed.

"When he throws you out on your—"

"Hey."

Looking up as Rand joined us, I noticed how big the man's smile was. The brilliant turquoise eyes were brimming with warmth and happiness, just dancing.

I was captivated.

"Did ya see me?" He waggled his eyebrows.

I shook my head, and the smile became absolutely evil. He was very happy with himself.

"We don't go around hitting people," I scolded him.

"Well, then, maybe people shouldn't go around hittin' people that other people think hang the moon." He cocked an eyebrow at me.

I stared up into mischievous blue eyes and realized that the way the man was looking at me, there could be no mistake about what I was to him.

Carly sucked in her breath.

He stood there staring down at me with possessiveness, heat, and plain old joy.

"Invite Glenn and Rayland home with us."

"I did already," he told me, reclaiming his seat beside me, lifting my broken leg back into his lap as Everett put a plate down in front of him. "They'll be right behind us when we leave, and Zach'll meet us there too."

Chris was there a second later with a small Ziploc bag full of ice. "Here boss, for the hand."

"Thank you," he said, eating with his left hand as he iced the knuckles of his right. Dusty brought his coffee and orange juice.

"Man, I am starving," he said, smiling around the table at his men as they all took seats, having moved from where they were sitting before to be close. "Hey, Ev, I saw the bull riding; not too bad."

"You would've won," he answered Rand.

"Yes, sir, I would've," he teased him. "But I don't suspect that Stef'll want me to ride the bull anymore, so we'll have to make sure you win next year."

"Yessir," Everett agreed.

Rand turned to Chris and then Dusty and complimented each of his men in turn. And I watched Carly listen and take in the scene in front of her, lingering, hovering there to see the men vie for the attention of the man who was their world. Because without Rand, there was no ranch, and without the ranch, they had no home. He was the nexus of everything, and the longer she stood there, the more she understood. The man was the same, and I was an extension of him to them. That I was a man made no difference.

Her concerns, the prejudice she was speaking of, might have mattered if Rand were dependent for his livelihood on one place or if he did business in only his town or the next, but he had been smart when he decided to grow his father's ranch, and made sure he explored all his marketing options far and wide. And whether people knew it or not,

Rand was a shrewd and disciplined businessman. He had good instincts, and he understood people, and lately, since he had a partner who knew acquisitions, he had become downright deadly in financial matters. There was nothing the man was missing except children. And he even had a plan for that with the help of his little sister, who was also my—

"Oh, shit." I jolted, remembering that I was supposed to call Charlotte.

Rand turned to look at me. "Did you just remember that Char's goin' to the doctor this Wednesday?"

"Yeah," I breathed, staring at him.

"Well, she called me when she couldn't get a hold of you, and I told her what you were up to, so she's comin' for a visit this weekend, and we can talk about things."

"Oh, God," I groaned. "Maybe I'll sleep in the bunkhouse, and you can tell her I ran away to join the circus."

He smiled at me. "She'll find you wherever you go, 'cause she loves you probably more than her husband or her mama or me."

I loved her just as much.

His smile was lazy and wicked. "She was fit to be tied."

"Crap."

"Maybe you best get her some jewelry," he offered, "or a car."

I nodded as he cackled.

"Rand."

He looked up at Carly.

"I hope you're happy."

"I am, thank you, and I wish the same for you."

She nodded fast before she turned and walked away.

"You take care now," he called after her before turning back to me. "I think when I explain things to Char, I'm gonna be in the same doghouse as you."

"Nope, death trumps secrets."

He brushed my hair back out of my face and looked at me before his brows furrowed.

"It's just a black eye. You should have been more worried about me on the bronco."

"You decided to ride the horse, Stef. That was your choice. You didn't choose to get hit."

"I—"

"Rand, you fuck!"

My cowboy turned his head and gave a sputtering, fuming, red-faced, pissed off Gil Landry his attention.

"I'm gonna call the sheriff and—"

"You won't do shit, Gil," he yelled over to the other man. "You hit Stef first, and I already stopped in town and saw Austin before I came out here. He told me to have you give him a call if you felt the urge to talk to him."

Gil was stunned.

"You know the sheriff here?" I asked Rand.

"Of course. We used to go fishing together when we was young. Now we hunt every winter. You met him before: Austin Cross. He has those speckled hunting dogs."

"Oh." I did remember.

"He looks flabbergasted," Everett said.

I turned to look at him. "What?"

"I don't have much call to use that word, and so… Gil Landry looked flabbergasted."

"That's a good word," Dusty agreed. "I like 'splendid.' I don't think splendid is used enough."

Everett nodded. "How 'bout, the boss threw a splendid punch."

"Yes." Dusty nodded. "It was splendid."

I rolled my eyes, and Rand started to chuckle while he ate.

"None of y'all is right in the head," Pierce muttered under his breath.

It was hard to argue with him.

After breakfast, Rand started ordering everyone around, and they moved fast since they were used to it, and then he and I went together to talk to the rodeo coordinators. Hud Lawrence was thrilled to see Rand, and Rand shook Katie Beal's hand for being the one to call and let us know about the rodeo in the first place. I watched her stare up at him in awe, and I got it. If you had an idea in your mind of what a cowboy was supposed to look like, with the hat and the Wranglers, the jet-black hair, and the killer blue eyes, Rand Holloway embodied that ideal. The look she gave me, like *good job landing that one*, was adorable. It never ceased to be interesting, the acceptance from some people, the anger from others. I myself had never cared who anyone slept with, and it still amazed me that some people did.

As Rand helped me back toward the trailer, his strong arm wrapped around my waist, I felt more like me than I had in days. And I got it. When I was with Rand, the tender, loving man he brought out in me was who I really was. I was still selfish, still opinionated and quick to get a rise out of, but with him, I was better. He brought out the best in me. What more could I ask for?

CHAPTER 10

GETTING HOME was indescribable. Rand put me on the couch to rest since I had fallen asleep in the truck on the ride home. I had no idea why it was that going someplace always took longer than getting back.

"We stopped a lot more times than you did," I told Rand.

"I'm sure you did."

"I was thinking I should cancel class tomorrow," I told him as Tyler came in the back door and yelled for Rand.

"I think that would be best." He smiled down at me, brushing my hair back from my face, the look in his eyes still the same as it had been for the entire ride home.

"I'm fine," I told him. "You want me to get up and make you dinner just so you can see?"

He shook his head before he leaned over and kissed my forehead.

"Rand!"

"What?" he snarled at Tyler, which was funny because he had been so tender only seconds before.

"Your mama called to say that she'll be here tomorrow, and Everett called to tell me that Rayland and Glenn are comin' for a visit as well—what the hell is goin' on?"

"I have things to discuss with everyone, even you, old man, and Stef here is fixin' to butt into your life as well."

Tyler turned to look at me. "What are you gonna do there, Stef?"

"I had no idea you had children," I told him.

He squinted at me. "And so you're thinkin' to do what with that information?"

"Invite them to the ranch, of course."

"They won't come."

I grinned slowly. "Oh, no?"

He rolled his eyes, and Rand chuckled above me.

"Stef is irresistible, you know that."

"I—"

"There's Glenn and Rayland," Rand interrupted him as lights illuminated the front windows.

I realized how much I wanted to close my eyes.

"Come on," Rand said, bending to scoop me up into his arms.

"What're you doing?"

"We're gonna all rest tonight. I don't feel like talkin' to everyone while we're all tired and short-tempered. I'll talk to Rayland and Glenn some, and then turn in."

I opened my mouth to interrupt him.

"Yes, I know, put out extra towels, washcloths, and the water pitcher with the glass that fits in the top that we use for company."

"Okay," I sighed, rubbing my eyes hard with the heels of my hands.

"Stop. Just close 'em."

"I missed you. I wanna see you."

"You can see me in the morning," he said as he picked me up and pressed me against his chest.

Leaning my head into his shoulder, I kissed the line of his jaw. "You don't have to take care of me. I'm not your wife."

"Where the hell did that come from?"

Instead of answering, I nuzzled my face under the collar of his shirt, inhaling his musky scent, licked salt from his skin—tasting him before I opened my mouth—and bit down gently.

"What're you doing?" he groaned, steadying himself on the stairs.

"I'm not weak. I can take care of myself and you if you let me."

"I know what you can do, Stef," he whispered, looking down into my eyes. "But just lemme take care of you, just this once."

The way he breathed in, the squint of his eyes, the press of his lips together, the cording of the muscles in his jaw, all of it together told me that I had scared him perhaps more than I knew.

"I want a hot shower, and then I want to get into bed with you."

"Will you let me help you?"

"I'm counting on it."

The shudder filtered through his strong, solid frame, and I felt like I could breathe for the first time in days.

Watching Rand made my heart hurt. He was so gentle, talking to me, gentling me like he did the horses, keeping up a running monologue as he explained about wrapping my leg in a garbage bag so I could shower.

Normally I would have tried very hard to seduce him. As he bent to wrap my leg in plastic, had I been a hundred percent, I would have shoved my groin into his face without invitation. As it was, the process of getting me into the shower and then back out exhausted me. I had existed on maybe three hours of sleep a night, and between that and my injury, I was ready to pass out.

Rand towel-dried my hair and then shoved me down on the bed. He had put me in a pair of sleep shorts and nothing else and swaddled me under the down comforter and tucked it over my shoulders and under my chin. He kissed my forehead and told me he'd be back with water. I muttered my agreement, and my eyes fluttered closed.

When I woke up several hours later, starving, I found Rand beside me, sitting there reading a book. First, he kissed me, which was amazing all by itself, and then he brought me food and made me take more drugs. Granted, it was only Tylenol, but since I had never been one for anything harder than alcohol, it was enough to keep whatever residual pain I had away. The roast beef sandwich was good, and sometimes plain potato chips are like a gift from heaven. The sun tea along with it, and I felt like a whole new person. Once Rand was back, I thanked him and asked if he would be able to read with me wrapped around him. He just patted his chest.

"Thank you for taking care of me," I said as I put my head on his chest, my hurt leg between his two good ones, and shoved my groin into his thigh.

He nuzzled my hair, and then when I tipped my head up, he kissed my nose. "I wish I had been there the whole time. Please, Stef, please don't ever leave without telling me where you're going again. I really need to know where exactly you're at when you ain't with me."

I nodded and pressed a kiss to the underside of his jaw.

He kissed my hair, inhaling me at the same time, and I could feel the tiny tremble snaking through the man's big body.

"I'm okay."

There was only a nod against my head. He loved me very much, and when I tilted my head back again to speak to him, he bent and kissed me.

His kiss was possessive, telling me without words who I belonged to. His hands were on my face as he moved my head so he could kiss my chin, jaw, and throat. It was wet and hot, and I whimpered as I rubbed my hardening cock against his thigh.

"What do you need?"

He reached down and gripped me through the thin cotton of the sleep shorts, and I made the garbled noise in the back of my throat. It felt so good.

I was rolled onto my back, and he slid the shorts down so that my now-leaking cock bobbed free. He bent my knees as he slid down between my legs, hands on the back of my thighs as he leaned over me and took my hardness down the back of his throat.

"Fuck, Rand." I arched up into him, gasping, my back bowing off the bed.

The man's mouth was wickedly talented, and he sucked all of me, and I could feel the muscles in his throat contracting. I had gone days without him, and my body knew what it wanted, what it had to have.

"Oh God, Rand, please turn me over and fuck me. I need hard. I want hard."

I was flipped gently to my stomach, and I lifted up on hands and knees, trembling with anticipation.

His hand went to the back of my head and he buried my face in the comforter at the same time there was the cool smear of lube on my entrance.

My whimper was loud as I felt the head of his enormous cock prod me.

There would be no foreplay, no preparation, no slow slide of fingers pushing into me, scissoring and stretching. There would be nothing but all of Rand's long, thick, erection thrusting deep inside me.

"Hurry," I begged him, even though it was muffled.

He plunged into me, and I howled with pleasure and release and need. No one would have ever believed that a man in pain, exhausted and bruised, would want to be fucked so hard he cried out. But to simply submit, to give up and let my body be ravaged so my mind could rest, to so trust another person that you gave them every little part of your soul, that was what I had to have. I took Rand Holloway into my body, my heart. There was nothing he didn't have, no part that was left unclaimed.

"Please," I cried and felt the tears flooding my eyes, rolling down my cheeks. "Oh, Rand, don't ever leave me."

He pounded into me, and the lovemaking became a blur of kissing and biting and licking and sucking and always, always, the deep, hard thrusting that made my world a rhythm of heat until I screamed out that I was going to come. His fingers, wrapped around my dripping cock, brought me to a shuddering release, and I closed my eyes so tight there was only black for long minutes before I was aware of hot come filling my ass and running down the backs of my thighs.

We stayed together, locked, my muscles rippling around him, his cock throbbing inside me, both of us trembling and heaving for breath.

"Rand?"

"You're the only one who makes me lose my fuckin' mind."

"I love you," I panted as his lips closed on the back of my neck, sucking hard.

"And I love you back," he husked, licking the sweat off my shoulder before he eased slowly, gently from my still-clenching channel.

He collapsed on the bed beside me, and I dropped down on top of him, curling my smaller frame around his massive one as he tucked my head onto his shoulder.

"Jesus, Stef, I love you more than anything. I will never, ever, let you leave me, and you gotta never think that's gonna change. We're gonna fight, but there will not come a time when I want you anywhere but at my side. You hear me?"

I nodded.

"Say it."

I smiled into the hollow of his throat. "Rand Holloway loves me."

"Yes, I do." He hugged me tight. "You're my whole life."

I fell asleep naked and sticky, wrapped in the strong arms of the man I loved. There was no better thing in the world.

CHAPTER 11

HE WAS surprised. Whatever Rayland Holloway had expected on the Red Diamond was not what he found. Breakfast had surprised him. I cooked, Rand made coffee, Tyler joined us, and so did all the unmarried men. The married men rode in from their houses, which were built on Rand's land far enough away to give them privacy. In the two years I had been there, Rand had added Tyler's house, and Mac's, since he was foreman, and Tom's, who had come to Rand with a family, and his cousin Chase's as well. Chase had met a woman in Winston, and because he and his wife were an interracial couple, it had been hard to find an apartment in town. So Rand had built them a house. All married men, he said, got houses. I thought Everett's might be next if he ever got his act together.

But Tom and Chase rode in, and they too greeted Rayland and Glenn when they reached the house. Everyone checked on me, winced at the eye, surveyed the cast on my leg, and said in various ways that they were glad I was okay.

"Can't have nothin' happen to you, Stef." Tom grinned at me. "I like my boss the way he is now. I ain't ready to have him back how he was."

Tyler had taken his brother and Glenn all over the ranch that morning, and Rand had shown him the website and the orders that came through at all hours. By webcam, he even showed off the efficient office in Dallas that handled Rand's business, introducing them to his sales manager, June Thomas; his accountant; and the other ten people who made certain that no one ever had to wait to buy beef from the Red Diamond.

"Congratulations again on the Grillmaster account, Rand." June smiled at him.

She was a very attractive woman who a lot of men made the mistake of thinking was only a pretty face and not a scary-smart financial shark. Her smile was predatory.

"Thank you."

"We look forward to doing much more business with you."

"Which is appreciated," he assured her.

"Give Stefan my regards," she told him since she couldn't see me across the room.

"Yes, ma'am." He smiled at her because he appreciated that too, that she included me as she did every other wife and every other husband of the people she did business with. I was Rand's partner; it was polite to hope I was doing well. In her mind, there was no difference, and my cowboy liked that about her so much.

Rand had to survey his ranch as he did every day, and Glenn and Rayland had ridden out to watch him, see the operation up close, and get a feel for the land. I checked my e-mail and got a nice message back from my boss at the college. She told me to of course take the day, take Tuesday, and rest, and to simply let her know if I needed Wednesday as well. I messaged her back that I would be in the next morning, but that I appreciated her concern. By the time lunch rolled around, I could tell from seeing the looks on Rayland's and Glenn's faces that the two men were overwhelmed with being on the Red Diamond. When Zach showed up, I watched them interact from the porch.

Zach was as tall and handsome as the rest of the Holloway men, but where the others had blue eyes, his were a lovely golden brown. From the little I could overhear, he was pissed that Glenn had used his need of Rand for selfish purposes. There was yelling and shoving, and Rand and Rayland had to break the brothers up. I was going to walk over to the fence when the profanity started flying, but Tyler showed up with May, and so I let them handle it instead, staying where I was, stretched out on one of the Adirondack chairs, my feet on the coffee table. I would have never done it inside the house, but on the porch it seemed perfectly acceptable.

"Everybody come on up here. I have something to say."

I sat up from my slouch as they all came clomping up the front steps, cowboy boots making a lot of noise, as Rand led them to me. He stepped around in back of me, hands on my shoulders.

"Oh my God," May gasped, crossing to me, sitting down on the loveseat, grabbing my hand. "Sweetheart, what in the world happened to your eye?"

"Mom," Rand said, and her eyes lifted from me to him. "Wait a sec, okay? Uhm, Zach, this here is Stef. Stef, Zach."

He was really the worst at introductions. He just basically said everyone's name, and that was it. "Nice to meet you." I smiled.

Zach seemed very interested in me from the way he was studying my face. "Same here."

"Okay, so." Rand squeezed my shoulders. "Mom."

Oh no.

"Wait." I turned my head to look up at him.

"I know Rayland's my biological father. Dad told me when I turned eighteen. I'm real sorry I never told you, but I was mad for a piece, and then by the time I worked through that, I just didn't have the heart to bring it up. Forgive me."

I turned to look at May.

Silence.

She just sat there, speechless, with her mouth open. As I checked everyone, I saw that Rayland had turned to stone, Tyler was holding on to the porch railing, Zach looked like a deer caught in the headlights, and Glenn, I was pretty sure, was going to be sick.

"That was fuckin' brilliant," I said, turning in my seat to look up at the man I loved.

He shrugged, shoving his hands down into the pockets of his jeans. "I ain't much for grandstandin', you know that. Sometimes the best thing is to just spit things out."

I knew that. "Yeah, but Jesus Christ, Rand."

And then all hell broke loose.

"You knew?" May screeched at her son.

"Your son?" Glenn roared at Rayland.

"Jesus," Zach breathed out, and the look on his face was hard to distinguish.

"You knew?" May's voice was increasing in decibel level.

"Your father?" Tyler barked at Rand.

I got up because I didn't want to sit there; I wanted to talk to my best friend. I missed Charlotte. Walking into the house, I grabbed my cell phone off the coffee table in the living room and called her. And because it was her, and because I had permission from Rand, which I had gotten that morning before we went down for breakfast, I broke the news to her about her brother.

"I know," she sighed.

My turn to be shocked. "What?"

"Yeah, Daddy told me when I turned eighteen. He wanted me to know, and if Rand ever told me, or didn't, he still wanted me to know."

"And?"

"And what? Rand Holloway and I have the same mom, and we grew up with the same dad, and so that makes us brother and sister. No one is ever taking him away from me, and even when I've wanted to kill him, I still claimed him as mine."

Of course the news had changed nothing for Charlotte.

"I'm sorry I didn't tell you."

"Oh, Char, that was not your secret to share."

"I should talk to him. Maybe I'll come early before the weekend and see you both."

I grunted.

"What was that?"

"Nothing."

"I saw the video, you know. I will smack you when I get there."

"Somebody already did."

"What does that mean?"

When I told her about Gil Landry and his sister and Glenn and how her cousin wanted to open a restaurant, she had me go back to where Gil hit me.

"I'll kill him!"

She was feisty, so she would try. "Rand already broke his nose."

"Oh, awesome. Put him on the phone!"

But when I went outside, I saw that Rand was no longer on the porch. When I looked, I saw him down by the large corral, leaning on the fence, and both Tyler and Rayland were with him. Rand had his arms crossed on the second rail down, forehead pressed to the wood. Rayland was standing close, closer than I'd ever seen them, and I could tell he was doing the talking.

"How about talking to your mom?" I offered Charlotte.

"Good," she said softly, and I could tell that the emotion of the moment was finally catching up to her.

When I offered May my phone and told her who it was, she snatched it from me and retreated into the house. I was left with the same stunned group of people I had left a half an hour before. They were sitting in silence, and I didn't want to intrude. Before I could turn to walk back into the house, there was throat clearing.

I turned to look at Zach.

"Do you think that, uhm, Rand would allow me to stay here with y'all?"

"Sure," I said softly. "But are you sure you'd be comfortable doing that?"

His eyes searched mine. "I think so."

I turned to look at Glenn. "I know that Rand will help set you up in your restaurant if that's what you want to do. He—"

"No," Glenn interrupted, taking a seat beside me, his knee bumping mine as he leaned forward. "My father and I are doing that together. Yesterday on the drive here, he fired me as foreman and told me to go start a restaurant or something."

I smiled at him.

Zach gasped.

"It's so like him."

"It surely is," Zach agreed. "He didn't tell you it was a good idea. He just threw you off his ranch, but he's gonna give you the money to start a restaurant, the same restaurant you've been talkin' about for the last four years."

"Yep."

"Christ."

"That's how he works."

"It is," Zach agreed. "He really is a son of a bitch."

"You could probably have my job as foreman," Glenn said to his brother.

"Not on a bet," Zach scoffed. "After I sell my ranch, I'm gonna come back here for a spell and work until I figure out what's next. And maybe bein' here will spark somethin'."

"Maybe," Glenn agreed, his voice hoarse as he leaned back, his shoulder against mine.

The three of us were quiet, watching the three men down by the large corral. Tyler was yelling, but I couldn't hear about what over the wind. Rayland was pointing at Rand and then patting his heart as he roared back, and my cowboy looked like he wanted to crawl out of his own skin. I stood up, moved to the porch railing, and yelled for him.

When his head turned, I waved for him, and he started toward me without a word to the other two men.

"What do you need, Stef?" Glenn asked me. "I can help you if you need something."

"Nope, only Rand," I told him as the man reached the porch steps and his eyes were on mine. "Your mother's in the house."

He nodded, but didn't leave, instead crossing to me and stepping close. His hand lifted to the back of my head as he leaned in and pressed his lips to my forehead.

"Everything will be fine," I promised.

He nodded before he left.

"That was nice."

I turned to look at Zach.

"You knew he needed a break, and so you gave him one without him lookin' like he needed it."

Exactly.

He gave me a slight smile.

I walked back over to them, taking my seat beside Glenn. When he turned to look at me, I didn't look away.

"I might be confused about who I want, but not what I want."

"I know." I patted his knee, leaning back, putting my feet up on the table, stretching out my legs.

After a minute, he put his feet on the table beside mine, and after another minute, Zach did too.

"All we need is some beer," Glenn sighed after several long minutes.

"We haven't even had lunch yet," Zach told him.

"We could drink lunch," I suggested.

Everyone agreed that my idea was amazing, but none of us moved. It was quiet out on the porch. The sky was gray—it looked like it might rain—and that crisp fall smell was in the air like a mixture of burning wood, wet earth, pine, and rain.

"This ranch feels like a home, Stef," Zach said after a while.

"It really does," Glenn admitted, head back, eyes closed.

"Does your arm hurt?" I asked him.

"Some. How 'bout your leg?"

"Some," I teased him.

He smiled, but didn't open his eyes.

"So are you okay about Rand?"

Deep male grunt from him. "Rand Holloway ain't my brother. The only brother I got is sittin' to my right. He'll always be what he is, my cousin I can barely stand… and that's all right."

Zach reached out and patted Glenn's leg, which pulled another grunt from the man.

"I'll come home for a bit after I get the ranch sold, and help you get the restaurant going."

"I appreciate that. Maybe you'll wanna stay and help me, you never know."

"Nope," Zach agreed, leaning back, pulling his hat low across his forehead. "You never do know."

I watched them, sitting there together, Glenn looking like he was asleep, Zach staring out into space, and wondered why they just couldn't say they were sorry for yelling at each other earlier and hug it out. But Zach stating he'd help and Glenn accepting was apparently as good as it got.

Tyler and Rayland walked up toward the house, and both men dropped down onto the sturdy chairs. They looked exhausted.

"So," I said to Tyler.

"You might have told me," he muttered.

"I had no idea until May told me while I was at the rodeo."

"And that there's another thing." Tyler turned on Rayland. "What the hell were you thinkin' lettin' your boy's partner get up on that damn horse? If you knew what Rand was to you and you knew what Stef was to him—what in God's name were ya thinkin'?"

"Like I could stop him!" Rayland pointed at me. "He don't listen to nobody about nothin'. He's just as pigheaded as you and Rand and Glenn and—"

"Just like a Holloway," May said as she stepped out onto the porch.

All eyes were on her, except Glenn who had fallen asleep, as she walked over to me, put a hand through my hair, and passed me my phone.

"Rayland, walk with me."

He got up fast and followed her off the porch and back down toward the large corral. We all watched them, walking side by side, Rayland having crooked his arm for May, and she holding on. I hoped they could find the closure they both needed.

"Hey."

I turned as Rand rejoined the group, taking a seat in the chair beside me, his feet beside mine on the table.

"I had a nice talk with her."

His mother, of course. "Good."

"I spoke to Charlotte on your phone as well."

I nodded. "You look beat."

"I think we all need a drink."

"I was saying that earlier."

He sighed deeply. "So you know, I am not giving those grazing rights in King to Rayland."

"But you said you'd think about it."

"Yeah, well, I thought about it, and it's no. After what he did to try and get them." Rand made a noise in the back of his throat. "And he told me that it was all him. When Glenn came up here, he was actually plannin' on going to Zach's ranch with me, just like I thought. That whole mess with us was just us, me and him, bein' our regular asshole selves to each other."

Beside me, Glenn started to snore softly.

"So he's a dick, but I knew that." Rand almost smiled. "But Rayland is the one who tried to take my land from me, not Glenn."

"He told me he didn't know when I got to the rodeo. I'm not sure if I really believed him, since he can be kind of a jerk."

"Because you were thinkin' he was a dick, he made sure to be one."

I nodded. "All you guys do that same thing."

"Yeah, I know it," Rand conceded with a grin. "Wake him up."

I shook Glenn's knee gently and made sure his eyes snapped open before I returned my attention to the man I loved. "But, Rand, with the grazing rights, you could give them to Rayland. You don't need to graze your cattle there."

"I might," he told me, "depending on how the Red continues to grow, but that ain't the point. He's still treatin' you like you ain't nothin', Stef, and after what you did and the men… I have a choice now that I wasn't gonna have because he decided to go behind my back and stab me. Where's the family in that?"

"I agree," Tyler chimed in, and I looked over at him. "You don't steal from a man and then want a seat at his table."

"Rayland is Rand's father."

"James was his father, and that's why he didn't turn out like Glenn or Zach."

"Screw you, old man," Zach snapped at him.

"You hide what you want," he said, pointing at Glenn. "As well as doing what you never wanted to do in the first place." He then turned to Zach. "And you're the same. Both of you made choices because you're afraid of your father."

"And if James were alive, you think Rand would have a man living in his house?"

"Oh, yes," Rand broke into the conversation. "Because I told him."

"What?" I gasped.

His electric blue eyes met mine. "We talked a lot about things, and when I started courting Jenny, told him I was gonna someday marry her, he wasn't sure that was the best idea. When I asked him why not, why marrying Jenny was no good, he said that maybe I should think about asking you to come live with me on the ranch instead, Stef."

I couldn't even breathe.

He sighed deeply. "And I did my best to deny it, and he smiled like he did and said okay. He knew I wasn't ready."

Leaning forward, I reached for him.

"He told me," Rand said and swallowed, sitting up to take my hand in both of his, "that whatever happened, that if I decided on you, Stef, that it was fine with him. He thought the world of you because Charlotte loved you so."

I cleared my throat. "How did he know about you and me? I didn't even know!"

"I suspect since I talked about you all the time that he knew."

"What did you say?"

"It wasn't nice."

"I'm not thinking it was." I smiled at him.

"I complained about you quite a bit, called you every word I could think of. Like I said, it wasn't good."

"And now people call you all those words."

"Which don't bother me half as much as I thought it would. I mean, don't get me wrong, I still have trouble thinking of myself as bisexual. I mean, I am, but I don't feel no different than I have all my life."

"Because it doesn't change who you are, Rand, just who you sleep with."

"You're still an asshole, gay, bi, or straight," Zach assured him.

"Nobody's talkin' to you," Rand groused at him.

"Fine," he replied irritably.

Rand looked back at me, and tugged me forward so he could kiss my forehead. "My father knew that if I ever pulled my head outta my ass, that it was gonna be you, Stef, so yeah, you bein' here on the Red—I wish my father was alive to see you living on his ranch."

I closed my eyes, clenched my jaw tight, and fought not to make a sound as I let his words find a place inside me forever.

"And that's the difference between my father," Rand breathed as I opened my eyes, "and yours," he told Zach. "So are you fine bein' here with me and Stef, or not?"

"I'm fine," Zach sighed. "I ain't got no problem with you and him long as I don't have to watch."

"Like I'd let you," Rand snapped at him, turning back to me, squinting.

"What's wrong?"

"You need to lie down. You look exhausted."

"I'm fine."

"No, you're not," he told me. "Get up."

I rose and he put an arm around my waist as I slid mine around his shoulders.

"I'm gonna put Stef in bed, make him some lunch, and I'll be back down to feed all the rest of ya."

"Take your time," Tyler told him, smiling. "You did real good with the rodeo, Stef. I'm real proud."

"I still want to talk to you about your kids, Tyler."

"Both those kids is older than you, Stef."

"What does that have to do with anything? I'm going to invite them out here to the Red."

"And for you, on Rand's invite, they might come," he confessed.

"Good." I gave him a grin.

He shook his head and settled back into his chair.

Inside the house, I told Rand that he needed to talk to Glenn and Zach.

"I know," he said as he bent, put an arm under my legs, and lifted me into his arms.

"I'm not an invalid."

"Just shut up and let me carry you in my own house if I want to."

As he mounted the stairs, I leaned my head into his.

"Better."

"Did you tell Rayland that you weren't giving him the grazing rights?"

"Yes."

"And what did he say?"

"He said that if he were me, he wouldn't give them to me either."

"And?"

"And I dunno, Stef. We'll have to see where we go from here. We ain't never gonna be a father and son since I already had one, but maybe we can get to be somethin' better than we are now."

"You're gonna let Zach stay, right?"

"Yes, I am."

"And what about Glenn?"

"I will help Glenn with the restaurant and whatever else he needs… to a point."

"What does that mean?"

"That means I ain't lookin' to let him have you."

I scoffed, leaning to kiss behind the man's ear.

He put me down, there in the hall, and when he was certain I was balanced, he bent and hugged me. I was pressed tight to him and wrapped up so that his face was in my hair and he was breathing me in.

"I love you so much," he whispered fiercely, squeezing tighter.

He really did. "I love you back, Rand."

We stood there, tangled together, each of us content until he lifted me up and carried me the rest of the way to our bedroom. I was put down, and pillows were shoved under my leg, propping me up, making me comfortable.

"Here." I patted the space beside me. "Lie down a minute."

He shook his head. "I got lots to do."

But I knew that Mac Gentry had everything under control. Rand's foreman had been pleased to see me like he never was when I got home, clapping me on the shoulder that morning at breakfast, telling me that all cowboys got thrown from horses at least once or twice in their lives.

"Just for a second, Rand, please."

He pulled off his boots and put his hat down on the nightstand and crawled up on the bed beside me. His head went to my heart and an arm curled around me. I stroked the thick black hair as I talked to him.

"Your mother and you, you guys must have talked while you were inside, huh?"

He grunted.

"Is she okay?"

Nod.

"Good, I'm glad. I want her to forgive herself for not telling you."

"I told her I was sorry, and she said she was too."

"I knew you two would be okay. I just didn't know about you and Rayland."

He pressed his big muscular body against me tighter, lifting so his face was tucked into the side of my neck. "Rayland doesn't get me and you. When he does, the day he does, he can be more."

And that made sense.

"I think the idea of you helping Tyler with his kids is real nice."

"We'll both try, Rand, all right?"

"Okay." He yawned. "You looked real nice at the bachelor auction, Stef. Did I tell you?"

"Yes, you did."

"Never again, though. You don't go nowhere without me."

"I won't."

He yawned again, nuzzling, and when he sighed the last time, I knew he was falling asleep. Big strong scary man, and he was wrapped around me, clutching tight even when he drifted off.

Bella came to check on me minutes later, coming into the room, jumping up on the end of the king-sized bed, and waiting for my word.

"It's fine, this once," I told her.

She lay down, head on her paws, and pushed her muzzle into the arch of my foot. I could feel her warm breath through my sock.

When her head popped up, I looked toward the door. May was there seconds later.

"Oh, there he is."

"He's kinda beat," I told Rand's mother.

She smiled gently. "He's kind of in love, is what he is."

"Me too," I told her as she walked over to the rocking chair in the corner of the room, picked it up, and carried it over beside the bed.

"I can't believe he kept this old thing."

"He loves it—that was your chair, wasn't it? He sits in it usually when he's planning something, when he has to think."

She chuckled. "I used to do the same thing."

We were silent for a few minutes, each thinking, I was sure, about Rand.

"So you talked to Rayland?"

"Yes."

"And?"

"And nothing's changed, but Rand knows and that lightens things between us."

"James was an amazing man."

"Yes, he was and I see so much of him in Rand."

"He really loved his father," I said, kissing my cowboy's forehead.

"Well, it went both ways. I mean, they never said such things to each other, but they both knew."

"I like being able to say it and hear it."

"Oh, Stef, I love that Rand is the kind of man who isn't afraid to speak his heart. He never did with Jenny and I was worried that he never would, before you."

"He tells me and shows me."

"I know." She nodded and I saw her eyes fill. "And I'm so happy that he can."

She reached for my hand, and I took it.

"If you hadn't gone to the rodeo, Stef, none of this would've happened. It's wonderful that you did that, for all of us, not just Rand."

"Well, I don't know if Rayland will ever accept me, and I don't know if he and Rand will ever be friends, but at least the air is clear between them."

"And Rayland sees the life that Rand's made for himself, his ranch, his men, and his life with you."

"Rayland hates me."

"He doesn't. He just doesn't understand how Rand can love you the same as he loved his wife or…."

"You." I squeezed her hand before I let it go.

"Yes."

"He might never understand, and that's okay. He just needs to accept it if he's ever really going to be a part of Rand's life."

"Well, he wants that badly. What man in his right mind would not want to claim Rand Holloway as his own?"

"Nobody."

She smiled at me.

"He's your son, too, ya know? James didn't raise him alone."

Quick nod from her. "I know."

I saw her scrutinizing me. "What?"

"You seem more settled to me, like you took off your parachute."

"What?"

She chuckled. "Stefan Joss, I know that you came into this relationship with Rand ready to bail out if things got rough, pretty sure that they would. You were making sure you had a good enough job so you had an exit strategy ready to go at a moment's notice."

"Oh God," I groaned.

Her laughter got louder. "But since you took that new job at the college, I feel like you've sort of thrown caution to the wind. You're committed to being here now, with him, and to staying. It feels like you're staying."

"I am."

"I'm so glad. I've never seen my son this happy, and because of that, he's not angry with me or Rayland. He's better at accepting faults and forgiving. Not that everything's perfect, but Rand's in a good place in his life, and I love seeing him like this."

"He and Rayland need to fix things between them."

"That's up to them, but we're not talking about that anymore. I'm talking about you, Stefan Joss. You have changed things in Rand's life, given him the home he always wanted, and now you have to realize, yes, everyone makes their own joy, but having you here adds to Rand's. You're the only one who can make him this happy. He's building his life around you."

I nodded because I knew that, and my throat had closed up hearing it out loud. Things you thought in your head always carried more weight when spoken.

"If you weren't here, Stef, the fallout from all this, from Rayland and I keeping secrets, would have been horrible. Rand has a number of good qualities, but before you were here, forgiveness, acceptance, these were not among them. You changed everything."

"I hope for the best."

"Oh, sweetheart." She smiled warmly, rising to kiss my cheek. "Of course for the best."

I watched her stroke her son's hair, put a hand on his cheek. "He's a good man," I told her.

"Yes, he is." She nodded before walking toward the door, taking a moment to give Bella a pat. "And I love how you being here has influenced life at the ranch, Stef. Even something as simple as having a dog here in the house in the middle of the day and not only at night—just those little things are what makes a house into a home."

She was at the door when she turned.

"Keep him up here as long as you can. He needs to rest. I can tell he's tired."

"May—"

"Charlotte tells me that she's going to help you and Rand have children."

I opened my mouth, but nothing came out.

"I'm tickled pink." She smiled warmly. "Now I'm gonna get lunch started. I'll bring you all up something as soon as I see what there is to fix."

"Yes, ma'am."

She blew me a kiss before she left.

My future stretched out in front of me, and I could see it clearly: my life with Rand, the ranch, the community he would create, all that he would achieve that was possible, amazingly, because I was there with him. He needed me to ground him, and I was thankful that I could mean that much to a man I loved with all my heart.

"Crap."

I looked down at Rand as he rolled sideways onto his back beside me.

"I fell asleep, didn't I?"

"Just for a few minutes."

"Shit, Stef, I got things to do."

I rolled over on top of him, pinning him under me to the bed. "Just stay a little while longer."

"That ain't fair. You know I can't say no to you."

"I know that, Rand Holloway, and it's one of the many things I love about you."

WHEN THE DUST SETTLES

Mary Calmes

As always, a thank-you to Lynn, and to Poppy
for getting things sorted out.

Chapter 1

"THERE, BOSS, take a left."

I took the turn as directed and the five other people in the pickup truck with me—three in the back seat, two in the front—yelled at the same time that it was the house on the right.

There were a lot of lights on, and clothes and stuffed animals were strewn all across the front lawn.

Crap.

I got out and heard the passenger's side door open, along with movement in the back of the pickup, at the same time.

"No," I barked, whirling to stare into the interior and the truck bed as I slammed my door shut.

Five pairs of eyes all between the ages of eighteen and twenty-two were pinned to me. A quarter of my staff had insisted they were going with me, cajoled, and finally flat-out refused to get out of my truck when I left to go pick up Josie Barnes. The rest of them, those old enough to know better than to leave a restaurant during the nightly dinner rush, stayed there, taking care of the place that had become home for all of us, not just me.

"Everybody stays in the truck," I ordered from where I stood in the street. "I don't want any of y'all hurt."

"But boss, her dad and her brother are up in there. We gotta go in with ya," Andy Tribble, one of my busboys, pleaded. "You didn't bring no backup."

"Kevin'll be here in a second," I explained quickly. "He's right behind us—he'll go in with me."

"Yeah, but—" Shawnee Clark began to argue.

"No!" I yelled and then included them all with a wave of my hand. "Any of y'all that gets outta this truck is fired, ya hear?"

"But I was the one that answered the phone when she called," Danny LaRue chimed in. "I should go in since I told her I was coming."

I sent up a quick prayer for strength. "What were her exact words, Danny?"

Silence.

"Time's a wastin'."

He coughed. "She said since you were still fishing that—"

"Since I was still fishing," I repeated. "Meaning that if I was there, I was the one she wanted, right?"

Nothing.

"D?"

He huffed out a breath. "Yeah."

"Well, then."

When he looked at me, his face was scrunched up. "You shouldn't go in alone."

Everyone nodded at once in support of his statement.

I knew why. I did. They needed me. I was the boss; it was my place, our restaurant, The Bronc. I'd pulled it out of thin air into existence, and they'd all taken refuge there with me in one form or another. I was the glue. Without me, if anything happened to me… they would all be adrift, and while for a few that would be a brand-new experience—some were too young to have lived totally alone yet—for others, it meant being without an anchor all over again.

So I understood that the fear was first for me, second for them, real and tangible and in no way self-serving. None of them wanted me in danger.

"Just nobody fuckin' move," I growled, those my final words on the subject.

There was lots of nodding and they all stayed put. I knew it wasn't the threat that kept them in their seats, though, but the look on my face. I had on my serious one.

I was almost to the porch when the screen door banged open and Josie's brother—she'd only ever called him Bubba—about twenty years old, came charging out with an electric guitar clutched in his fist. Since I knew from our Christmas party eight months before that it wasn't his, I surprised him and grabbed it out of his hand.

"What the hell," he roared, reaching for it as I put two fingers on his collarbone to keep him still.

"Step back," I growled, and then keeping my eyes on him, I yelled, "Kev, get over here!"

My head bartender, Kevin Ruiz, was a little taller than me, hovering around six three and had twice the muscle. He'd followed my pickup in his Chevy Avalanche that dwarfed my ancient Dodge. I'd heard him pull up while I was crossing the yard.

"You best get off our porch before I call the cops," Bubba threatened.

I didn't move, just held the instrument out to Kevin until he moved up behind me and took it. "Look around for the amp," I directed.

"Yeah, boss."

"Who the hell do you think—"

"Shut up," I warned, bumping him hard as I walked by, up the porch steps, and into the house.

"What the fuck are you doing?" he shouted, catching me as I stalked into the living room.

It was a horrific sight that sent a chill down my spine. At the same time I felt a quick swirl in my stomach. The desire to pivot and punch a hole through a wall, any wall, was nearly overwhelming.

Josie Barnes, born Joseph William Barnes—which I knew because when I hired her, we had to do paperwork together—was on the floor at her father's feet. Mr. Barnes had his clippers out, and her hair, which had hung to the middle of her back in thick chestnut layers, was now sticking up in ugly uneven tufts, shorn down to her scalp. Her face was scrubbed clean of the normal simple makeup she wore, the sprinkle of freckles on her cheeks stood out in stark contrast against her pale skin. She was sitting there naked, panties and bra on the floor, holding her legs tight together and her hands clutched over her chest.

I saw red.

I charged across the room, grabbed Mr. Barnes's neck in one hand and the clippers in the other. I hurled him back so hard he fell down onto the couch, and the clippers I turned and flung against the wall as hard as I could. They exploded in a shower of plastic and metal.

"Ohmygod, who is this man?" Josie's mother, Miranda, standing by the mantle clutching a Bible, shrieked at me.

"I'm her boss," I bellowed at the woman whose name I only knew because it was on the emergency contact form in my office. I was betting we'd be replacing her name before the day was out.

All Holloway men were big and loud; it's just how we were made. We were also black haired, square jawed, hard muscled, stubborn, and rude. And even though I was the smallest of the family by far, I was just as ornery and noisy. It was not up for debate. Those were the facts.

So when I roared from my diaphragm, she recoiled, slid sideways, and hugged the wall.

"You know he's a boy, don't you, you dumb fucker?" Mr. Barnes spat as he got unsteadily to his feet.

"I don't see a boy," I said frankly, and suddenly I felt a hand on my calf. Looking down, I saw Josie trembling.

I could only imagine what my eyes looked like when I turned to Mrs. Barnes. "Get me a blanket, ma'am, and I will take your child up outta here and you won't never be bothered again."

My drawl, normally not that pronounced, got really thick when I was mad.

"I know you," Mr. Barnes snarled, taking a step away from me. "You're Joey's boss, that fag that runs The Bronc where he works."

He didn't know I was gay. He threw the "fag" in for good measure, but like I cared. "Yessir, that's me."

"So you gonna take him home and fuck him?"

The bile rose in my throat. This was the man's *child*, whom he had held as a baby, played with, held hands with…. It defied all understanding and human compassion.

"Actually, no, sir," I said hoarsely, my voice nearly bottoming out, as furious as I was. "Josie's a girl. I only fuck boys."

He swung at me and I put him on the ground. Mrs. Barnes was screaming when I threw Bubba down on top of her husband a moment later. One redneck throwing roundhouse punches at me or two, it didn't matter none. I was raised on a ranch; I had been breaking horses and driving cattle and tussling with anyone who wanted a piece of me since I was a kid myself. Compared to Josie's out-of-shape father and spindly brother, I was a god.

I took the blanket her mother shoved at me from the couch, bent, wrapped Josie up, and lifted her into my arms. The desperate wounded sobbing began instantly.

"Is there anything in this house you need? Tell me now, 'cause you ain't comin' back."

She heaved out a breath. "He-hee-he broke my guitar! I can't—"

"No," I soothed, pivoting and heading for the door. "I got the guitar, it's fine. Kevin has it. Where's the amp?"

Her face went from catastrophic to filled with light and hope in a second, even though still awash in tears. "You saved my guitar?"

"Of course I saved your goddamn guitar," I groused, scowling. "Where's the case?"

She pointed. "Right there by the door."

"And your amp?"

"At work. I never bring it home."

I grunted.

Kevin was right outside on the porch, and when I opened the screen, I dumped Josie into his arms and grabbed the case in time to see Mr. Barnes, red-faced and sweaty, closing in on me with a baseball bat.

"Rethink your course, old man," I warned. "I will feed you that fuckin' bat along with every one of yer teeth."

"You—"

"You think I don't see them bruises on her neck and face? Her right eye's about swoll shut and her lip's bleedin'."

"Stop saying she!" he thundered. "That's a boy! He was born a boy and he'll die a boy and—"

I cut off his rant. "She sings like an angel, you know. Gonna be big someday, and y'all are gonna be terrible sorry when everyone knows what you did here."

"At least he looks like a boy now!"

"No, sir." I shook my head. "*She* looks like a baby bird that you put under your boot."

"You—"

"I'ma say this once," I began, drawing myself up as big as I could. "I don't never wanna see none of y'all up at The Bronc. If I do I'll have you arrested for trespassin'."

"And where will he live? Who will pay for him to go to school or—"

"That ain't your concern no more, how she pays for anythin'," I said and turned, kicking the screen door down as I left. Walking over it, I scanned the porch once I was outside.

I found a makeup bag, a broken blow dryer—not that, unfortunately, she'd need one for a while—and lots of thongs, panties, and bras. I gathered it all up and was striding through the now-empty yard moments later.

Everyone screamed at once.

"No!" Josie's fractured voice rose above the others.

I looked back over my shoulder and saw Mr. Barnes on the porch with his rifle. Wheeling to face him, I ran through every scenario I could imagine, but all of them came back to the same conclusion.

I was dead.

He could shoot me and claim self-defense because I was in his yard. My people would watch me bleed to death, and that would be their last memory of our time together. Or… I could play the last card I had.

"You know Rand Holloway?"

He squinted at me. "Everyone in Hillman knows Rand Holloway, you ignorant—"

I put my hand over my heart. "Glenn Holloway."

It was fun to watch the color drain from his face. Rand was the kind of man nobody wanted to cross. But it wasn't really Rand—my cousin, well… half brother—who was so frightening, but his ranch was like a small town now, and there were some men who worked for him, Mac Gentry most notoriously, who had dangerous reputations. Even the police were no better deterrent than the men who called the Red Diamond home.

I saw the rifle shake, and I spun on my heel and walked to the side door of the pickup.

Shawnee zippered open a duffel bag and I dropped all the underwear in. I saw Josie was dressed, and when I got in the truck, I took off my Stetson and shoved it down onto her head, low over her eyes.

"We're fixin' to stop by Caffrey's and pick you up a hat for work tomorrow."

She was in my lap then, sobbing into the side of my neck, and I figured we were never getting out of there if I just didn't leave her where she was.

We drove away fast after I took a breath and my heart started pumping again.

BACK AT work an hour later, I had Eric and Jamal rig up a makeshift shower so Josie could take one. She needed to get all the fine little hairs off her body so she didn't scratch herself to death. Kevin used the clippers we had in the office and evened out what was left of her hair, shaving it all to the same one inch off her scalp. On the way to The Bronc, we had stopped and picked up three long scarves for her to tie around her head, a cowboy hat for work, a pleated purple cap, and a pale blue Army hat with silver stars on it. We also bought neon blue hair dye so what fuzz there was, was at least an interesting color.

After a thorough inventory, all of Josie's things were accounted for, the guitar and amp being the most important of all. She must have thanked me about nine hundred times when I had carried her out of my truck, her arms and legs wrapped around me as though she were a young child and not a seventeen-year-old girl.

The boys attached a hose to the sink in the employee bathroom, ran it out the back door, and because a lot of the girls sunbathed on the roof before work, they had towels to hold up to give Josie some cover. It took time, but finally with her body washed and clothed, hair dyed, makeup applied, then being fed and hugged over and over, she stopped shaking and breathed. I realized I finally could as well.

I got a call from a sheriff's deputy because the Barnes' swore out a complaint against me.

"So what's our next step here?" I asked him,

He cleared his throat noisily on the other end of the line. "Nothing at all," he informed me, sounding nervous as hell. "Just—if you might see your way clear to letting Rand know that we let this whole incident drop…then that would be good."

"Yessir I will," I replied, putting the drawl in my voice. "He'll be mighty pleased I reckon."

His exhale was audible.

People living in deathly fear of Rand Holloway was working for me.

By eleven Josie was taking a nap on the couch in my office while I sat at the bar and talked to Kevin, Callie, and Marco. I closed up early at midnight instead of two in the morning and had everyone on the floor in the employee break room a half an hour later. They were all looking at me.

Two days.

You wouldn't think the place could go completely to shit in two days, but it most certainly had. Without me there, my restaurant exploded in anger, frustration, name-calling, and backstabbing. And while I was glad to finally know all of what was going on and have everything that was bubbling below the surface out in the open, I could have done without the drama.

I really hated drama.

"If one person doesn't pull their own weight," I said, addressing my staff, "the whole team gets dragged down."

The room exploded in noise. People turned on each other, there was pointing, there was yelling, and I let it go because I could feel the tension in the room dissipate with just the volume.

Kevin walked over to me, and after a minute I nodded and he blew the air horn, which startled the hell out of everyone.

I stood, lifted my hands, and told them all to shut the fuck up. Once I had silence and fixed stares, I started again. "Why didn't anyone tell me that JT was bangin' every single woman that came in here?"

Abruptly, no one could look me in the eye.

"He's gone."

And that fast, everyone was back to looking at me, suddenly hopeful, and of course I understood why. JT had been taking my money and doing no work for it, and they'd all thought he'd had my blessing to be that way, when the truth was far more ridiculous. I'd had no idea. I'd thought he was a good guy, but it turned out he was lazy and cruel and a total womanizer. When Kevin and I busted him in my office having sex with a guest from the hotel, I fired him on the spot. Jamal and Eric really enjoyed carrying him out the back. Callie Pena, my office manager, had his paycheck under his windshield wiper, calculated out to the penny.

She was thorough like that.

They waited.

"To replace him, as of today, Kevin has been promoted to manager," I told them. I then tipped my head at Bailey Kramer, who was sitting in the back holding Josie's hand. "Bail, you're the new assistant."

She was stunned, and the smile I got, slow, sheepish, spreading over her features, showing off rows of perfect white even teeth, made me break into one too.

"So now we're good," I announced. "Marco is taking over the head bartender spot."

There was applause as he stood and bowed, promising he wouldn't let me down. This was his home. After prison, a lot of people wouldn't take a chance on him. The fact that I had gambled meant the world to him and his family.

It was the same for many of the people who worked for me. My head chef, Javier Garza, was—they said—let go from his last position for stealing and—he said—for being Mexican. The reality was that his changes—brisket in pecan and mesquite marinade and turkey legs for the kids added to the steak plates and hamburgers we started with made us crazy successful in a very short amount of time.

Two years ago, because Mitch Powell, the builder and owner of the Kings Crossing Resort and Spa, owed Rand Holloway a few favors, he paid off one of them by giving me a throwaway location for my new restaurant, The Bronc, next to the golf clubhouse. We weren't in the main area where all the other restaurants were, and because of that, people had despaired of our chances for success. The thing was, though, it was my dream, and I had been thinking and planning it for years. So when it came time to execute, I did.

We covered the parking lot in the same rubber they used for play areas for kids at school, put poles up so no one could drive in, filled the entire space in picnic tables, and built a counter ledge all the way around it. Only families got to sit at the tables. It was funny how many times single parents, or two men or two women, made the choice to think we didn't count them in our definition of "family." How many times was I stopped and thanked, told that a member of my staff had brought them to a table, sat them down, and explained that, yeah, if you had kids, you got to sit and take a load off. If you had grandparents with you, you got to sit. But two on a date, or a group of guys, that's what the ledge was for, just wide enough to put a plate on. You had to shovel your food in while standing up. But for people with strollers, people with teenagers, there was a table with an umbrella over it just waiting for you.

The comments on Yelp, Zomato, and TripAdvisor, on our Facebook page, on our Twitter feed, as well as in the *Lubbock Avalanche-Journal*, were all wonderful. The service was fantastic, everyone said across the board. Whoever owned The Bronc really knew how to take care of people. All the comments were really nice to hear. When Guy Fieri showed up to tape an episode of *Diners, Drive-Ins and Dives*, I nearly passed out. And even though I wasn't the one in the kitchen cooking for him, I could not have been more proud when I shook his hand and he thanked me for having him there. It was my place, after all. The Bronc Burger, made with ponzu sauce and buffalo meat, was apparently one of the best things Guy had ever had. I was thrilled, so was my staff, and the influx of new patrons staggered us all. As a result of all the good feedback, press, word of mouth, and independent foodie blogs, the business took off and the money came rolling in.

It was, in my opinion, the coupling of amazing food and great service. When we first opened, all we served was a steak plate—cubed pieces of meat marinated in garlic and red wine sauce—and hamburgers. That was the extent of our selection, except for the sides. There were tater tots, sweet potato fries, coleslaw, mac 'n' cheese, and chili. We didn't have a kids' menu. You could order a half, though, and what kid didn't like mac 'n' cheese? Soon after we added this amazing tofu burger. It sounded gross when we added it to the menu, but holy crap, did we sell a ton of them. I had my own chef for that, Han Jun. His mom was East Indian, his dad was from Okinawa, and he was the one who added the ponzu sauce to the steak too, which made the garlic taste even better. Because the tofu burgers were so popular, instead of opening up a second grill in the back, I made it the vegetarian area. The grill was new; it had never had any meat cooked on it, ever. We even had a sign over it that read: *If you're packing meat, get the hell outta here.*

Really, the tofu burgers, made with all the same stuff as the steak except for the cow, were a bigger hit than I thought they would be. What started out as a "maybe" changed into a great addition, another dimension to the restaurant, and the vegetarian window three of my girls painted and decorated so it looked like an entrance to a secret garden was what a lot of people made a beeline for.

Inside we had a full bar, and seating was basically a huge island for drinking along with eating. There was no place to park yourself inside unless you were drinking. The food part was all outside.

In the winter we tented the parking lot and got space heaters and blowers. In the summer we had misters and fans. What was nice was that Stefan Joss, Rand's partner, negotiated everything for me when I first moved in. He was scary, and that had surprised me. He looked sort of sweet, but then all of a sudden, you found yourself faced with a predator, all teeth and claws.

Stefan negotiated the one thing I had no idea I would need—a flat utility rate. For seven years. I almost passed out.

"How?"

"Gifted." He smiled at me and his pretty emerald-green eyes glinted.

I was so thankful at that moment, I sold my soul to the devil and told Stef that whatever he needed, I was his guy. I owed him and no task was too much, no favor was too great to pay. And now, after two years, Rand was collecting on what I owed his partner.

It was why I went away for a few days of solitude.

I needed to be in a calm place before I had to submit to taking orders from Rand and listen to his foreman, Mac Gentry, tell me how stupid I was. I needed to be cool and grounded before I left with them for a long weekend of driving a small herd of cattle—only two hundred head plus calves—from grazing land up in the Panhandle back down to the Red Diamond.

At least, that's where I *thought* we were going. I wasn't positive. They weren't Rand's cattle, meaning they weren't born and raised on the Red; instead, he'd purchased them at auction when the ranch they were living on was seized by the federal government in a USDA raid. Apparently tainted beef was tracked to the Bannon Cattle Company in Montana, and when undercover FDA agents went in to investigate, they found gross violations everywhere from the stockyards to the slaughterhouse. The cattle were being treated inhumanely, and more importantly, killed painfully and sloppily. At auction, no one wanted to put the time and money into grazing the cattle or seeing if the two hundred head left could be salvaged. Except Rand.

Rand bought them all, had them trucked from Montana to Texas, and they'd been grazing for the past six months separate from his own herd. It was easy to pick out Rand's cattle from any others. He didn't castrate, dehorn, tail dock, or perform tongue resection on calves. At the Red Diamond Ranch and Cattle Company—he added to the ranch's name when he started shipping beef internationally—he had also done away with branding the year before. No one stole cattle from Rand Holloway. He had too many men—normally, just not this weekend—and he had become his own law. All Red Diamond cows were healthy, strong, and treated like a gift. No one mistreated anything on Rand's ranch, and though there were people who found killing animals to eat them an abomination, even they could tour the Red and find no instance where any livestock suffered.

People were another matter. I, for one, would be suffering this weekend.

Between weddings, childbirth, and vacations, Rand was short-handed, so he called in my marker with Stef. I had to go sit in a saddle from sunup to sundown for three days, beginning early Friday morning and concluding late Sunday night, and look happy about the whole experience.

So, I had needed to relax and fish before I rode into hell.

The drive was starting out early the next morning, so after the meeting broke up, I offered to drive Josie to her friend's house, where she would be staying for a week. I also had to stop at my place and grab my gear since I had to report to the Red in only a few hours.

"Aren't you going to be tired?" Josie asked.

"Maybe I'll sleep through the bullshit."

"What?"

I shook my head because I didn't want to start talking about my family.

She got in the truck with me and I drove us to my house. As she stood in my living room glancing around the bungalow, I got the feeling I was being judged.

"What?"

She coughed. "Oh no, nothing."

I realized I needed to throw away the five empty food containers on the coffee table in the living room. "Just spit it out."

"You, uhm, live here alone, don't you?"

"Yeah, why?"

She shook her head and gave me a big smile. "I was just wondering."

I rolled my eyes and left the room. She followed me into my bedroom after a minute, hovering in the doorway, afraid, it seemed, to trail me any farther.

"What?" I snapped.

Her eyes were wide and round as she caught her breath. "Do you smell that?"

"What?"

She peered around the corner. "Did you kill something in here?"

"You're hysterical," I said as I checked my clothes.

She put her hand over her nose and gagged.

"What the hell's the matter with you?"

"Are you kidding? You just sniffed that shirt before you stuffed it into that duffel bag."

"Well, yeah," I said absently, picking other clothes up off the floor. "I don't know if it's clean or not."

She pointed at the chest of drawers in the corner. "Clean clothes go in there, boss."

I grunted.

"Ohmygod!" she shrieked, which startled me, and I swung around to face her.

"What's wrong now?"

"You're a grown man, for crissakes!" She was horrified, going by seeing her nose scrunched up and her brows furrowed and the look of disgust all over her face. "We walked by a perfectly good-looking washer and dryer. Do they not work?"

"They work."

"Well, then?"

"I—"

"Your kitchen reeks," she said flatly. "This is your home, boss, not a dump."

"I was fixin' to—"

"Seriously, this house is so cute from the outside, but"—she grimaced so I couldn't miss it—"the inside looks like ass."

"I ain't never here," I defended myself.

She crossed her arms and tipped her head, staring up at me. "So how about this," she began. "Instead of playing musical houses for Josie, maybe I should stay here and get this place shipshape. You have that apartment over the garage that could be mine."

"It's full of tools and black widow spiders."

"Yes, well, the tools can go in the garage and the spiders can die."

"Yeah, but—"

"There's a shower and toilet up there, right?"

"Well, yeah."

"I mean, we all saw it when you moved in."

"I—"

"It's a studio apartment, so enough room for one."

"You don't wanna live with your boss."

"I do, actually," she said pointedly. "I feel safe, and oh dear God do you need me."

"You—"

"Then it's settled," she announced cheerfully. "You go off and ride horses, I will make this place a home, and by the time you get back, it'll be livable."

"No, I—"

"And for rent I might even cook, but for certain I will work on the house and the backyard that could be great if you, you know, mowed."

"I can't have a girl living with me. What would everyone say?"

"They would say, boy, that Glenn Holloway is a soft touch, but everyone needs a little sister to take care of them."

I threw up my hands, got out the spare key for her, and told her not to drink my beer or eat all my leftovers.

The wince of apparent pain over the suggestion made me laugh.

"As if any of those leftovers will still be here when you get home." She retched. "I'm getting a hazmat suit on and then I'm bleaching everything."

I could only groan.

"And as far as me drinking your beer—I hate that stuff, so really, you don't have to worry."

"No boys over here 'cept the ones from work, you hear?"

The look I got, as though I had lost my mind, no one could have missed. Clearly boys were *not* on her agenda at the moment.

I finished packing and told her she could sleep in the spare bedroom until the studio was cleaned out. "Get the guys to help you."

"Like I'm doing all that by myself."

"And seriously, kill the spiders first."

"Yeah, no kidding."

She trailed after me to the kitchen, and when I opened the refrigerator to get a bottle of water, she gasped.

"It ain't that bad."

She pointed. "Is that *green*? Ohmygod, what *is* that?"

"You—"

Hesitantly she took a step closer before pointing at what I was pretty sure used to be potato salad a very long time ago. "I think that has fur on it."

I locked the door on the way out.

Chapter 2

It was three forty-five in the morning by the time I made it out to the Red Diamond, towing a horse trailer that was in better shape than my truck. I'd driven over to the Blue Rock Stables where the owner, Addison Finch, let me keep my horse. There was no way in the world I would ask Rand for room in his stable. What was great was that Addison was the one who took care of the horses for the resort, so the walk over there at night from my restaurant so I could ride Juju was short. I had a routine down. Jog over, work out my horse, and then run the long way home to my bungalow. What wasn't so great was I'd made my horse as nocturnal as I was, so when I got there in the early morning and loaded her into the trailer, she only had one eye open, just like me.

The house was lit up when I pulled in, so I knew people were awake. That made sense. Rand normally started his day at four, and we had at least a five-hour drive to get to the cattle.

Sitting there, I debated just calling and telling him that I'd come down with pneumonia, or the plague, or just *anything* to get out of the drive. It wasn't even his fault, really; it was mostly that Rand was larger than life and everything he did turned to gold, making it damned difficult to ever measure up to him.

Rand owned the largest legacy property between Dallas and Lubbock and had made said ranch self-sufficient out of necessity. Basically, he'd been booted from not only his seat on the community board of directors of Winston—where the Red Diamond was technically located—but from the town itself when the county had been rezoned. So even though his home sat in Winston, the house was, by boundary, part of Hillman, as was the resort where my restaurant had been built. I had never understood how they figured the boundaries, because Rand's three hundred thousand acres stretched over close to four hundred and seventy miles, well beyond one county and into the next and the next, but apparently it was where the main house sat that determined "home"—and Rand Holloway was no longer welcome in his.

The reason for the ousting had been Rand coming out and bringing the man he loved—Stefan Joss—to live with him on the Red. The town of Winston could not handle one of the pillars of the community being gay and so had taken steps to ensure they were separated from Rand and the land he called home. It had been a colossal mistake: the ranch was more profitable than anyone could have imagined, giving Rand the power and the funds to make changes in Hillman as well as to turn his property into a small self-sufficient town in and of itself. The ranch boasted hundreds of Quarter Horses, thousands of cattle, and I had no idea how many acres of land now devoted to farming. There was still only one main compound, but the ranch also now hosted more than fifty private homes and an unknown number of cowboy camps that I had neither the time nor the inclination to ask about.

He was a force to be reckoned with and everyone else, including me, paled in comparison. Since it was exhausting to try to measure up, to keep my sanity, I steered clear of him, his husband, their son, and the idyllic life they lived on the Red Diamond.

But now I was stuck because my marker had been called in, and even though I was sure they could get along without me, paying my debt so it wouldn't be hanging over my head anymore was too much of a temptation to pass up. After this, Stef and I would be square and I'd never have to return to the Red and feel crappy about myself. We'd be even and I wouldn't have to see Rand ever again, I'd never have to find myself desiring things I couldn't have, coveting the idea of his life, his lover, and the peace he seemingly felt down to his bones.

I could be more pathetic, I knew that, but at the moment, sitting in my truck in the dark, not moving, staring at the house, I couldn't imagine how. It was time to make a choice. Taking a deep breath, I made it and got out, heading for the porch.

I got no answer when I knocked on the screen door, so I opened it and stepped into the living room. Instantly an enormous Rhodesian ridgeback tromped around the corner toward me, the welcoming bark, just one, making me smile before the whimpering began. I knelt, which, with an eighty-pound dog, wouldn't have seemed smart, but she knew me, as was evident from the whine of happiness, tail wagging, and the cold wet nose that got shoved into my face. The tongue on my chin sealed the deal.

"Hey, Bella," I greeted, rubbing under her chin and scratching behind her ears. "Where are all your people?"

"Glenn? Is that you?"

Thankfully it wasn't Rand calling out to me, but his partner, Stefan. And he was late determining if there was a stranger in his home, but because he'd heard no screaming, which meant his dog was not tearing me limb from limb in the living room, he had to be confident it was either me or my Uncle Tyler. No one else walked into the huge Folk Victorian home without permission. As much of a family as everyone was on the Red Diamond, this was still the boss man's house, and since the baby was born, since Wyatt James Holloway arrived two years ago, no one walked in unannounced to Rand Holloway's home. No one.

"It's me," I called back to Stef as he came out of the kitchen, dish towel over his shoulder, carrying a platter of cooked bacon.

"Hey, take this out to the table, will you?"

I moved fast to do as he asked and grab the dish, closing the distance from the living room to him, marveling as I always did at the man Rand loved. Before I met Stef, I had no idea men could be that pretty. I never dreamed that I'd meet a man with such beautiful, delicate, angelic features, golden skin, and thick blond hair that fell to his shoulders. It had been, it turned out, the final brick in the wall. Me seeing Stef, noticing everything about him, his face, his skin, the way he moved and the sound of his voice, all of it, even my long-dead desire for him, had finally made something crystal clear in my head. I was tired of wrestling with the whole question of whether I was gay. Meeting Stefan Joss, the partner of the man I'd *thought* was my cousin, sealed the deal.

Again, Rand was a sore point with me, beyond his having the ranch and the monogamous partner and basically everything I'd thought I wanted. Two years ago I found out my father, Rayland Holloway, sired not only my brother, Zach, and me, but also Rand Holloway, the eldest child of my Uncle James and his wife, May. It was bullshit someone should have told the whole family years ago. It took Stef looking at Rayland and looking at Rand to figure it out—which was just ten kinds of stupid, because who looked at someone and thought, "Hey, those eyes of yours ain't right." It had mostly been Stef thinking he knew something and his assumption being correct. Which pissed me off to no end, because like he was frickin' Sherlock Holmes or some shit. It was really giving him way too much credit, the whole uncovering of the big hush-hush family secret. But without him talking to May and Rand, neither would have ever come clean, and the rest of the family would have remained in the dark. So while I appreciated what Stef had made everyone admit to, I was still really annoyed that Rand and I now shared a closer biological bond—and that my bond with Zach was no longer unique. It was like I got Rand, whom I'd never taken a shine to, and lost my one claim to Zach, who I'd always thought was my sole blood brother. But now I had two siblings, neither liked me, and both got on together just fine, leaving me firmly out in the cold.

Worst of all, Rayland was trying so hard to mend fences with Rand that he'd forgotten I was alive, and Zach was now working on Rand's ranch.

It had hurt me in more ways than one. My father, who promised to help me with a down payment for my restaurant, backed out to expand the family ranch, the White Ash. He was exploring the land for mineral reserves and oil and that took cash. It was, he said, an opportunity he couldn't pass up, and the money he promised me was quickly committed elsewhere. Zach, at least, had an excuse I understood. He couldn't help me because he was working for Rand, and the Red took up all of his time. In the end I sold everything I owned but my horse—I could not be parted from her—and had just enough to get the restaurant off the ground.

So my life basically boiled down to coming out, telling my father I wanted to open a restaurant instead of work on the White Ash, and my family—such as it was—abandoning me. I always missed my mother; there was a hole in my heart where she had been, but I had not felt her loss as sharply as I had when I was first trying to get my dream to take shape and she wasn't there to stand beside me. My father and Zach abandoning me would not have been so crushing if she'd been alive to take their place. As it was, I grieved all over again and felt the pain of her passing like it was brand new.

Had the restaurant not taken off like it did, everything would have been shit. The fact that it had, though, the realization that I was part of a whole new family and didn't have to bother with my old one no more—that was my salvation.

"What are you doing?"

I realized I had not moved from the time Stef put the platter in my hands.

He was squinting at me.

"Sorry," I grumbled, stepping around him to head toward the kitchen and out the back door to the picnic tables.

He moved fast, getting around in front of me. "What's wrong?"

"You're letting Rand use me for a cattle drive, Stef."

"A baby drive, not a real one." He waggled his eyebrows at me. "And this way you can bond with Rand and reconnect with Zach."

I scowled. "I ain't fixin' to do shit but drive them cattle."

"You could try and put forth a little effort."

"Pardon?"

His eye roll made me smile. "Just take the bacon out, and don't give any to the dog, no matter what."

That made no sense. "No matter what?"

"She'll try and tell you she's starving to death and that only bacon will save her. These are silly torturous lies."

He was weird and that was certain. "She's only a dog, Stef."

"That's what she'd like you to believe."

Snorting out a laugh, I brushed by him and left the house through the kitchen door, Bella trailing after me. I stopped quickly, gave her a slice, and then continued on, walking around the side of the house to the picnic tables set out under the huge English oak. Normally the tree gave off an amazing amount of shade and the temperature could be counted on to be several degrees cooler beneath the canopy, but at the moment, so early in the morning, it was simply cool everywhere. Rand's men yelled greetings as I put the platter down, and people reached for it, adding bacon to the eggs, biscuits and gravy, grits, hash browns, fried green tomatoes, and country ham. There were lots of pitchers of orange juice and pots of coffee. It looked like a special occasion, but it wasn't. The hands ate there daily, and every Sunday Rand and Stef had breakfast for everyone who lived on the ranch. It was a family on the Red, and while I appreciated that, I had my own. Finally.

I turned to go back to my truck but was yelled at to stop. Pivoting around, I found Rand Holloway himself standing there, arms crossed, scowling at me, looking big and somewhat scary, with the extra four inches of height he had on me.

"And where are you scuttlin' off to?"

"To my truck," I said shortly, leaving him there.

As I walked, I looked up at the hills and saw the silhouettes of the wind turbines I knew were there. Between those and the solar panels on all the houses on the ranch, The Red Diamond was completely self-sufficient, no longer dependent on the county grid for electricity. I didn't know the difference between a windmill, a wind pump, or a wind turbine, but Rand did. And of course since I had to know, I had asked him what if it rained every day for a month and the solar power went kaput, and what if his pinwheels couldn't spin? What were they going to do then?

Apparently energy could be stored, and more importantly, he was working on using the waste from the stockyards for methane gas that would aid the wind power he already had at his disposal. That was next on Rand's agenda, and fruition was apparently imminent. Rand was always thinking, and he had Stef to do the cost analysis and basically help him make whatever dream he had into a reality. They made a great team, and while I had been very thankful for Stef's help myself, it was disappointing that I was going to have to pay for it with three days of sheer torture.

"I thought you didn't drive stock anymore."

My day was getting worse and it hadn't even really started yet. First Rand, and now, somewhere behind me, talking, giving me shit so goddamn early, was Mac Gentry.

And honestly, his smoke- and gravel-filled voice, sultry and sexy at the same time, would have gone right to my dick if he wasn't the biggest asshole I knew aside from Rand.

"Glenn?"

I ignored him, continued on to my truck, got out my duffel, pulled on my shearling-lined denim jacket, put my phone in the glove compartment, and closed the door. I knew I didn't have to worry about the truck while I was gone. On the Red everything was safe.

When I turned, Maclain "Mac" Gentry was standing in front of me. He was tall like Rand, six five, and 240 pounds of hard, heavy muscle. I knew that because I overheard him tell one of the other men once. It was funny; it never bothered me to have to look up to Rand, but it bugged the hell out of me that Mac was bigger, more thickly muscled, with broader shoulders and a wider chest. I felt small in comparison to the foreman of the Red Diamond, and I didn't like it one bit.

"Move," I groused, meaning to brush by, only to have him take firm hold of my bicep. I snapped my head up and my eyes met his smoky gray gaze.

"I don't want you on this drive if you're going to whine the whole time."

Even though he was giving me the same grief he always did, I found myself focusing on the way the faint light from the porch caught in his dirty blond hair, sparking over the stubble on his cheeks and upper lip, caressing his brows and the tips of his long lashes. With the dark hair and eyes I shared with all the Holloway men, I was lost in the shadows. But not him, not in all his golden glory.

"Don't worry," I snarled, mad at myself for even noticing how roughly handsome the man was, yanking my arm free with much more force than needed. "I swear that none of y'all will hear a word outta me."

He scowled and I walked away. I didn't have time for his regular macho bullshit. We had established from our initial meeting, when Mac looked at me like I was the most useless person on the face of the planet, that we would never get along. Zach he liked because he worked on the ranch with Rand. My father he liked because he owned a ranch just like Rand. But me, the guy who quit ranching to own a restaurant, me he didn't understand, and so didn't like. Not that I cared. Maclain Gentry was a dick and I had no use for him either.

Returning to the tables, I put my gear down by everyone else's and took a spot at the end so I could eat. It was going to be a long drive and I at least needed sustenance.

I DIDN'T ride with Rand and Mac and Zach because I didn't want to get into it with any of them. Instead, I rode in the truck with Pierce and Chase, Tom, Dusty and his son, Rebel—I swear to God, only in Texas—who was driving the truck and horse trailer back to the Red after dropping us off. I had no idea who was driving Rand's rig back.

We were missing one of Rand's best guys. Everett and his wife, Regina, were brand-new parents and he wanted to stay with her and their new baby girl. Since his daughter was just three days home from the hospital, Rand said of course he could stay home. I was sure he remembered bringing his own son home and what that felt like.

Rand's half sister, my cousin Charlotte, had given him the gift of an egg, and he and Stef had a surrogate carry the child for them. Wyatt James Holloway was born in the middle of July and just celebrated his second birthday a month ago. I didn't see him often, as I was not much for being at the ranch, but it was cute how he waved good-bye to all of us as we got into the trucks. He was an adorable little boy, even if he did look just like a miniature Rand with his same jet-black hair, but with the dark blue eyes Charlotte shared with her father, not the turquoise Rand shared with mine.

I could tell the leaving was hard on Rand. The tightness in his jaw, the way he held his son and clutched at Stef… he didn't like going one bit. He was the kind of man who would stay home all the time if he had his druthers; it was his favorite place to be. Being away from Stef was always hard for him, and now there was his son as well. All things considered, I was looking at pain when he turned to leave with us.

When Stef called him back, he whirled around and ran. They made a nice picture there on the porch, Stef with his hand on Rand's chest and Rand's on his cheek, the toddler between them as Rand bent and kissed Stef's forehead. He seemed better when he finally joined us, but then everything was gone—sadness, yearning, all of it—as his mask slid into place. He was the kind of man who wouldn't let anyone see him vulnerable, except Stefan. He was all walled up before we got underway.

Since I didn't have to drive, I pulled my hat down over my eyes and took a nap. We stopped for lunch a few hours later, and I was surprised when Zach came over from eating with Rand and the others and took a seat beside me. His scrutiny was unnerving because he looked so much like my mother, and I still missed her. He had her same big brown eyes; it was too bad he had his own mouth.

"You lost a shitload of weight, Glenn. You sick?"

"Not at all," I answered tightly.

He rubbed the back of his knuckles over my beard and then, before I could pull away, jabbed at my mustache with his finger. "And what's with all this hair on your face?"

Holloway men were usually clean-shaven, so the facial hair—though the beard was barely that—I'd let grow in was just another way to distinguish myself from them. "I'm busy," I said defensively, hating that he'd even brought it up.

"How busy can a restaurant be?"

I didn't take the bait since the comment was just plain ignorant.

"It was a joke!" he crowed, whacking me hard on the back. "For fuck's sake, Glenn, not everything is meant to be taken so serious."

My back hurt a little because he was stronger than he gave himself credit for, but I didn't want to fight. "How're you doing on the Red? You still like it?"

And he was off, telling me about the calves that were born and how many, and the horses he'd helped break and how good they looked, and how one of the Red's bulls was just sold for some ungodly amount of money.

"It's hard to be away, but this drive will settle Rand up with Hawley McNamara, and it's a short trip, and since we'll have regular folks with us—"

"Regular folks?"

"Well, yeah. The cattle have been grazing on McNamara's dude ranch since Rand wanted to keep 'em separate from the regular herd."

I was bored already. "And?"

"Can you hold on a minute?"

I grunted.

"So," he said loudly. "Since all our land was full, Rand reached out to McNamara to see if he could pay to graze the cattle there."

"Sure."

"But he said he didn't need money. He needed Rand to take his guests with him and drive the cattle down to the Red."

"I see."

"Easy enough, right? And it oughta be nice to break things up."

"Break what up?" I asked honestly.

"Doing the same ole shit, of course," he replied, squinting at me. "Man, you are a prickly piece of crap."

"I wasn't trying to—"

"Yeah ya were, you know you were."

"You know what, Zach," I snapped. "I think your master's callin' you."

"Fuck you, Glenn," he retorted, getting up, but not before knocking my glass of ice water into my lap, just to be a dick.

Everybody laughed, and I was left with a wet spot on my crotch that made me look like I pissed myself. And people wondered why I didn't spend more time with my family.

Walking back from the bathroom over loose, rocky gravel, I tripped and would have done a nosedive if someone hadn't closed their hand tight around my arm.

"Careful."

I would have rather wiped out than talk to him twice in one day.

"Watch what you're doin'."

"I'm fine," I growled at Mac, cursing my annoyance and the sort of daze I was moving around in. I was usually more coordinated.

"No," he contradicted. "You were about ready to fall on your face."

"Yeah, so? Ya wanna medal?"

He shook me and I lifted my head so I was gazing up into his eyes.

"You should go home, Glenn. Go back to your restaurant where you belong."

"I can't," I griped. "I'm covering for Everett and—"

"We'll get along just fine without you."

I knew he would, they all would, but I was paying Stef back, and that was more important than anything else. "Oh, I'm sure you will," I said snidely. "But I'm here to do the job that was asked of me."

I tried to tug my arm loose, but he was bigger than me, and stronger, so until he wanted to let go, I wasn't going anywhere.

"We don't need you to do nothin'."

I sucked in a breath because the silver flecks in his eyes were really something to see.

"You hear?"

I'd never asked Mac where he was from because, honestly, wherever it was, he should have stayed there, but it was definitely not West Texas like the rest of us. His voice was softer, richer, with a sprinkling of something in it that only came out when he was mad.

"What?" he asked suddenly, scrutinizing my face as though something had changed.

I shook my head because there was no way I was ever going to tell him the warmth of his voice could have gotten me right out of my clothes. For one, straight men didn't tend to enjoy hearing things like that, and for two, he was a prick.

He jerked me closer and I had to lean my head back farther—he was so damn tall—and his stormy eyes narrowed to slits.

"How come you're so skinny?"

"What?"

"You heard me."

"I ain't skinny," I assured him. "I've just been busy. Most days I don't get a chance to eat."

Slow nod from him. "But other days you run?"

"Pardon?"

"I've seen you running at night."

"How?" I asked, trying to wiggle my arm out of the death grip he had on it. "Aren't you in bed at like nine or so since you gotta be up by four?"

"Sometimes," he answered. "And other times I can't sleep, so I drive over by the resort and I see you running after midnight, or riding your horse."

Strange that he would know it was me in the dark, but he was right: I ran when I could. I knew I'd dropped a lot of heavy muscle for a leaner frame, but I was still strong and not at all wasting away. It was simply that he and Zach didn't see me often enough to realize it had been a gradual change, not an overnight one.

"I—"

"That ain't good to be workin' that horse at night; you'll screw him all up."

I was so stupid. For a split second I'd been about to speak to him like he was a normal human being, not a complete asshole, full of nothing but judgment, like my cousin. "She," I emphasized, "is fine. But thanks for your concern."

He shook his head and still didn't let go.

"And I promise I ain't sick or nothin'," I told him. "I used to work real hard to be as big as my dad and Zach, and even Rand." The steroids I'd injected bulked me up as well, but I stopped all of that when I left my father's ranch. I was healthier now because I ran and swam, which was more natural for me and burned off my nervous energy. Plus the steroids had made me kind of a dick, and with them out of my system for more than twenty-four months, I saw a change in my temperament as well, where most people were concerned. Most people being those who didn't treat me like a five-year-old.

He nodded slowly.

"Never mind," I grumbled, trying to pull loose. "I don't know why I even—but I ain't sick, so you can just not worry, all right?"

"Say thank you."

"For what?"

"Keeping you from falling."

"Oh yes," I bit off. "Thank you so much."

He shoved me away, and I stumbled before I got my footing. Of course I turned and flipped him off and then headed back to the truck. I settled in, survived a few more taunts about my wet pants, flipped them *all* off, and went back to sleep.

I had read somewhere that if you could sit for fewer than five minutes and nod off, then you might be sleep-deprived. I wondered what less than a minute meant.

CHAPTER 3

GREEN LEAF was, in my opinion, not a good name for a ranch. Tea? Sure. A nursery? Yeah. But not a ranch. So when we rolled up on it a couple of hours later, I was thinking we were stopping someplace to eat or visiting a health food store or something. But no, it was a dude ranch, which made a little more sense, but still, I was amazed.

On a real cattle drive, you started before dawn. On a fake one, apparently middle of the day was normal. I was again cursing Stef and the fuckin' payback until I saw the man who crossed the porch of the house everyone had come from. Beautiful did not do him justice. He was shorter than me, slender and loose-hipped with a fluid stride that was a pleasure to watch. His smile lit his big cornflower-blue eyes, and when he walked over to Rand with a woman and another man, I understood they, along with many others, were coming with us.

Of course, once everyone was mounted up, the pretty man and I were nowhere near each other. Apparently he was not too experienced, so instead of riding at the back with me, he was at the front with Rand and Mac and Zach. Being separated by two hundred head of cattle from a guy I wanted to get to know was not my idea of fortuitous. But at least when we stopped for the day, I could go talk to him.

I was ready to find someone, and not simply for a one-night stand. In the past two years, I really tried to go to bed with someone to see what being a gay man was all about. But every bar I went to in Lubbock, and the couple I visited the last time I was in Dallas for a convention, were not what I expected. The men there moved faster than I was used to. And no, fucking in a bathroom was not what I wanted for my first time. The bar scene really made no sense because none of those men lived where I did. And how was I supposed to have the conversation about the topping I saw myself doing and how careful I would need to be with the guy who was bottoming if they were bent over a sink or shoved into a stall? I wanted to talk things out with someone, because even though I knew I would top—of course I would, without question, because that would need to happen so I could still be me—but… I had questions. So many questions. Starting with how *they* felt about it, bottoming, being under me, having my weight on them, pressing them down into the bed and feeling me move inside them. I needed that. I wanted to hear about the readiness in another, I needed to *be* someone else's desire.

The craving in me could be traced back to Rand. I blamed him. I wanted what he and Stef had. I wanted the monogamous, go to bed at night and wake up in the morning with deal. A guy who would look at me like I wasn't stupid, who thought I had a lot to offer, who would actually just see *me*.... That's what I craved. But so far, all the boys I saw at bars or my restaurant or around the hotel were just passing through. I had lots of offers for steamy sex with no strings attached, but since all I'd ever wanted was to belong to someone, I had, as of yet, not gone to bed with a man. I wanted at least the potential for permanence.

When we stopped for lunch, I went to find Rand and tell him the pace was too fast for the new mothers and calves toward the back. He was showing some of the kids how to make a lasso, boys and girls clustered around him, and I saw the looks on the faces of the mothers. He made quite the picture there, and when I glanced over at the guy I wanted to get to know and saw his parted lips, yearning all over him, I got that I was right about him. No man who wasn't gay looked at another guy like that. Now all I had to do was get him to see me.

I was about to cross to him when Mac moved from behind Rand over toward where the food was. At that moment I understood my guy was not lusting after the boss man, but instead the foreman of the Red Diamond. He moved really fast to get into line behind Mac for chow and then slid a hand over his forearm to get his attention. When Mac turned, he furrowed his brow as he regarded the guy, who was either oblivious or didn't care, too intent on what he wanted. And I got it: the small, pretty man was interested in big, strong, and gorgeous, and he'd found it in Mac. Whatever the foreman of the Red Diamond's faults were, he was still stunning. He and pretty boy would have made a beautiful couple if he was gay. I would have given the object of my latest fantasy the heads-up that he was barking up the wrong tree, but since he didn't see me at all, I doubted he could hear me either.

"Glenn!"

My eyes flicked to Mac, who had yelled.

"You need to eat!"

But I had a granola bar in my pack, so I was fine. I turned and left to go back to where Juju was standing with the dogs. She wasn't tied, she never needed to be, Juju stayed where she was put unless I called her.

Walking by Zach and some of the others, I heard him telling the story of the last time I went bull riding. It had not been one of my finer moments. Since my name was still on the list for my father's ranch, when we had to compete in the annual rodeo, I had to go.

The year before, Stef had been at the rodeo with me and I'd broken my wrist, but the year after, I broke the same wrist, three ribs, and my nose. It was sheer luck that my legs hadn't been smashed when I was trampled, but the enormous heavy hooves had missed me by inches. No one mentioned that, of course, not even Zach, and hearing everyone laugh, again, like they all hadn't done it enough the first time once they knew I would live, was another reminder that I didn't belong in their company anymore. As if I ever did.

"Don't tease ole Glenn, y'all," Zach cackled. "He's sensitive."

I picked up speed, and by the time I made it to Juju, I could have spit nails. The look I got from her, though, like where the hell was her treat, made me even more pissed that I forgot to grab her an apple.

"I'm sorry."

Of course, she did what she always did and turned her back on me.

"Oh, come on," I whined.

When I walked around in front of her, she turned her head until I ripped open the granola bar and she heard the foil go. Then she bumped me with her head, doing the whole bitey grabby give-it-to-me-now thing and I chuckled as she delicately took the entire thing, chewed a couple times, and swallowed it down. She was lucky I had one more, or I would've been really annoyed about going hungry.

"Can I eat this one?" I asked.

It was like she shrugged, and I realized how tired I was. My horse was basically talking to me.

Good lord.

I pet her, hung on her neck, and she let me like she always did before, blowing air softly into my face. It was gentle, the way she was with me, always, and I wasn't surprised when she nuzzled my chest with her nose for a moment, ending with her head resting on my shoulder. The affection she showed me, along with her possessiveness, like the way she tried to take a bite out of me if I ever rode another horse, were just some of the many reasons why when I left the White Ash, I took her with me.

She was beautiful, all black except for a white pattern on her forehead that was cataloged as a star but to me always looked more like a skull. When she was born, for whatever reason, her mother had taken an immediate dislike to her and, in fact, tried to kill her by biting and kicking at her with her back legs. We separated them immediately, and I was tasked with keeping the foal alive.

Her mother, Voodoo, was pure Arabian and was purchased to breed with my father's Arabian stallion, Hamza, whom he'd traded land for three years earlier. Rayland Holloway loved Arabians, but there were so many top breeders in Texas already that it was hard for him to find a good mare. When he finally did, unfortunately, Voodoo wouldn't have any part of Hamza, and the artificial insemination route had been unsuccessful. The first time didn't take and the second, she miscarried because the vet said she was overly stressed by the whole process. The third time they were ready to try, one of the new hands put her in the wrong stall, and instead of running into Hamza's corral, she went in with Medallion, my father's Foundation Quarter Horse. From what happened after that, it was clear that Voodoo did not dislike stallions as everyone had assumed; she just had no interest in Hamza. Medallion she liked just fine, and so my father ended up with Juju, who was a mix and not pure anything. No one was all that worried about Juju when she was born. If she didn't make it, it was okay; he was going to try again with the two purebred horses anyway. But when her mama didn't want her and I was the first one in the stall, picking her up, cuddling her and carrying her away, I got attached good and hard.

I slept beside her, fed her, walked with her, finally ran beside her, and by the time she was a filly named Juju—'cause it was bad juju what happened to her—and not a foal anymore, we were bonded heart and soul.

She was mean to everyone but me, crazy smart, like diabolically clever about getting out of a stall, corral, or anywhere she didn't want to be, and did not ever allow anyone else to ride her. She didn't buck; that would have been way too much trouble. Instead she would just lie down. First she'd go down with her front and back legs folded under her, but if that didn't work, she'd start to tip over until you moved because she was so damn heavy and no one wanted their leg trapped under her. My father could not believe it the first time she did it, or the second, or third, but finally he threw up his hands in defeat. He'd never seen a horse that stubborn. If she'd bucked, he could have broken her, but her whole passive resistance routine, he had no idea what to do with. When I got on and she stood right up, ready to go do whatever I had in mind, he announced she was mine. As if there was ever any question.

Now, as I stood beside her, she bumped me, moving me until I got off her so she could munch a bit more grass in the cool shade. She was grazing, not really chowing down since she was so picky that where we were standing would never do as actual sustenance.

It was good that I was in the back, so no one had to talk to me. The dogs were spread out in the shade and I went over and sat with them. One after another I was greeted, with Beau, Rand's lead canine, putting his head in my lap. Petting him, talking to the others with Juju there close, keeping an eye on me, I finally felt some of the irritation dissipate.

Had I been at home, at my restaurant when the guys teased me, I bantered right along with them. In my place I was considered a pretty damn good sport. But my family and the men who worked with them brought out the very worst of me. And since petulance wasn't sexy, I put the pretty man out of my head. I just needed to concentrate on living through the drive. I promised myself I would never, ever again put myself in the position to owe Stefan Joss anything.

Live and learn.

THE RIVER we came upon late in the afternoon wasn't that deep, but that didn't mean the calves could move through the water without drowning. Most of the others drove the cattle across, but I dismounted, left Juju drinking, and started the process of carrying the babies. Once they were in the water, it was fine; it was just getting them to edge. I got kicked a lot and went under more times than I could count, and it took forever to get all twenty of them from one side to the other. The mothers followed dutifully behind once they saw me carrying their babies.

I was sitting on the other side, pouring water out of my boots, when Rand came riding up along with Mac and Zach.

"What the fuck is taking you so long back… here… and where the hell are Pierce and Tom?" Rand asked like I should know.

I looked up at him, squinted, and waited for him to figure it out as I wrung out my shirttails.

"You're supposed to have two more guys with you," he insisted, scanning both sides of the river, turning around in the saddle to check the area before returning his attention to me. "Did you send them away?"

"Like anyone would listen to me," I groused.

"Well, then where the hell are they?"

"Your guess is as good as mine, boss man," I replied, clipping my words.

Zach moved his horse up beside Rand's stallion and glowered down at me. "Why the hell are you wet and… oh." He groaned, turning in this saddle to look at the calves prancing around their mothers fifty feet from us. "Jesus, Glenn."

I got up. "Dead cattle would've made a helluva good impression on them kids, Zach."

"Where the hell are Pierce and Tom?" Rand demanded, for once his annoyance directed at someone besides me.

"I thought you told me they were supposed to ride lead to help watch over the parents and kids," Zach explained, glancing at me and then back to Rand, meeting his glare.

"No," Rand replied brusquely, gesturing at me. "They were supposed to help Glenn."

"Why didn't you just call us on back?" Zach growled. I knew why he was angry. Rand was pissed at him and he had to take it out on someone.

"I dunno," I said flippantly, "y'all ain't been all that concerned up to now."

"Did you once say the pace was too fast?" Zach berated me.

I hadn't. I'd meant to, but got diverted with my quarry and Mac. "No."

"Well, then, how the fuck were we—oh, for fuck's sake, you're bleedin'."

I had a scrape over the swell of my right hip, but I would live. "It's fine."

"You're gonna be black and blue tomorrow."

"The fuck do you care," I snarled. "Just get on back up to the front and lead."

He spurred his horse toward me and his look was murderous. "You—"

"Quit," Rand ordered harshly, his tone brooking no protest. "Go get the guys who're supposed to be riding drag back here with him."

"Rand, I—"

"Now," he bit off curtly, turning back to me, not giving Zach a chance to defend himself.

Zach shot me a murderous glance and was gone seconds later, leaving Rand sitting tall in his saddle, frowning at me.

"What?"

"We'll have some guys back here to help you."

"Don't do me any favors."

"You're such a dick," Rand barked. "Why ya gotta be such an asshole all the time?"

"It's a gift." I smirked up at him.

He left me then, but Mac dismounted.

"Oh, for fuck's sake, what?"

"Unlike Rand, I *will* deck you," he warned, his voice hoarse and low. "Now lemme look at your side."

"It's nothing," I told him, taking off my hat and raking my fingers through my shoulder-length wet hair to get it out of my face before I put my hat back on.

"Just lemme see."

I yanked my flannel and undershirt up and shoved my waistband down so he could see the wound. "There, see, it's fine."

"Are you serious?" He was using that tone, the one filled with disdain. "Jesus, Glenn." He touched the reddening skin. "We gotta stitch this up."

"It's a scrape," I argued.

"It's a gouge," he corrected me. "And it needs to be closed up."

"You are out of your mind if you think—"

"Shut up," he said gruffly, hand on my hip, holding tight. "God, you're a pain in the ass."

"Then don't worry about it." I squirmed out of his hands, stalking away and shoving my shirts back down.

He moved much faster than I thought he could and had me spun around and facing him, only inches separating us. "You will let me take care of this," he said, then paused, his gaze meeting mine, and the pleading I saw there was unexpected. "Please."

It was strange, but his hands on my arms, holding tight, the way he was staring down into my eyes, the fixed regard, it was very settling. "Okay," I agreed, taken off guard, not minding so much the fact that he'd just manhandled me, finding that the dominance—because he could simply lift me and throw me over his shoulder if he wanted, he was that much bigger and stronger than me—was doing warm, fluttery things to my stomach.

He'd been holding his breath, and the glower I got that made his gray eyes darken to charcoal was really something. "Good. Follow me back to the wagon."

"But the calves." I waved a hand toward them.

"You heard Rand, he'll have Zach send Pierce and Tom on back here."

"All right, then," I conceded.

He turned away, and I was faced with his wide back and broad shoulders, saw the muscles rippling under the shirt, hugging his triceps, traps, and delts. The jeans he had on clung to his narrow hips and tight round ass, and they cleaved to his long, powerfully hewn legs. Mac was built nice, but I would take the observation to my grave.

"You're so odd," he said, rounding on me.

Lost in admiring his solid, carved frame, I almost walked into him, and because I was embarrassed, I bristled. "Don't insult me any—"

"Shut up. I didn't mean nothin' by that."

"Then what did you mean?"

"I mean," he said irritably. "That you whine and complain more'n any two people I know, but without even a word, you jump into that ice-cold river and walk those calves across one by one. What the hell?"

"I don't complain."

"Watch you don't turn into a pillar of salt, lyin' like that."

"I—"

"You didn't want to ride drag even though you're one of the only people who can, with all your experience," he said. "You think Rand is making us all carry too much gear." I realized he was making a list. "You're tired and hungry, but when it's time to rest, you pet the dogs instead of closin' yer eyes, and when we stop for chow, you don't eat nothin'. And that's all just this mornin', for crissakes! I won't even get into how much you bitch whenever you're out at the Red."

I felt my face get hot. "Well, don't worry. I won't be back after this."

He growled, grabbing hold of my arm. "You're such an idiot."

I yanked free and stalked away toward Juju. "I really love being told that all the fuckin' time!"

"Get your ass back here!"

I mounted and looked back at him over my shoulder while riding to catch up with the now-wandering cattle. With the help of the dogs and fast and nimble Juju, I got all the calves and their mothers rounded up and moved my charges farther down the trail. I would keep up if it killed me, because dealing with Mac or Rand or Zach was not something I wanted to do. I just wanted to get the job done and get home.

After a few hours, between the rub of my jeans, the belt, and the cramp in my side from trying to sit awkwardly, I was in pain. I took off the T-shirt I had on under my flannel, folded it up, and pressed it between the waistband of my underwear and my skin, over the scrape. With the grinding sensation gone, I felt better. I was a little lightheaded, but I figured it was because it was so hot and I'd barely eaten anything. When we crossed the next part of the river, after I got all the calves from one side to the other, I let Juju rest and have some water while I splashed some on my face.

"Glenn!"

Jesus. His voice could cut glass.

Rand brought his horse closer but still stayed well out of touching distance of Juju, and once I was mounted again, I rolled my head to look at him.

He was silent.

"What?" I asked curtly.

"Stop moving the stock and wait on Pierce and Tom."

"Why?"

His jaw clenched. "Goddammit, Glenn! First you're pissed that you're back here alone, but when I say to hold up because I'm sending you help, you want to go on and keep moving. You make no bit of sense."

I groaned irritably, squeezing Juju with my legs, and when I did, she moved on her own, walking quickly sideways.

Both horse and rider were looking at us. The stallion was nickering, clearly chafed, and Rand was scowling.

"What?"

"What?" Rand repeated, incredulous. "The hell is that? Is she a circus horse or something?"

"No," I snapped, because I didn't like how he said it. It sounded derogatory. "She was just doing her sidestepping thing she does when she knows I'm on edge."

He pointed at us. "That's not normal."

"Says you with your beast of a stallion," I fired back.

His head shake was full of disgust. "You realize that you're following so far behind you don't even know where the goddamn line is."

"Lemme get my compass," I muttered and was going to dismount to get into my saddlebag, but Rand stopped me with the sharp command to stay in the saddle. I bristled. "So you like me being lost or—"

"Just shut up," he instructed me. "Christ, it's a wonder you've lived this long."

I threw up my hands, waiting on him.

"Jesus."

"Are you *done*?"

"Mac said you're really hurt," he retorted.

"Mac worries like an old woman."

"There's blood on your shirt, idiot," he huffed.

"It's dry. I ain't bleedin' no more."

"Just follow me back to the chuck wagon, lemme give you a shot of penicillin and a pain killer, and we'll tape it all up."

"Too bad we don't have a stapler."

"I do back at the Red," he told me.

"Yeah?"

He nodded. "More importantly, we got us a doctor and a nurse to go with it."

I chuckled. I couldn't help it. "You're gonna have a whole town on the Red pretty soon, ain't ya, Rand? You won't be dependent on no one for nothin' at all."

"That's the plan," he said and actually smiled at me. "Now come on."

I followed him back because he was being nice to me, and it was really hard to say no to him when he was.

We dismounted when we got close to the wagon carrying food that now contained medical supplies as well. I noticed tents were being set up, and that surprised me. On a real drive, we stopped for lunch and that was it. But with regular people along and some kids, there had to be a lot more resting.

"We got us a first aid tent now," Rand informed me, "and a cot to lie down on."

"Well, that'll be nice not to have to drop trou to get a shot of Penicillin leaning up against your horse."

"You're such a smartass."

I shrugged, trailing after him, and once we were in the tent, he shoved me forward. Dropping onto the cot, I lay down on my side.

"Oh, for crissakes, Glenn, you bled through your T-shirt."

I loosened my belt, unfastened the button-fly, and then tried to shove my jeans to my thighs. I was surprised at the feeling of being stabbed when I tried. "Fuck."

"Okay," Rand sighed. "This isn't gonna work."

Groaning, I told him to yank my jeans and underwear off the wound fast.

"Oh, I'm gonna have to do that too, but you need stitches."

"No, I—"

"It's too deep and too wide."

I really could think of nothing worse at the moment than Rand taking needle and thread to my skin. "Just—"

"Shut the fuck up," he ordered. "It needs cleaning and stitches and—if you could see it, you'd agree with me."

"I can see it," I said. I had forgotten this part of driving stock, the part where pain factored in. "Tape'll do just fine."

"It's too deep for—fuck."

"You're making a big deal outta—"

"I'm gonna give you a local anesthetic," he said, ignoring my comment.

"How do you have that?"

"I just got through telling you that I have a doctor on my ranch."

I was done talking to him.

He gave me the first shot, the painkiller, in my left hip and then the second, the antibiotic, in the other.

"Gonna brand me next?" I teased.

"We don't brand nothin' on the Red no more, ain't ya heard?" He sounded exasperated so I made a point of not answering him. "Glenn?"

"Stop talking. I'm bleeding here."

His noise of disgust was not lost on me.

"I think I need a nap."

"Among other things, I would say so," he agreed. "You need a week at the Red just eatin' and sleepin'."

"Like that'd happen. You'd put me to work in no time."

He was quiet for a moment. "I wouldn't, though. You could just *be*."

It was possibly the weirdest conversation I'd ever had with him, and I didn't realize I was dozing until I was poked with something. "Can you feel that?"

"I can feel pressure, but it don't hurt none."

"Good 'cause I'm poking you with a needle."

I grunted.

He started grabbing stuff to clean the scrape out with, water and soap, and he was really taking his time and being careful, which surprised me.

"You can do it faster. You ain't gonna hurt me."

"Just shuddup."

I finally closed my eyes and put my head down, and I must have dozed off until I heard Zach mutter, "Oh shit." I hadn't realized he was even there. It would have jolted me, but I was really very sleepy, and I had to wonder what exactly was in that first shot Rand gave me. I was a little more drugged up than I should have been.

Maybe.

Possibly.

The fact that I didn't care should have been a concern. But I could not force myself to bark at either one of them.

"That's worse than I thought it was," Zach said from what sounded like a distance but couldn't have been.

"Yeah, he did a good fuckin' job," Rand griped.

"He's gonna be all right, yeah?" Zach asked Rand, and I was surprised at the fear I heard in his voice.

"He'll be fine once I get this cleaned and closed."

I felt a warm hand on my bicep, holding gently but firmly, not letting go, and then another between my shoulder blades, rubbing circles like my mother used to do. "God, I don't worry about no one like I worry about Glenn."

"Don't I know it," Rand admitted, his voice thick. "I wish he'd just move onto the ranch so I could keep an eye on him."

He did?

After a minute Zach sighed deeply. "I'd love that."

He would?

"So would Stef."

Stef too?

"But he won't."

"No. He's a stubborn piece of crap."

I was most definitely that.

"I wish he'd stop mixin' up what he thinks we want him to do—or be—with what we actually give a damn about."

"He's always had that problem," Zach explained. "And while it was true with Daddy, it weren't with nobody else."

Rand grunted.

"There's no pleasing Rayland Holloway exceptin' if we was you."

"Rayland Holloway is not my father."

"Your blood says different."

"You know what I mean," Rand muttered irritably. "James raised me. He's my father. You and Glenn can keep Rayland."

"Awful gracious of you, thank you," Zach replied snidely.

After a moment Rand exhaled sharply. "If I could, I'd move my mother back into the house and have her bring Tate. I'd build Charlotte and Ben a house on the ranch, as well as one for Glenn, and we could all be there together."

"What about Tyler, since you're dreamin' and all?"

"Tyler's happy living with his daughter and her family for six months and his son and his for the other half of the year. He don't never get bored, he says, and he gets to spend time with all his grandchildren. I would never mess that up by invitin' him back to the Red, especially after all the work Stef went to, to bring that family back together."

"Sure."

"But Tyler knows he's always got a place with me and Stef."

"Yeah."

"And you. You know that."

"I do."

"I don't know Cyrus or his lot well, and Brandon punched Stef that weekend Char got married," Rand said tightly. "I don't reckon I've ever forgiven him for that."

"I ain't heard that story."

"Have Stef tell you. The part where later on Stef has to carry Brandon up out of a ravine is funny when *he* tells it. I don't find it quite so amusing."

"I'll have to remember to ask, that sounds like quite the story."

He made a noise. "If I could get Glenn on the ranch, though—that'd be good."

"It ain't like he couldn't be, and he could keep that fool horse of his there too."

Rand growled. “Why in the hell that horse ain’t on the Red is beyond me.”

“He’s proud, you know that.”

“I do. It’s how we were all raised. To not ask no one for nothin’.”

“Yep,” Zach said quietly.

“You’d think family wouldn’t count, though.”

“Yeah,” Zach scoffed. “You surely were not raised by Rayland Holloway.”

“Thankfully not.” Rand sounded somber as he said it.

“Hey!” Mac yelled, but he sounded far away, too, like Zach, so I let the sound wash over me without any fuss.

“Why’re you shoutin’?”

“I just—you’ve got a lot of blood on you.”

“It’s not mine,” Rand informed him. “I’m cleanin’ Glenn up, as you can see.”

“What’re you doin’?”

“I’m fixin’ to stitch him up, Maclain,” Rand said sarcastically. “What the hell does it look like?”

“Yeah, okay.” Mac coughed. “Just be careful.”

“Be careful?”

“Please.”

Momentary silence before Rand spoke again.

“Mac?” Rand sounded confused.

“Yeah. What do you—Zach, move, lemme in there.”

“Mac, I can take care of—”

“Just slide over.”

“What are you doing?”

I heard a throat clearing, and both of Zach’s hands were replaced by a bigger one sinking into my hair, massaging my scalp. Another touched my side, warm and strong and callused, languorously sliding over my skin.

“Mac?” Rand asked.

“What?” he answered gruffly.

“Something you wanna tell me?”

“No, I don’t think so.”

“Okay,” Rand said, and the cleaning was rougher, faster, but it was fine because it didn’t hurt in the least.

Lulled by the languid stroking of my hair, I was asleep seconds later.

"GLENN."

I jolted awake, but a gentle hand on my shoulder quieted me, and when I looked up, squinting in the light, found myself staring into a gorgeous set of quicksilver eyes.

"Maclain?" I said, making a conscious decision to use his full name to keep whatever warm, quiet intimacy we had between us going. He was there, with me, beside me, close enough that I could feel the heat rolling off his big hard body, and because I'd always dreamed of having him in my space, and now he was, I didn't want to do anything to disturb the delicate peace.

He cleared his throat. "Since when?"

"What?" I croaked.

"Why 'Maclain'?" he asked, his voice a lazy, sexy rumble.

I held his gaze. "You're treating me nice, so I figured I shouldn't use the name of the guy who hates me."

"So Mac hates you?"

I nodded.

"No," he corrected with a sigh. "I don't hate you."

"Seems like it."

"Okay," he said, his voice bottoming out as he leaned down closer to me. "From now on you use Maclain so you know the difference."

I smiled. "That sounds good."

"So." He sighed, stretching out beside me on his side. "How ya feel?"

"I'm all right. How long was I out?"

"Maybe an hour."

"I can ride," I assured him, getting ready to sit up.

His hand on my shoulder kept me where I was. "Just lie there for a bit longer. We're settled in for the night already. We can't push these folks like we can our own."

That made sense, but I would have argued that I needed to get up and help do whatever, but he reached out and pushed my hair out of my face. I had no idea something so simple could make my heart race and my pulse jump, and even though both of those sensations, reactions, were brand new, they also made total sense. While half of me had always been on the lookout for a man just like Stef—small and delicate and beautiful—the idea of Mac throwing me up against the side of the barn and having his wicked way with me had been just as, if not even more, appealing. I was afraid of submitting, but there had never been any doubt to whom I would consider going ass up for. I had thought about Mac's hands all over me many a time.

"Is Rand pissed at me?" I managed to get out.

"Actually he's madder at himself for leaving you alone. I think we all thought someone else was back there with you."

His hand was so warm, and the thought hit me that I wanted it much, much lower. "Maclain?"

He grunted softly.

"You know you're touchin' me, right?"

"I do," he whispered, and his easy grin made me catch my breath.

This was so dangerous. He was trouble for me and I should have gotten up and run. The smart thing to do was to put a lot of real estate between me and the gorgeous sexy man with the sinful mouth and wicked glint to his eyes, but holy God, he smelled good. How did a man smell like that after a full day in the saddle? Like leather and smoke, a trace of soap and the sun on his clothes, and freshly cut grass. I wanted to inhale him, press my face to the side of his neck and taste his skin even as my brain screamed at me that it was a mistake. He didn't know what he was doing, by allowing this present communion, because he had no clue what was really going on in my head or what I truly wanted from him.

"Maclain," I whispered and found that his name sounded good coming out of my mouth.

He grunted.

"How come?" I fished, swallowing hard.

"How come what?"

"You know."

"Why ya think?"

He really had a great smile. It crinkled the deep laugh lines in the corners of his eyes and curled the corners of his mouth. He was very handsome. Not the breathtaking kind or the movie-star kind, but rugged, like he could have been a sheriff in the Old West. He seemed concrete, strong, and man, did I need some of that. It was really too bad he wasn't for me.

"Glenn?"

Even though I could feel the ball of fear in my chest, I answered, "I dunno."

"You wanna guess?"

I could, and I really hoped it didn't get me beat up. Mac had easily fifty pounds of muscle on me, all of him looking like roped steel. If he wanted to hurt me, I'd be in real trouble. But I couldn't help myself. I had to know. So I cleared my throat and threw caution to the wind. "I thought you were straight," I mumbled.

"Nope," he said flatly.

My mouth went dry, and just for a second, I thought time had stopped and I would live forever in this moment of complete and utter disbelief where everything I thought I knew turned upside down and inside out.

"Pardon?"

"I suspect you heard me just fine."

The hell did he say?

His chuckle was a little bit evil. "You should see your face."

I couldn't for the life of me remember how I was supposed to tell if I was dreaming or not. It would have been good to check since I was really unsure if I was awake.

Mac Gentry was *gay*? How the hell had I missed that all these years?

The shudder went through me fast, and then I got my bearings and met his gaze, holding it, not looking away. "How come you never mentioned that before?"

"Because you never asked."

I coughed softly to give myself a moment.

"Rand called Everett and he agreed to drive up here and pick up you and your horse with the stupid-ass name."

It took a second. "What?"

Immediately he was scowling at me. "You heard."

"Why am I being sent home?"

"'Cause you can't ride when you're all tore up. Don't be an idiot."

Of course. As usual, I was the idiot. Sitting up, brushing his hands away when he tried to stop me, hold me down, I asked when Everett was coming.

"He'll be here at the ass crack of dawn, I reckon."

"And you all just decided this."

He pointed at my side. "No, Glenn," he said crossly. "The gash in your side decided this."

I shook my head.

"You didn't even want to be here," he reminded me. "You hate the ranch and driving cattle and everything else. Now you don't have to have nothin' to do with any of it."

But that wasn't the deal I made. "I made a promise to Stef."

"Rand said that you don't make no promises to family. You shouldn't have to."

"Stef's not my family."

"The hell he ain't," Mac griped. "He's married to your brother, you damn fool."

It took everything in me not to yell. Idiot. Fool. All the different names he applied to me that basically all meant the same thing.

Mac thought I was stupid, plain and simple. It could not be made any clearer.

"Why are you here?" I hoped my tone was as cold as I felt.

His glare was icy, any tenderness he'd felt for me evaporated like it was never there. "I have no idea."

It felt different in the tent when he stormed out a moment later—like all the heat went with him—but I didn't care. It had just been demonstrated to me again, for the billionth time, that I had no place in the world of the Red Diamond.

What did it matter if Mac was gay? He certainly wasn't for me. He found me lacking, just like my family did, just like all the hands did, just like anyone attached to the ranch did. I was useless, plain and simple. All the things Rand had said while I dozed, and Zach too, they only did so because they thought they had to, or because they felt sorry for me. There was no real affection, no kinship, no love or respect or genuine feeling. And even though they'd thought I was asleep, and I could have assumed they were speaking from the heart, clearly they hadn't been. Because my real worth came down to what kind of cowboy I was, and since I didn't want to be one, I was of no use to any of them.

I couldn't wait for Everett to come get me, because I was never showing up at the ranch again after this. I was so very done.

CHAPTER 4

I COULDN'T sleep.

Thinking about Mac and Rand and Zach and then Stef's hope that there would be bonding and my own bullshit getting in the way—as well as all of theirs—it came to me that something had to give.

The more I thought about it, the worse I felt. So in the early hours of the morning—the illuminated display on my G-Shock Mudmaster told me it was just after two—I finally gave up wrestling with my conscience and got up from the bedroll I was sleeping on. I gave Juju an absent pat that made her grunt like she was irritated—probably because I woke her up—and walked back toward the circle of lanterns. Other people might have worried about snakes, spiders, scorpions, or other critters bothering them, but with my horse standing vigil over me—even though she'd been sleeping—I didn't. Her hearing was better than mine and I'd seen her crush a lot of creatures under her hooves over the years. She was bloodthirsty even though she was a vegetarian. Herbivore. Whatever.

I pretended to sleep through dinner so no one felt the need to speak to me or check on me, but now that I knew it was only hours before I'd be leaving, and God only knew when I'd be back out to the Red… if ever… I felt the urge to make amends.

My brain had not turned off overnight. Over and over, again and again, I had thought about what Rand and Zach had said. The reality was that like it or not, we were family, and the bond of blood was a real one. It would keep us in each other's lives forever. I needed to get that through my thick skull. I also needed to pull my head out of my ass and realize that just because the ranch wasn't my life, that didn't make it bad. I didn't need to vilify them to make what I did better. The fact of the matter was that the people in my restaurant were just like the ones on the Red Diamond, each set depending on either me or Rand. We weren't as different as I made it out to be.

It had been Mac telling me who he was that made me recognize the truth. For better or worse, Mac spanned the gap between Rand and me. I could have fit Maclain Gentry into my world, but he already had a place at the Red Diamond. We could all coexist if I would stop being so defensive and angry and just breathe. Not that Mac and I would ever be anything more than passing acquaintances, but still, there could be a ceasefire. It all started with me, I was the one carrying the banner into battle, I had to be the one to call the truce. It was what Stef had wanted the whole time, for bridges to be built and crossed. Communication had to start somewhere.

Walking around the camp, I checked the tents and finally found the one Rand and Zach were in.

Slipping inside, I moved over to Rand's bunk and knelt down beside his head. Beau was sleeping under the cot, but he didn't stir even when I had my knee down next to his nose. I shook Rand gently and his eyes fluttered open.

"Hey," I said, smiling down at him.

He squinted a second and then jerked under my hand. "What's the matter? Are you all right? Is your side hurtin' you or—"

"I'm fine, don't worry," I soothed. "I just wanted to say I was sorry for being a dick earlier, and I'm sorry I got hurt."

He stared at me for a moment. "Am I awake?"

I snorted out a soft laugh. "Just—accept the damn apology, will you?"

"Yeah, all right," he agreed, smiling sleepily up at me. "I wanted you on the drive, Glenn. You make it easy for me."

"No, I don't. The opposite is true and we both know it."

He shook his head. "No, sir. I didn't worry one time today until I knew you were hurt."

It was a nice thing to say. "This just ain't me no more."

"I know it," he said, studying my face. "But that don't mean you got no home on the Red. Working it and living on it are two different things. You go on and ask Stef if that ain't the God's truth."

I nodded.

He reached up and patted me gently on the cheek. "Just visit, for crissakes, will you, please? It ain't like seeing you pains me or nothin'."

"I'll keep it in mind," I promised as I got up. "Thanks for taking care of me."

"I know you won't see a doctor, but will you lie and say you will?"

I grinned down at him. "You bet."

He shook his head and I headed for the tent flap.

"It wouldn't kill you to come out and see me."

"We're all busy, Zachariah," I said, turning toward the sound of his voice, unable to see him. "But since you get Sundays off, maybe you can find it in your schedule to go fishin' with me or watch a game or such. I'll even drive out and fetch you."

He cleared his throat. "I'd like that. Call me, would you?"

I would definitely make an effort because it was time to bury the hatchet. It was my ax to grind, after all. They all responded to me, to my anger, my hurt; they weren't carrying it around for anyone else.

Outside, I took a deep breath and felt better than I had all day, even with the twinge of pain in my side. Since I needed to talk to Mac as well, I went looking for his tent, and when I came around the corner of the encampment, nearly collided with the pretty face from earlier in the day.

"Shit," he gasped, flustered, as he grabbed at me to steady himself. "I'm so sorry I didn't see you there."

"Course not. No way you could have," I said gently, lowering my tone in hopes he'd follow my example. It was very early in the morning and his voice was loud.

"I was just—I—" He stopped and his eyes searched my face as he let go of me. "May I ask what you're doing out here so late?"

I nodded. "I was looking for Mac's tent."

He inhaled sharply. "I just came from there."

"Oh" was all I could think of to say before I turned to go.

But he slipped around in front of me, barring my quick retreat and stepping in close—too close—pressing up against my chest, staring up into my eyes, the scrutiny intense. "Are you the reason I wasn't allowed to stay?"

"What?" Seriously, the man could have knocked me over with a feather, because what the hell did he think was going on between me and the foreman of the Red Diamond?

"I mean, a man like Mac Gentry," the pretty man began, "you know he's not for keeping, right?"

I was stunned, a deer caught in the headlights, paralyzed, completely out of my depth because what he was assuming, what he was saying, had nothing to do with me except for down deep in the secret place where the truth lived.

"Mac is just for fun," he continued. "He's the guy you fuck around with and throw back, but still… I figured I'd at least get one more night out of him."

One more night? Was he insane? If he was lucky enough to get Mac into bed, he sure as hell should have kept him there. I most certainly would have, without question.

Of course, if Mac could have—and by the sound of things had already had—a man as perfect as the one standing in front of me, why in the world would he ever look twice at me? I was not the stunning creature this man was.

"Right?" he asked, grinding against me, his hands on my hips.

I had no idea what I was supposed to say, but I was certain of one thing. He was not the sweet thing I'd taken him for. This was a predator, not a bunny.

"No one ever says no to me," he purred.

It made sense. I was betting he'd never heard "no" in his life.

"So I have to wonder," he said, narrowing his eyes, looking me up and down. "Who are you?"

"I'm no one to him."

"Are you sure he—"

"You're drunk, Robin, go sleep it—oh," Mac said as he walked out of his tent in sleep shorts and a long-sleeved T-shirt.

Even though it was summer, it was early in the morning out on the prairie, so still very cold, which was why I had my jacket on. Mac must have been in his sleeping bag. He looked rumpled and sleepy, with his hair standing on end, slitted eyes, and furrowed brow. I'd never seen him look better.

He was stunning, but really, I shouldn't have been attracted to him. Beautiful, delicate like Stef, guys who were fragile were what did it for me. I had a type and I'd been looking for men who fit that idea in my head. What was odd was, when I was propositioned, when offers were made to fulfill my desires, to go to bed with some gorgeous, breathtaking man… I turned them down. And while I told myself the whole one-night stand component was a deal breaker, looking at Mac, I had to wonder if there was more to it than that. The foreman of the Red Diamond had mesmerized me from day one, from the first time I saw him riding up toward the house to speak to Rand. He dismounted, and I was introduced and made a horrible first impression as my tongue was stuck to the roof of my mouth.

I was rendered mute just watching him walk. His stride made me wish I could write poetry, and those strong capable hands of his should have had songs dedicated to them.

Mac looked like the kind of guy who would hold me, or whoever, down in bed, so… that was wrong. And it was stupid, because when I looked at Rand and Stef it was clear, just spending a few minutes with them, that there was no way Stef was topping in the sack. But maybe I was wrong and they switched it up. But with a man like Mac….

My brain raced through everything, all the time, it never stopped, and the worst part was that once I'd come out, told people I was gay—my father, Zach, Rand and Stef—I'd thought the hard part was over. But it turned out just because I was gay didn't make me any less messed up.

"Glenn?" Mac said softly. "What're you doin' out here?"

I was surprised at the look on his face, somewhere between discomfort and anger. I was going to say something shitty—something about him chasing hot men out of his tent in the wee small hours—when his gaze met mine… and softened.

His eyes warmed in the lantern glow, those massive shoulders of his fell, and he exhaled as he crossed his arms over his wide chest.

He calmed.

It probably had nothing to do with me, but as I cataloged every bulging, rippling muscle on his cut, toned form, I saw him curl his bottom lip slowly, decadently, until I realized what I was getting was just a trace of a smile.

He wasn't pissed at me. The frustration, irritation, or whatever it was—had nothing to do with me. It was, in fact, focused on the other man in our midst. That was good, because I'd gotten a glimpse of gentleness in Mac, and God… how easy would it be to get used to seeing that every day?

"Maclain?" I breathed out.

His heated gaze hit mine. "Come here."

Without thinking I dropped my hands from the pretty man pressed up against me and would have taken a step toward Mac, but Robin stopped me as he clutched at my shirt.

"Wait."

I could not take my eyes off Mac; I'd never seen him look so warm and inviting with a trace of danger all at the same time. A current of need ran through me and I had to keep myself still and not go to him.

"I'm so embarrassed," Robin whispered.

It took a concerted effort to drag my eyes off of Mac's delectable form to meet Robin's gaze.

"I thought he wanted to play," he said, leering at me.

"What'd you do, go in there and try an' attack him?" I teased even though my throat tightened and my mouth went dry.

His big blue eyes widened almost comically. "I—no, not exac—"

Lifting my hand, I stopped him and he relaxed against me. "He can't, not on a drive. He's the foreman of the Red Diamond; he's in charge of all these men and basically everyone's safety. He can't do anything that would compromise that."

His gaze flicked past me to Mac and then returned to my face. "It's more than—it's not just because of the drive. I've been out to the Red Diamond before."

"Oh," I managed to get out. I wanted him off me. Now. Clearly Robin was already a notch in Mac's bedpost.

"Tell him how long ago that was," Mac ordered, his voice icy.

"What?" Robin asked, and I took that moment to drop my arms and take a step back.

I'd walked into a lover's… what, discussion? I needed to get out of there so they could talk. I was a giant third wheel. "I should leave you two alone so—"

"No," Mac demanded, striding forward, taking hold of my bicep so I couldn't leave. "There's no reason for you to go," he clarified, then pinned Robin with his stare. "Tell him."

"I—" He was squinting at Mac. "—what? Why?"

"Because I said so."

"Screw you, Mac," he snapped, and I saw him wobble just a bit, unsteady on his feet. "I don't owe you a goddamn—"

"This here is Robin Halsey," Mac explained, talking over the inebriated Robin as he eased me sideways, closer to him, back toward the flap of his tent. "And he coordinates vacation packages for the resort."

"At King's Crossing?" I asked even as Mac drew me forward, stepping around me so I stood between him and the tent.

"Yeah," he said, tipping his head at Robin. "We met when he came out to the ranch with Mitch Powell before anything was even built out there."

I looked back and forth between the two. "Well, I didn't mean to interrupt," I said quietly. "I just needed to talk to you right quick."

Mac nodded and gestured into his tent. "Come inside, then, and talk to me."

"Yeah, but—"

"You're not interrupting anything," he assured me before glancing back at Robin. "Ain't that right?"

"No," Robin said with a shake of his head. "That's not right at all. I told you I wanted to talk to you and—"

"And I told *you*," he growled. "We're done."

"You make no sense."

"Go sleep it off, Robin."

"Are you kidding?" His voice rose angrily. "How could you possibly want him instead of me? That's insane."

"No, it's really not," he conceded, shoving me into the tent.

When I rounded on him, he was zipping up the flap.

"I'm sorry," he said gruffly, then closed the distance between us, taking my face in his big, rough, hard callused hands.

I suddenly could barely breathe.

"Tell me what you wanted to say."

Talking? Was he kidding?

The half grin I got flushed me with heat, and that was nuts because all he was doing was stroking over the curve of my jaw and staring into my eyes.

"Glenn?"

The rumbling purr in his voice sent a shiver through me that was impossible to hide, along with the smell of the mint on his breath and the soap on his skin. The warmth of his hands wasn't helping matters either.

He sighed and shook his head. "Waiting on you to figure shit out is exhausting."

"What?"

"Lemme enlighten you," he husked before he drew me to him, lowered his head, and kissed me.

I whimpered in the back of my throat and opened for him, parting my lips as his tongue found mine. Why or how, what was going on, none of that mattered at the moment. I had wanted to kiss Mac, to see what all that power and heat tasted like, and while I was confused, it didn't matter. I would take advantage this once.

He stepped into me, slipping one hand around the back of my neck as the kiss ramped up, became urgent and grinding, devouring and mauling, like he wanted to eat me. Not that I cared. I was his for the taking, whatever he wanted, ready to yield.

I wrapped my arms around his neck, surrendering my weight, leaning as he dipped his other hand to the small of my back and pressed me against him, rubbing, pushing, parting my legs with his thigh as I tried to stay standing.

The kiss made me dizzy but I gave as good as I got, needing to sate my curiosity, to see what having Mac's mouth on mine, his tongue exploring, teeth nibbling, and hands, now, on my ass, squeezing, felt like.

"Fuck," he snarled, breaking the sublime, euphoric connection, the drugging kiss ending as he shoved me back.

I was lost, staring at him, watching him pant, seeing how swollen his lips were, how red, noting the clenched fists and the slight tremble to his broad shoulders.

"I should throttle you."

"What?" I asked, taking a step toward him.

He lifted his hand to keep me away. "We're gonna get something straight first."

"I don't—"

"You're not a top."

I had no idea what we were talking about.

"God, look at your face and your big, dark, beautiful blue…. Fuck, Glenn," he groaned, then pounced, gathering me to him in a rush.

I took him in my arms when he grabbed me, tipped my head back, and laid a kiss on me that I felt from head to toe and all parts in between. His tongue tangled with mine as he fisted a hand in my hair and held tight as he used his other to get into my jeans. The belt surrendered easily, the snap next, the zipper making a quick sound before he wrapped one scarred, strong, beat-up hand around my cock and pulled.

I nearly made a wet mess right there as I bucked into his grip, but I held on, squirming, hands in his hair as he stroked me firmly but gently. I needed to be closer to him and so tugged on his T-shirt, wanting it off.

"Jesus, Glenn," he rasped, pulling free, only to grab my bicep and haul me over to his bunk. He shoved me down and I sat hard, looking up at him and waiting.

He squatted in front of me and gingerly picked up one foot, pulled off my boot, and then repeated the motion with the other. Once that was done, he stood back up, grabbed the bottom of each leg of my jeans, and shucked them down and off fast.

"You see this," he said, gesturing at me. "You… waiting… looking up at me with those pretty eyes of yours, ready to take direction…. This should clue you in."

I was lost, but I had to touch him. That was the most important thing. "Please get naked. I wanna see all of you."

I would have thought he was a stripper, the way he took off his T-shirt, reaching down his sides, sliding it up and slowly off, letting me see the hard, flat planes of his stomach, the wide, carved pectorals with dark-brown nipples, the sexy angles of his collarbone and his chiseled arms and massive shoulders. He was built powerful and strong, and I wanted him all over me.

His cock was erect under his sleep shorts, tenting the soft cotton, making a wet spot, and before he could do as I asked and divest himself of every stitch of clothing, I leaned forward and pulled at the drawstring. They dropped to his hips, holding there for a second before falling to his cock, caught on his long, thick length like they'd been hung up on the end of a club.

"Glenn," he whispered as I lifted them off and let them drop to puddle around his ankles.

"Just let me," I groaned, my breath catching as I wet my lips before parting them, opening for the wide mushroom head of his gorgeous cock.

He was silky on my tongue, hot and slippery, and his taste, bitter and salty at the same time, combined with the smell of soap on his sleek skin, the musky, earthy scent of his groin, the thick curls, all of it combined, the sensations overwhelming, made me ache to have him.

"You have no idea what you—fuckin' Glenn, you're so—just give in already. Lemme have you."

Funny. That was exactly what I wanted myself.

I had no gag reflex at all, never had, and from practicing on the toys I had at home—locked safely away from the prying eyes of any houseguests—I had confirmed how good at swallowing I would be, if nothing else. At the moment, though, I was glad there was no hesitancy in me because the filthy choked moan that came up out of Mac's diaphragm when I swallowed him down the back of my throat told me all I needed to know.

I had no technique, had in fact only been on the receiving end of this maneuver, but my rough, fumbling, untrained enthusiasm was apparently more than appreciated. His fingers in my hair, tugging as I licked and sucked, laved, dragged my teeth carefully down the side of his heavily veined shaft, directing my movement and pressure and pace, let me know he was enjoying my efforts.

"Jesus, Glenn, I'm gonna kill whoever taught you how to do these things with your mouth right after I thank them."

"Why—" I began, licking him from balls to head, only to suck hard and sloppily on his glans a second before deep-throating him once more.

"Fuck!" he huffed, jolting in my mouth, driving down a second before he sucked in air through his nose. "It's like you're a virgin with the skills of a whore."

I snickered, smiling around his cock, humming a second, making his balls vibrate before I let his shaft slip from between my lips. "I haven't been a virgin since I was fifteen years old."

"You've never been with a man," he clarified, sliding his precum- and saliva-dripping cock across my bottom lip.

I opened and he pushed in and out as I felt my cock thicken to an almost painful hardness at what he was allowing.

"How the fuck do you—stop," he croaked out, fingers threaded in my hair, holding tight. "I'm gonna come if you—"

I made the suction stronger, faster, and took hold of his ass, grazing his cleft with my fingers, parting his cheeks slightly as he hammered into my mouth.

He was gorgeous when he came, head back, eyes closed, biting his bottom lip, all those beautiful muscles clenched at once as his gorgeous chest froze with his held breath.

The hot spill against the back of my throat was thick and briny but not bad, and I drank him down and stayed there, still, until he slowly withdrew.

When his eyes fluttered open, I smiled up at him, more than a little proud of myself.

"You made a huge mistake," he informed me, cupping my face in his hands as he dropped to his knees before recapturing my lips.

Mistake? As far as I was concerned, with how I was being rewarded, I couldn't think of one wrong turn I'd made.

The kiss was to taste me and rub his tongue over mine, and when he took me in hand, sliding his thumb over the dripping head of my cock, the mewling cry that tore out of me was involuntary.

"What—" I gasped, "—mistake?"

He broke the kiss to look at me. "You gave in. Ain't never lettin' you go now."

That didn't sound like anything to be sorry about.

"Does your side hurt?" His voice was filled with concern.

"What?" I breathed in his air, inhaling his scent, wanting him all over me but unsure how to get him there. Did I shove him down, take what I wanted?

"Are you in pain?"

"Only from blue balls," I teased.

He was not taking the bait. We would not be engaging in our normal banter. "Have you ever been fucked?"

I was startled and tried to put more distance between us so I could see his face. "I—no. You have to let me have you."

He studied me a second. "If that's what you want," he said, kissing me again until I forgot what we were talking about, lost in the taste of him.

I was always a top, and yes, I'd only ever been with women, but I figured there would be a guy, beautiful, smaller like Stef, and I would be…. But I'd watched a lot of porn, and even though I knew it wasn't like that in real life, what I saw were some huge Hulk-sized guys mounted by men considerably smaller and not built like body builders. So I knew size, in and of itself, was no indicator of anything. There were power bottoms and submissive tops, and if you saw them walking down the street together, you would have maybe thought the reverse was true. But really no one knew.

I had an idea of what went on in Rand and Stef's bedroom because of what I knew of them as men, and I knew what everyone else thought, but maybe we were all wrong. Maybe my big scary half brother liked Stef to have his way with him. Maybe they switched, and not like it mattered, not like I truly cared, but all of it had wreaked havoc on what I thought I was supposed to do and be and made me think I was looking for one thing when something else—or someone else—was what I needed.

Pushing him back, I stared into Mac's now dark charcoal eyes, clouded with passion, heavy lidded with blown pupils.

His breath hitched. "Why're you waiting?"

I had no idea what I was supposed to do. "Maclain?" I understood the mechanics of the act, the lube, that there was prep involved and not simply me shoving myself inside of him. There were steps, but initiating them was lost on me.

"Honey," he rumbled. "It's taking everything in me to not attack you, so if I'm what you want, get the lube out of my pack right there and fuck me."

I concentrated on keeping my voice level. "You'd let me do that?"

"I would beg you to do that if that's what it would take."

Jesus.

He wanted me so bad that it didn't matter if he had me or I had him. How fucking hot was that? It didn't matter to him even though the first thing he'd said to me was that I wasn't a top, which must have meant that his plan was for me to be on the bottom. And when he'd said it, I had been excited, not scared, not questioning, not anything but made of yes. "But you don't even… like me," I ground out.

"Idiot," he murmured before he lunged at me, knocking me back down onto his bunk, and I was caught under 240 pounds of rugged, hard burled man.

Even after such a short time, I was already used to the ravenous toe-curling, spine-melting kisses and returned each and every one as I took the tour with my hands, touching him everywhere I'd always wanted to, his thick dirty-blond hair, his wide, sculpted back, my fingers tracing down over his ribs before moving to the solid, defined chest. When he had to breathe, I kissed him everywhere else, across his clavicle, up his throat, over his jaw, my kiss-swollen lips abraded by stubble before they settled, again, over his.

"Wait," he insisted, about to lift away.

I caught his bottom lip so he couldn't, tugging on it with my teeth, making it clear he had no choice but to kiss me.

"That was fast," he sighed as I rolled him to his back, sitting up, straddling his thighs.

"What?"

"You showing me what you wanted," he answered, taking hold of my thighs so I couldn't move. "Now why don't you tell me what's on your mind so I'm not the only one naked."

"I like looking at you," I confessed, slipping my hands on his chest down to his abdomen. "And I never thought you'd ever let me touch you."

"Any man would let you touch him, Glenn," he assured me, "and beg for the privilege. You have no idea how lethal that smile of yours is, how much I've wanted to touch them thick lashes of yours when they're restin' on your cheek, and how many times I've stopped myself from putting you flat on your back 'cause I knew how bad you needed to be kissed."

I sucked in a breath. The revelation that he thought I was appealing surged through me, and it felt so good. But I pushed it aside, needing to be clearheaded when I talked to him. "Listen, I don't wanna be fucked and just left after—I've been runnin' from that."

"You've been runnin' from everything."

"What's that supposed to mean?"

He shook his head. "You realize you're usually mean enough to hunt bears with a hickory switch, right?"

"Me?"

"Hell yes, you." He snorted. "I ain't never seen a man piss off so many people so fast who only want to keep him 'round."

"Keep me?"

"For fuck's sake, Glenn," he replied almost angrily, "all any of us wants is for you to be out on the ranch."

"What're you talking about?"

"You know."

I shrugged, thinking of my conversations with both Rand and Zach and what they'd also said when they thought I was asleep yesterday. "Maybe a little. Now."

He rolled me to my back and settled over me gently, as to not put any pressure on my side, but holding me down at the same time so I couldn't get away.

"Rand wants his whole family on the Red, and you're the one who's missing that he could have right now."

"I don't—"

"Take this off," he prodded, working open the buttons on my shirt. "We all hoped, me included, when you started out with the restaurant that it wouldn't go well so you—"

"Oh?" I bristled, trying to move him.

"Stop wigglin', you ain't goin' nowhere."

"I—"

"We wanted The Bronc to go up in flames so you'd come back to the ranch."

"You did?"

"We all did," he assured me. "But now we see the success you've made of it, and we're all real happy for you because it seems like, when you're there, that you're in your element."

"Oh?" His words were designed to give me heart failure, as good as that sounded.

"You're real good with people."

I was, as long as they weren't related to me or foremen on ranches.

"You have a way of gettin' folks to follow you, just like Rand does."

It was a really nice compliment, and one I had thought myself, that Rand and I were more alike than I'd ever thought. "Thank you."

"You're very welcome," he said, smiling at me. "But that leads us right back to what Rand wants, and that's you on the Red."

What he was saying was good, but more than that, to me, for me, was the way he was gazing at me with the softest expression I'd ever seen. It felt quiet and connected, like we had moved from somewhere apart to something closer with just new moments between us. It was like every second something was changing right there in front of me, and I knew, beyond a shadow of a doubt, that he was fond of me, into me, wanting to spend time learning things and being around. Now that I was certain what I was seeing, could distinguish what true interest looked like on him, I'd never miss the possessiveness on his face or the heat in his eyes or the arrogant smile on his lips, ever again.

"He wants you to move your restaurant onto the Red."

"What?" I asked, lost in cataloging the signs of wanting on Mac.

"Rand wants The Bronc on the ranch," he reiterated distractedly, helping me out of my button-down and the T-shirt underneath. "But barring that, he'd at least like you living there."

"But I—"

"Zach wants that, too, you right there, accessible as well, and me."

"You?"

"Yes, me," he growled, running a hand down my abdomen, tracing over the ridges of the six pack I'd worked hard to achieve. "Because unlike the others, I can insist that you come stay with me."

"Are you drunk? Is that what all this is?"

He scoffed and his slow smile made those eyes of his glitter like mercury poured into a glass. “No, sir. I just want what I want and I’m fixin’ to have it.”

“Oh? What is it you want?”

“That’d be you, Glenn Holloway. Just you.”

Chapter 5

I COULDN'T breathe. He was trying to kill me with naked confessions.

"Maclain, you—God."

He'd reached under the elastic band of my briefs and drawn out my cock, hence the momentary loss of my words.

"Every time I see you and those blue-green eyes of yours settle on me and my heart goes up in my throat, I know that you're supposed to belong to me."

But how could he have his life figured out when I had no idea what had been happening?

"You're so confused about things," he said, leaning sideways to reach into his pack and retrieve the lube. "Everything that you face, all your issues, are in your head."

"I don't understand."

"I know, honey," he soothed, sitting up, reaching for my briefs and sliding them down and off my legs, leaving me as naked as him. "Damn."

"Keep talking."

I got a flashing grin in response. "Sorry. Your skin is very distracting."

Mine? "It is?"

He scowled at me, but instead of it being irritating, I found it ridiculously hot. "I just realized something crazy. All that swagger and bravado I see all the time, that's all fake. You have no idea what you look like at all."

"Are you kidding?"

"Do I look like I am?"

He didn't, no. "C'mon. I look like my father and Rand and Zach and my Uncle—"

"No. You don't."

"Maclain, I—"

"Rand and the rest of the Holloway men are big, scary alpha-dog type guys, and you are not that."

But I *was*.

"Maybe you *were*, maybe you used to be when you were shooting poison into your body and—"

"How did you know about the steroids?"

He rose and sat up, and I had Mac where I never thought I ever would—straddling my thighs.

I immediately moved my hands to touch him, stroke his skin, and map the contours of roping muscle that made up his legs.

"Look at me."

But I was savoring the feel of him.

"Hey."

I lifted my eyes to his.

"I knew you didn't lose weight. You just lost all that bulky 'roid-rage muscle that was never you but was probably more about fitting in on the ranch than anything else."

"I don't belong on a ranch," I told him.

"Not as a cowboy, no," he agreed. "But that's not what Rand needs, anyway. He needs you because you're a member of his family, and he wants you around him and Stef and Wyatt, and he needs your skills with people because he has none."

I chuckled.

"Don't get me wrong, the man inspires lifelong loyalty from his men, but that ain't what I'm speakin' of."

I knew that too.

"You know as well as anyone that Rand has a very direct way about him that puts people off right quick, and trying to talk to him about it is like tryin' to walk snakes."

God, he was beautiful, and listening to him felt so natural, like we'd been doing this forever. I was going to say something, tell him how I felt, when he squeezed my hips with his thighs and I jolted in pain.

"Oh shit," he gasped and in seconds he had us trading places, me on top and him below me on the thin padding on the cot. "Better?"

I was sitting with his wide, thick cock nestled between my ass cheeks; I was light-headed, with just the feel of him, that's how much better it was.

"Maclain," I whispered.

"Lift up," he directed me. "Push back just a bit and take the lube in your hand and grease yourself up real good."

But looking at his length standing rigid and dripping between us, I had other thoughts.

"You're going to need to lift my legs up on your shoulders when you shove inside me, and I need you to be—"

"Maclain."

"Glenn," he said playfully, smiling up at me.

"It doesn't make you feel…." How was I supposed to ask this?

"Talk to me," he prodded, reaching up to trace over my left eyebrow.

I smiled down at him. "You like my face."

He nodded. "I do. I trip over things when I'm walking whenever you look at me."

"No. That's me. I trip all the time."

"When you're tired and worn out, yes," he agreed. "But not normally. You run at night in the dark, honey. You're pretty fuckin' coordinated."

I glared down at him. "How come you're only saying nice things to me now?"

He reached behind me and pinched my ass. "Because you're naked, and I don't just mean that you've got no clothes on."

"What?"

"I *see* you," he said pointedly. "You try so hard at everything. And some of it's shit like trying to be as big as the other men in your family when clearly you were made leaner, smaller, with them long lashes and big eyes and that mouth that makes my dick hard just lookin' at it."

A pulse ran through me, and the lube I'd squirted out and dumped in my palm got slathered on his dick instead of mine. I wanted to stroke his flesh, not my own.

"You try to carry all the people who work for you on your back."

"How do you—"

"I've been in there to eat. I talk to them, but mostly I listen."

"I've never seen you."

"You're always running. Literally."

"Are you stalking me?" I asked hopefully.

"I check on you," he conceded.

"What's the difference?" I asked, squeezing his cock, tugging gently, watching as it seeped pearlized drops of precum.

"I—" He closed his eyes for a moment and I watched him take a breath in and hold it, wetting his lips before he opened his eyes. "What?"

Curling over him, I took his mouth, made him open for my tongue, and I sucked on his as I kissed him long and slow and deep.

His throaty groan was full of yearning and I chuckled against his lips.

"You know you have power over me and you're getting off on using it," he said hoarsely, hands fisted at his sides, griping the metal sides of the sturdy cot.

"Why aren't you touching me," I teased, taking hold of his now-slippery cock and pressing the head to my entrance. "Don't like me anymore?"

"If I put my hands on you, hurt or not, virgin or not, I will flip you over and bury myself to the balls in your ass."

"No, I don't think you would," I said, confident in my belief even as I pushed back, taking in only his glans, the stretch and burn sucking my breath away.

"Can we not talk anymore," he pleaded, rough and shaky. "I really can't—oh please, Glenn, honey, take me all in."

But it hurt and my own erection was flagging until he put his hand there, jerking me back to hungry need in seconds, making me crave his touch and even more, wanting him inside.

"I won't hurt you," he promised, leaning up, kissing my eyes, my cheeks, my nose, and finally my mouth, so tenderly I felt the ache for him blossom in my chest and storm through my body like sparks of lightning.

I bucked against him and pressed back farther and farther each time, taking more of him inside me until finally his groin was flush with the curve of my ass.

"Take a minute to let your body adjust to—Glenn!"

I couldn't wait. His cock was dragging over that spot I'd read about, and my body, which had been hesitant, was quivering with fresh arousal and a renewed sense of urgency. I wanted to impale myself on him, get him in harder and faster, so I leaned forward, letting him slide out, and then eased back until he was buried to the hilt again.

"You are so tight," he marveled, hands on my face as he stared into my eyes. "And slick, and I need you to let me put you on your hands and knees."

"Can you do it faster like that?"

"Yessir, I can," he swore, his voice whiskey smooth, edged in smoke.

Scrambling off him, I dropped to the tent floor and into position, waiting only seconds before he was behind me. Hand on the small of my back, he spread my cheeks and speared inside, thrusting deep in one smooth stroke.

"Oh God, why would anybody ever wanna top," I mewled, taking a trembling breath as he eased out and then rammed back inside, pounding into me again and again, piston fast, exactly as I wanted.

"Because you feel amazing, that's why," he answered me. "I have dreamed about having you wrapped around my cock, and I cannot wait to get you in my bed."

His bed?

"In my house, on my sheets, under my blankets—tell me I can, tell me you're going to come home with me and sit on my porch and eat in my kitchen and sleep in my bed."

My heart, in the midst of the best sex of my life, threatened to explode. "You're sayin' you wanna see me?"

"I am," he said plainly, grabbing hold of my ass, careful with my wounded hip, his fingers ready to leave bruises on the opposite side. "A lot. Just me, just you, *us*, no one else. So say I can."

"Oh yes."

"And swear you won't do this with anyone else until one of us says."

"I promise," I rasped, in absolute lust and like with Mac. The lusting was not new, of course, but the liking certainly was.

"Good," he said, laughing softly in my ear before kissing me there and turning my head so he could ravage my mouth for a moment before I was ordered to grab my dick. "I need you to come before I do so—"

"Just let go and hammer me."

"Oh yeah, fuckin' made for me," he growled as he pummeled inside of me as my muscles clamped down around him.

"Maclain!" I yelled, coming apart beneath him as I splattered the ground beneath me.

He emptied into my ass and I realized at that moment I had never felt closer or more connected to another person, ever. Sex wasn't love, I knew that, but I was changed because of this, and not merely because now I knew what I'd been missing. He knew me, truly saw me, and he was the only one who had ever cared enough to look.

"Oh Glenn," he croaked, lifting me up from my hands so I was upright but still on my knees with his cock pulsing inside of me. One of his hands was wrapped around my throat, the other pressing down on my abdomen. "You are so fucked."

I scoffed. "Well, yeah, I was."

"No," he whispered into my hair. "You have no idea what you just did."

"And what did I do?" I asked, leaning back, letting my head bump his, our cheeks scraping together, my short beard and mustache on his stubble.

"You gave yourself to me."

I had. "It was stupid, what I thought before."

"Tell me."

"I thought I wouldn't be a man anymore if I was on the bottom."

"You thought you'd be less."

"Yes."

"But now you know that's stupid because top or bottom has nothing to do with being a man. You're doing what you want and what feels right at the time."

All I could do was nod.

"But that doesn't mean that we can't switch it up next—"

"No," I said quickly, my voice thick with lingering passion and emotion. "I'd like to have you—I want it just this same way again."

"Whatever you want," he husked, easing gently from my sensitive channel.

The feel of his slick cum brought another thought to mind. I cleared my throat. "Maclain?"

"You're worried about the condom," he said, taking my face in his hands so he could ease me to a sitting position.

"Not worried, just—I mean, I've never been with… and it's been well over some years since there was a girl and I've been tested and I'm fine but I should have told you that and I have the results in my e-mail if you—"

"I have mine saved on my phone," he explained, pushing my hair out of my eyes and tracing over my cheeks with his thumbs. "I can show it to—"

"No, I just wondered why you didn't put one on."

"Well, because I know there hasn't been anyone for you, and I'm always careful, so I wasn't worried about it."

"How did you know there was no one for me?"

"Remember how I told you I've been keeping tabs on you?"

I did. "Yeah."

"What I didn't say was that any guy lingering around your restaurant waiting for it to close, waiting to get a chance at you… I've quietly discouraged them."

"You're lying." I chuckled, my heart beating wildly, hoping it was true. To someone else it might seem a bit scary; to me, staking that kind of claim was crazy, stupid hot.

"Oh no I ain't," he promised me, his eyes, still dark with hunger, riveted on my face. "And since just thinking about being inside of you has forced me to take more cold showers than I can possibly ever count, I was sure as hell not going to offer to glove up for no good reason."

"Because you knew we were safe."

"I did," he admitted, his gaze never wavering as he drew me in for a kiss. It was tender but thorough, and when he was done checking my tonsils, he gave me a smug grin. "I would never put you at risk for anything. Not ever. I swear."

"I believe you," I sighed, so sated, so calm, realizing that being in bed with someone who knew what he was doing and wanted me as much as I wanted him was a blessing to go to church and light a candle in thankfulness for. "As long as it's just us, we should never use a condom, don't you think?"

"I agree," he sighed, brushing my hair back again. "This got long, huh?"

"Yeah. It needs to be cut."

"Awful pretty to cut," he said wistfully before he kissed me again. "I like the beard and the mustache too."

I smiled at him. "You seem to like a lot of things about me."

"No 'seem,' I do like everything about you," he said adamantly, and I got another kiss. "Now don't move. I wanna take care of you."

"You did already," I told him, and that time he bit my ass, a quick nibble, to shut me up.

I stayed frozen as he pulled everything off the cot and arranged it on the ground before prodding me to lie down.

Sprawling out, sighing deeply, not remembering when my body had ever been so sated or my mind so still, I grinned when I felt the T-shirt being used to clean me up.

"I'm still gonna smell like sex and sweat and have your dried cum all over me," I remarked cheerfully.

"Yeah, that's really not a bad thing," he said, falling down beside me, bumping me, snuggling tight, his mouth on my ear and behind it, on my skin, sucking, licking, trailing lines of endless, rough kisses that, along with the bites, were going to leave marks. "You can go around with me on you all the time."

"You're a possessive man, Maclain Gentry."

"You have no idea, Glenn Holloway," he said, snorting out a laugh as he nuzzled the hollow of my throat. "Man, I knew you were gonna smell good."

"You thought a lot about me."

"Night and day."

"How come?"

"Simple things."

"Like?"

"You're nice to look at."

"You too," I sighed.

"I'm addicted to those eyes of yours."

His storm-washed-sky ones were nothing to scoff at, either. "Ditto."

His chuckle was sexy, low and seductive and dirty in that way where now I knew carnal pleasure awaited.

"You're making my dick hard again when you laugh like that," I drawled.

"Oh, I knew you were gonna be good in bed too. Hell if I didn't."

"What're you talking about?"

"How fast you get mad, all that passion, plus watching you eat, the way you devour your food and suck all the meat off a chicken bone—it's hot."

I laughed at him, and he rolled me to my back to bury his face in my belly, kissing me there before scooting up to lay his head on my heart.

"It is. You enjoy your food and your beer, and watching you eat strawberries last summer was a religious experience."

"Same as watching you walk," I sighed, my hands in his hair as I tugged him up to kiss me. "I love to watch you walk."

He opened for me and I kissed him lazily, taking my time, because I could. He didn't belong to me… yet… but I had a great start.

After rolling him to his back, I spread myself over him, loving the feel of all that virile male power lying dormant under me.

"We'll be back from the drive on Sunday afternoon. I want you to be at the Red when we get there so you can come home with me."

"Yeah?" I asked anxiously, almost holding my breath because he sounded so good, like he was making plans, making *promises*, and I was excited just thinking about spending long periods of uninterrupted time with him.

"Say you will."

"I will."

"Good," he said, reaching up to squeeze my ass and dip his middle finger into my crease, making me shudder with the contact. "Now tell me truly, do you feel all right with what you did? What I did?"

I made a noise that could not be classified as speech and rolled to my good side so he could spoon behind me.

"Glenn?" he asked. I heard the cap on the lube snap open. "Tell me."

"How can you even ask that when I've never felt better in my life?" I said gruffly, bucking forward as he curled two fingers inside of me and rubbed over my gland.

"Am I hurting you?"

"No."

"I have the need to gorge on you in case I wake up in the morning and this is all just a really fuckin' hot dream."

"Not—" I gasped as he withdrew his fingers and replaced them with the head of his long, beautiful cock that already I needed inside me again. "—a dream."

"That's good," he said, going slow, pressing forward, stretching me, filling me, and not stopping until I was clenched around him.

He slid out a fraction and then pushed back in, gentle, tender, and with an agonizing languor that built a ravenous need in me almost instantly.

"Don't stop. Please don't stop."

"Then tell me now that you're okay," he ordered, slipping his hand down my hip, careful not to touch where the stitches were before taking hold of my straining, twitching cock. "Or not, and we'll talk about it, but I want this settled between us."

"Nothing needs to be settled," I confessed. "I'm good."

"Yeah?"

"I thought, before…." I moaned, the feel of him stretching me and filling me so good, the slide and the push more exquisite than I could have imagined, making it hard to keep a coherent thought in my head. "That bottoming would make a difference, that I'd care what I did, but it doesn't because I'm still me, nothing's changed at all." Nothing was taken from me by giving myself to my lover. I was still me, no less powerful, no less a man. Inside, I was the same except for knowing what my body was capable of feeling. "I just didn't know, and there's so much bullshit everywhere and it messes with your head."

"You didn't know how you'd feel, and there's a misconception that the guy on the bottom isn't just as strong or powerful, that submitting somehow makes you weak."

"Which is stupid."

"Yes," he agreed, his voice cracking as he surrendered to his own need. "And remember, however you want me, however you need me, I'm all yours. All of me… just yours."

I had a feeling we were talking about more than his body, but I had a confession. "Maclain?"

"Yes, honey," he said gruffly as he ground into me, deep, increasing his rhythm, stroking me faster, his breath stopping and starting.

"I like it like this." The words tumbled out of me as I came over his fingers and wrist. "I love it like this."

CHAPTER 6

I WOKE up in the morning, sore everywhere, but it was amazing, the change to my outlook when I lifted my head up off Mac's chest to look down into his gorgeous eyes.

"Yeah, all right," I allowed, grinning at him. "This is the best way to start a day ever."

And he kissed me, morning breath and all, and even better, hugged me tight to his heart and buried his face in my hair.

"Sunday around four I need you there when I come in from the stockyard."

"I wouldn't miss it."

"You swear?"

He was worried that away from him I would change my mind about us, and that was a slice of heaven right there because it was me who mattered and that was brand sparkling new.

"Yes, baby, I'll be there."

"Oh yeah, that's good. I will most certainly be your baby."

"So tell me, where's your family?" I asked. "I've always wanted to know."

He brushed my hair back from my face; it was already getting to be a habit of his, even in so short a time. "When I told everyone at home in Jackson Hole, Wyoming, that I was gay, they wasted no time in throwing me off the ranch."

I drew him into my arms and squeezed him tight, because what words could I offer him that would come close to helping.

"I suspect," he sighed, cuddling tight, "that if my mother were alive, that would not have been the case, but she passed when I was ten, and that was the last we saw of my father's heart. I think he buried it with her."

"Jesus, Maclain, I'm so sorry."

"It's all right. Sheridan Gentry has five other sons to take care of him, so he ain't missing me."

"I would," I blurted out, tipping his head back to kiss him. "Miss you."

It was scary how ready we both were to belong to another person, to start a relationship. It was like we'd both been waiting for the other to notice that forward, together, was the place we both wanted to go.

"Well, what I'm hoping is that we'll get to where missing me will never cross your mind because you can't even imagine letting me go at all."

"I don't think you have to worry about us getting there."

His smile was wicked. "Well, well, now, ain't we a pair, gettin' attached so fast."

Fast was an understatement, so the time apart when Everett picked me up to take me back to the ranch was probably a good thing.

AS EVERETT'S truck sped away, everything I'd thought about just an hour before, how we should handle things, how we should keep things under wraps until we made concrete decisions about our future… seemed stupid. I didn't want to pin Mac down, but I realized in the whirlwind of activity that was my leaving that I hadn't actually gotten around to asking him what he did or didn't want. I'd assumed things, and that was never good.

"You forget something?" Zach called over to me as I walked back past where all the men and guests were sitting down to breakfast. I hadn't been hungry, and since Everett wanted to get back to his family, we had skipped the meal to leave for the Red. But it turned out I wasn't quite ready to go, and I made Everett stop his truck and trailer so I could get out and run back to Mac, who hadn't moved from where he was when I left him not ten minutes prior.

He was still standing there, glowering, arms crossed, brows furrowed, a study in irritation with maybe even some anger thrown in for good measure.

Darting over, big smile on my face, I stopped directly in front of him and slipped my hand around the back of his neck, massaging gently. "Hi," I greeted, as though I wasn't insane and wasn't right back after barely being gone.

I had no idea his glower could get any darker. "What're you doing?"

I slipped my right hand over his hip. "Remember when I was leaving and told you that we should probably keep this to ourselves?"

"I seem to recall that," he said coolly, his tone as frosty as his gaze.

"Well, I was trying to think about you and how private you are and how maybe you didn't want everyone knowing your business, but

I realized that you could have taken that to mean that I didn't want everyone to know."

He grunted, but I saw a glimmer of warmth start to infuse the quicksilver of his eyes. I was definitely seeing some thaw.

"So I came back to tell you, Maclain Gentry," I said as I eased his head down even as I lifted for his mouth, "that I want everyone to fuckin' know about us."

The kiss I gave him was filled with longing, but more importantly, hope. I'm sure it also left no doubt in anyone's mind that Mac was very much with me. Taking a step back from him, I was very pleased when he followed, not wanting to sever the contact.

"Turns out I suck at keeping secrets," I told him, smiling up into eyes that were no longer sad but heated pools of molten silver.

"That's good," he agreed, sighing deeply, pulling the brim of his hat back down low. "I'm the same, and as you know already, a bit too possessive for most people."

"I'm not most people."

"No, you ain't, not at all."

"You'll miss me, right?"

"You have no idea."

I was smug as I walked away, and when I waved from the truck, he was waiting to wave back. It was nice. A man who could show he was invested.... Very nice.

The ride back to the Red Diamond was a bore because Everett didn't want to talk, he simply concentrated on the road, watching for state troopers and scaring me into ordering him to slow the fuck down. I didn't want me, him, and Juju to end up splattered all over the highway.

"You shouldn't have come," I groused.

"It was me or Stef," he said, clipping his words. "And have you ever seen Stef drive a truck and trailer?" He raised his eyebrows and I chuckled. "Terrifying just don't do that situation justice."

"No, I bet not."

"And Rand woulda been madder than a peeled rattler if I let that happen."

Possibly. "Well, if you could slow down just a bit, I'd appreciate it."

He did so without any further pestering, and so in appreciation of that, when we got to the Red, instead of making him take the time to drive me up the long road to the house, I told him I'd unload Juju and ride her to where my truck and trailer were parked.

"Thanks, Glenn," he said sincerely, giving me a wide smile. "It's my first baby, you know, so… all I'm wanting to do is stay home with both her and my wife."

I nodded, and as I led my girl out of the trailer, before I could saddle up, Everett took hold of my shoulder.

"Ev?"

He took a breath. "I just want you to know that Mac is a real good man, and I ain't never seen him chase no tail."

I had no idea what I was supposed to say to that. "Okay."

"You and him." He stopped and thought a second. "I can see that."

He could? "You can?"

"I reckon so. He's scary and mean, and you're kind and soft-spoken like Stef. Y'all will balance each other out real nice."

He thought I was kind? "Everett, when have you ever known me to be kind?"

His scowl was funny. "You take care of all them orphans that work for you up at The Bronc, I watched you carry Bella three miles through the brush when she got out that time and tangled with them coyotes, and you ain't never got no hurtful word for no one but members of your own family."

I smiled at him, overwhelmed by how he saw me and how maybe I should start seeing myself. Perhaps I was more of a nurturer than I realized. There could be more of my mother in me than I ever suspected.

"And everyone knows the only people you can complain on is your own."

"Yeah."

"So if you end up on the ranch, living on the other side of Tyler's old place down by the creek… that'd be just fine," he finished, offering me his hand.

Amazing how people could surprise you.

IT WAS almost eleven when Juju and I came cantering up the drive. She was happy to be out of the trailer and I was just happy, period. The stitches in my side hurt a bit, a twinge now and then, but when Mac had checked it, there was no redness or any signs of infection. Rand had done a really good job, and the hug I gave him when I left—which startled the hell out of him—was my thank-you.

"Don't—" He coughed. "—stay away so long, all right? I'd like to see you some."

"Yessir," I teased, and he did a really odd thing and put his hand on my cheek and studied my face. "Rand?"

"Just—come around."

I *heard* him that time, because I'd believed in Mac the night before when he told me how things really were. People actually wanted me around, so maybe I could quit being a prick and thinking everyone was only saying what they were saying because they thought they had to, or because they felt sorry for me. My father didn't give a good goddamn about me, but that was not a surprise. To have the others care was more than I would have ever imagined possible.

So as I came up on the house, I was in a really good mood but not blinded with happiness enough to not find the two unfamiliar cars parked in front of the house odd.

That made no sense.

Most parked cars would be down by the stables, sure, down at the front office, again, yes, and even farther out by Mac's place if someone came to call on him—that would not have given me pause. But here in front of the big house, where I'd only ever expect Stef's car or Rand's truck, cars parked here would mean someone there to specifically see one of them, and while it was possible—Stef had friends in town—it simply wasn't likely. In fact, normally when Rand was on a drive, that was when Stef took the opportunity to get off the ranch and visit Charlotte or other friends scattered across the country. As I ran through different scenarios in my head, I realized he could have been having company, and maybe someone had driven in from the airport in Lubbock to visit him.

But the cars weren't rentals, and neither of them was the vehicle belonging to Rand's mother, May, because I knew the scary pink Jeep Wrangler on sight.

I was probably overthinking it. Stef certainly must know all kinds of people I didn't have any clue about. But then I saw Bella outside pacing on the porch and the hair on the back of my neck stood up.

What was the dog doing outside?

That thought came from being brought up on a ranch. Nothing ever changed, and everyone got a weird, ridiculous hypersensitivity to anything out of the ordinary. Like, why was the Mullins boy driving so fast? Or did the Ballards get a new truck? Or, like now… why the hell was there a Toyota Highlander and a Prius—of all the cars on the planet—in Rand's driveway? Vehicles out on the ranch were all American-made—except for Stef's car—as well as everywhere in the county, and always had been, I was sure. My own truck had come over with the Vikings, a hand-me-down from my father I hadn't bothered to replace yet, as it still had some life left in the ancient engine. But imports in Rand's driveway were strange. Again cars at the main house just made no sense.

Maybe I was being stupid, but still, who would be visiting Stef in the late afternoon on a Saturday when all the men who would normally be on the ranch, including Rand, were gone?

For a second I thought maybe it was a robbery, because maybe Stef wasn't there either, but his new Volvo S60 was in the driveway, so I knew he was most likely there, plus, again, the dog was there, and Stef was rarely without her.

But… the dog was outside. What the hell?

So instead of going up to the stairs, I rode Juju up behind the thick hedge to the left that had been planted to camouflage the concrete bunker that hid the sewage tank, and twisted her reins in the branches to keep her from drawing attention.

I darted around the west end of the porch and went to the far side window on the left, where I was immediately joined by a whining Bella.

Kneeling down, I pet her and ordered her to be quiet, a command she knew because it was how Rand trained the dogs to either herd the cattle or move between them silently. So she understood me, which was lucky considering what I saw inside the house.

Stef was in the living room, Wyatt asleep in his arms, standing with a young guy, maybe nineteen or twenty, bookish, in slacks and a button-down; a girl who looked about the same age wearing Daisy Dukes and a fuchsia crop top that showed off a great tan, gorgeous abs, and a belly piercing; and two guys who were both older and bigger. One of them had on a camouflage baseball cap and a denim shirt the sleeves had been ripped off of, and the other was in a straw cowboy hat and a gray T-shirt about two sizes too small that showed off every muscle in his abdomen, chest, and arms. He was taller and bulkier than me, but I wasn't worried about that. It was baseball cap guy who gave me pause. He was the one with the gun.

I was too afraid to leave Stef and Wyatt alone to ride back to get whoever was down by the stockyard, and sending Bella to find Everett might have worked if this were a movie, but it certainly was not. I figured once I got the gun, the others would scatter. I wanted them out of the house and away from Rand's family. We could find everyone later; the county wasn't that big.

I debated going around through the kitchen, but the screen door on the back creaked loudly and the boards on the deck squeaked. Since they would all see me coming through the front screen door or any of the many windows that led in from the porch, instead, since all the windows were open—the English oaks around the house shaded it well, so even in high summer, it was easily twenty degrees cooler under them—I jumped off the porch and darted around the left side of the house, that which faced the hills and the wind turbines, to the window in the first of two sitting rooms, the one that had been converted into Stef's office a few years back.

Making a short jump up for the ledge, I grabbed on to it, lifted myself, put my feet on the molding that ran around each wall of the house for decoration, and balanced there. It wasn't hard to move the screen, simply lever it up and push in and place it gently on the floor inside. Then I hoisted myself up and folded over, pushed the screen to the side, and wheelbarrowed my way in on my hands until I could slowly, gently put my feet on the floor. Two years ago I wouldn't have been able to get in quietly. I'd been heavier, carrying a lot more muscle, and wasn't half as flexible then. But now lighter, more limber, I did it easily.

Leaning out, whipping my Stetson out onto the grass, I gave Bella a harshly whispered order. "Get inside, girl. Get in!"

She lost her mind.

"The fuck was that?" I heard someone ask.

"It's the stupid dog he put outside."

Slinking against the wall, still hearing Bella howling outside, making enough noise for them to worry someone would hear her, one of them finally suggested what I wanted.

"I'm gonna shoot that dog."

"Oh no, please don't," Stef begged.

"She's makin' a terrible racket."

"She just wants to see me."

"Well, I'm gonna put a bullet in her head if she don't stop."

Reaching the open doorway of Stef's office, I leaned out into the short hall that connected it to the second small sitting room. Moving quickly, I slipped into that room and climbed on top of the couch, onto the coffee table, and then walked along the chaise to the wall. I'd learned early in an old house with wood floors that the best way to not make noise was to get on top of things already sitting heavy on the boards.

Leaning only inches out that door into the living room, I could see reflections in the glass of the grandfather clock against the wall to my right. When I turned my head back and forth, I could see everyone.

They were all clustered more toward the back of the house, almost to the kitchen, which made sense. Whoever these people were—burglars, kidnappers, God knew—they'd invaded the home and were smart enough to want Stef away from the front porch where anyone driving up would have seen him. It was also why they hadn't seen me on horseback coming up the drive.

"Mr. Joss, I'm so sorry," Button-down lamented, trying to take a step forward, but the girl yanked on his arm. "I'm so stupid."

"You ain't stupid," Straw Hat told him. "You went along 'cause you knew nobody would get hurt." He turned back to Stef. "And nobody will as long as you listen and do exactly what we say."

"Just shoot him and take the baby," Daisy Dukes said flatly.

"No!" Button-down was aghast.

"Not kill him, honey, just shoot him in the leg so we can take the boy. That'll be a lot easier and we can keep him quiet real easy."

Stef clutched Wyatt tight, and I reached behind me and took hold of the antique fireplace poker standing in the holder beside the leather tufted chair near a decorative antique writing desk that as far as I'd ever seen, no one used. The house had been built pre-central heat and air, and since Rand had never converted it, there was a fireplace in every room but the kitchen and dining room downstairs, and one in the master upstairs. It was a sweet house full of quaint charm that Stef balked at updating, keeping Rand's plans for an open-flow renovation on ice. So at the moment, it was still a box inside with smaller rooms and lots of walls to hide behind. Since the setup was serving me well at the moment, I was thankful for Stef's sense of tradition.

"I think we should all go into the kitchen," Baseball Cap commented. "I want us right at the back door in case we have to make a run for it."

"All right," Straw Hat agreed.

"What is this room over here? Did you check all these when we came in?" Baseball Cap asked as I retreated a bit, seeing him coming my way.

When he walked around the corner, I swung the poker at the back of his head, caught him in the neck, and he tripped forward noisily into the room, screaming for help before falling over the couch that matched the chaise and clunking his head hard on the coffee table.

I scrambled for the gun he dropped, but Straw Hat was there, jumping me from behind and driving us both out into the living room into another wall.

"Stef, get to the kitchen and let Bella in!" I yelled.

He bolted by me, Daisy Dukes right on his heels, with Button-down bringing up the rear. I tripped him, even though I was grappling with Straw Hat, who then caught me in the shoulder with a knife I didn't know he had.

"You fuck!" I swore at him, enraged. It was a nine-inch switchblade, not legal at all, and I was thankful it was buried in my rotator cuff instead of my heart.

I swung with my still-good right arm, caught him in the jaw with my fist, and when he stumbled back, I kicked him in the knee and saw it bend the other way, hearing the pop at the same time. His scream was deafening in the small space, and I left him writhing on the floor.

I knew the gun was somewhere in the sitting room, but I also knew that Baseball Cap was out like a light and Straw Hat was in way too much howling pain to go looking for it, so I bolted after Stef, moving fast down the hall, made it to the kitchen, and was there greeted with the lovely sight of Daisy Dukes, standing next to Button-down beside the counter with her hands up. Both were there, frozen, not moving as a very pissed off Bella stood in front of them, snarling, hackles raised and head down, ears back, and lips curled up so teeth and gums were visible. She was not fucking around.

"Good girl," I said as I staggered in, seeing Stef on the phone as Wyatt lifted his head, blinking and bleary.

"Ungen," Wyatt said when he saw me, smiling big and leaning out a little for me to take him. Ungen was me: uncle and Glenn without the L the sweet little boy had trouble pronouncing.

I wanted to grab him but I couldn't; my left arm had stopped working. I couldn't lift it at all, but more troubling was all the blood.

Grabbing a dish towel from the handle of the oven, I pressed it above my heart and leaned on the counter to steady myself.

"Can you call off the dog?" Button-down said. "She's freaking us out."

"No," I snapped. He'd tried to kidnap a baby but the dog was being a psycho? Jesus.

"Is my boyfriend okay?" Daisy Dukes asked, tears welling up in her eyes. "Did you kill him?"

"*I'm* your boyfriend!" Button-down gasped.

Poor bastard. He'd been so used.

"Mr. Holloway?" she prodded.

How did she—ah… it took me a second in all the excitement. "I'm not Rand Holloway."

Her and Button-down's eyes got huge.

"I'm his teeny half brother," I added with a cackle, watching with great satisfaction as they both turned a lovely shade of white.

"Ohmygod, you're bleeding," Stef croaked.

The towel was getting a bit damp, it was true. But more importantly, I had just thought of myself *first* as Rand's brother instead of his cousin. Amazing how many things had changed so quickly.

Stef moved into me then, into my space, just closed the distance between us and put his head on my good shoulder as Wyatt wiggled and complained because he was getting crushed between us. "Thank you for saving me and my son."

"You could've," I assured him, because I knew the man well. "We both know you're scary as hell."

"I will be," he said icily, turning to look at Button-down and Daisy Dukes. "I'll put Wyatt on the counter and you watch him while I go get my baseball bat upstairs."

Thank God all the guns Rand owned were on his saddle with him, very far away from home. I was guessing that the two people in front of me would have been in trouble if Stef could have gotten his hands on a firearm. To say he did not look happy was the understatement of the year.

"Is the sheriff coming?" I asked.

"Yes."

"That's good," I told him. "'Cause I think I'm gonna pass out."

The last thing I heard was Wyatt calling my name.

Chapter 7

Waking up in the hospital was never fun. Waking up with a stressed-out Stefan Joss was just odd.

"What's wrong with you?" I asked. It came out all croaky because my voice was weird. I needed some water.

"Oh thank God, you're awake," he whispered, deflating with relief, leaning forward in his chair to take hold of my hand and wrist and give me a brave smile.

"For crissakes, Stef, I just lost some blood," I groused. "I'm not dyin'."

He stood then, leaned over, and hugged me tight. I let him clutch at me for a second before I told him to get the hell off.

"You fainted," he barely got out, eyes swimming with tears.

"Shit," I grumbled. "I'm sorry I scared you."

He sucked in a breath. "I've never seen anyone pass out from blood loss before."

"It sneaks up on ya."

His mouth fell open. "It's happened to you before?"

"I grew up on a ranch, Stef; of course it's happened before."

"Oh God," he moaned. "I really don't know if I even want Wyatt to learn to ride a horse."

I snickered. "I reckon that decision's been made already, huh?"

He shrugged, like, *perhaps*.

"Speaking of horses," I began.

"Juju's in the stable at the Red," Stef told me. "She's fine. I had Elliot, one of the new grooms, make sure she was all settled in."

"I'll get her moved as soon as I get outta here."

"Or you could just leave her where she is."

There *was* that possibility, with changes, a thaw in my and Rand's relationship for one, to consider. But I didn't want to talk about that. "How long was I out?" I asked, changing the subject.

"Almost two hours."

"Oh, that ain't bad," I said, grinning at him.

"Not bad?" His gasp and how big his eyes got told me he was a bit horrified.

It was nice, how worried and scared he was, but really, I'd been out longer when I was thrown while breaking broncs or riding bulls or the time I was riding a new horse while barrel racing and he drove me into a wall when I overcorrected.

"It really ain't," I assured him, reaching out to touch his cheek and give him a little pat. "But so yanno, I'm all right now, so can I have some water?"

He had to call the nurse to ask—he wasn't taking any chances—and after he did, a young RN with a name badge saying "Paisley Chambers" showed up, with a perky little blonde ponytail and pink scrubs. She explained, even though I knew already from Stef, that I'd been out a couple of hours, but my color was back and I looked much better.

"We had to give you some fluids and glucose to get your blood sugar up," she said sternly, her voice full of authority for one so young, giving me the judgmental brow. "Why were you dehydrated and why aren't you eating?"

So I explained about the cattle drive and how I normally did eat but hadn't been just for the day but how I should have, what with being in the saddle the whole time.

"Yes, you should have," she agreed. "Now, I'm sending a meal up in here, and you better eat everything on that tray, ya hear?"

"Yes, ma'am," I agreed.

"Good boy," she said with a smile before telling Stef that she'd find the doctor and that yes, I could have some water. Not a lot, but some. I was not to overdo.

Once she was gone and Stef poured ice water into the little plastic tumbler for me, I asked him the obvious. "Who in the hell were those people, Stef?"

"The guy in the long-sleeved shirt, his name is David Lawrence, and he's one of my former students from the college."

I waited for him to go on, sipping my water.

He cleared his throat. "The girl is Kree Walton, and they wanted to—"

"Oh, I know what they wanted to do," I told him. "They wanted to kidnap Rand Holloway's child and hold him for ransom."

He nodded.

"So what, this David just called you up out of the blue?"

"Yeah, he said he needed a reference letter, and… God, Glenn, it's just—" He inhaled sharply. "He was one of my teaching assistants, you know? Why would I ever have cause to doubt him?"

"No, you don't blame yourself for that, Stef," I insisted. "None of that's on you."

"I feel really stupid."

"For wanting to help out an old student?"

His eyes searched my face. "You could have been killed."

"So could you," I volleyed, not bringing up the fact that Wyatt had been in danger as well. "But we're both fine, so let's not fuss on it no more."

His smile was beautiful. "Yes, Glenn."

I tipped my head as I looked at him. "You realize the security out there at the ranch is about to go through an overhaul, don't ya?"

He rolled his eyes. "Oh yes, I already had this discussion with Mr. Holloway half an hour ago when we talked."

I chuckled. "Is he on his way back?"

He grimaced as the door opened and a cute little candy striper brought in my late lunch of hospital food complete with hot tea, apple juice, and milk. I thanked her, and as I started in, could not help smiling over at Stef as he flopped into the chair and told me that Fort Knox would have nothing on the Red Diamond once Rand was done.

"You and Wyatt," I sighed, "are the two most precious things in the world to him. How could you expect anything less, Stef?"

"I guess if you think about it that way," he said softly, looking at me hopefully. "Then it's sweet all the changes he plans on making."

"Sure," I agreed, with a grin. "I doubt it'll feel like a prison at all."

"Oh God."

"Maybe tell him to go easy on the barbed wire and motion sensors and automatic lights huh?"

Apparently I wasn't as funny as I thought I was.

When Stef tried to call Rand for the second time, he was out of range which made sense. There were so many dead spots out on the prairie and since Rand had loaned his satellite phone to Charlotte when she was on a trip to Paris with her mother, Stef didn't have that to get back ahold of him on. So he couldn't talk to Rand again and I couldn't talk to Mac. I hoped Rand shared with the guy I was ready to start a life with that I was fine, but I had no way of knowing.

To get back at me about the prison cracks, when Stef returned later Saturday night to check in on me, he told me that he'd called over to The Bronc and told whoever answered the phone that I was stabbed but in stable condition at the hospital in Hillman.

"You ass," I whined. "Do you know what's gonna happen now?"

He only smiled and nodded before he turned on the TV and started flipping channels.

"They're all coming," I told him.

"Not tonight they're not," he said cattily. "Visiting hours are over, they can't get in."

"Then how come you're here?"

"I'm family, asshole."

Nice. "Shouldn't you get home to your kid?"

"He's with Morgan and his wife, he's fine."

"I don't know Morgan whoever."

"Morgan Sowers, he's our new blacksmith, he's a really nice guy."

"What if they drop him on his head?"

"Morgan's wife is the pediatrician out on the Red; I'm not really worried about it."

"Rand just can't keep collecting people Stef, law enforcment'll start to think he's a drug lord or some shit."

He turned off the TV and twisted around in his chair to look at me. "So?"

"So what?"

"Did you bond with the boys?"

I stayed quiet.

"Did you and Rand and Zach work things all out?"

I grunted.

His eyebrows lifted before he smiled. "You did."

"We had us a bit of a come to Jesus meeting, yeah."

"And?" He prodded me.

"And I might come visit the Red a bit more often."

He looked so very pleased with his scrunched up eyes and lips pressed tight together and clasped hands.

"It's a work in progress, right?"

"Yes. Good. I'm so glad."

"You like putting the Holloways back together, don't you, Stef." He'd done it with Tyler and his family.

"I do," he admitted. "Your father and you, Rand, and Zach are next on my list."

I would not hold my breath.

IT WAS early the next morning, just after visiting hours began, as I knew it would be, when my bed was jostled and there were whispers of "shut the fuck up," and "you're gonna wake him up," before I did, in fact, open my eyes.

The room was crowded with people—way more than I was sure was allowed—and ten or so of them surrounding the bed so I couldn't even see the door of my room. "Shit," I grumbled, squinting up at all of them. "Why aren't you guys gettin' ready to open The Bronc? Sunday's one of our busiest days."

A wall of noise came at me, everyone speaking at once, each voice trying to be louder than the last.

"Stop," I half yelled before turning to look at Josie, who was closest to me, both of her hands on my right forearm, squeezing tight as she sucked in breath after breath. Only when I studied her face did I notice that her eyes were red and puffy.

"Oh for fuck's sake, you can see I'm fine."

She sniffled. "You were hurt. When Mr. Joss called the restaurant and Kev took the call, it scared the hell out of all of us."

Which had been Stef's intent. He was going straight to hell if he didn't watch it.

"We were all really worried," Callie said tightly, and I watched her bite her bottom lip.

"You've never passed out before," Kevin explained, coming around the girls to stand on my left and touch the bandage there. "And you never had to go in an ambulance before."

"I've done all that many, many times," I corrected. "Y'all just never knew me when I was working the ranch."

"Your doctor said you lost a lotta blood," Shawnee chimed in from where she was at my feet, ignoring my comments entirely. "Your doctor told Bailey that between the stitches in your side and the stab wound, you had to stay here a couple days."

"Which means I'll be out first thing tomorrow morning," I explained.

Lots of exhaling and smiles, they were all visibly relieved and happy.

"How did you talk to my doctor?" I asked Shawnee.

"Oh, I didn't, Bailey did. You know how persuasive she can be when she wants something."

I was well aware. She looked all sweet and soft on the outside, but inside she was all tiger. "Is that who's at the restaurant?" I asked, turning to Kevin. "Bail?"

"Yeah, it's her and Jamal, Sandy, Esteban, Marco, Deshaun, Kelly, and oh, we might have a problem."

"What's that?"

Callie and Kevin exchanged worried glances.

"What?"

Callie took a quick breath. "Well, it turns out that the resort is being sued for racial discrimination."

"Okay, and? What does that have to do with us? You already told me that our staff should be in an ad for—what is it?"

"The United Colors of Benetton," she stated with a smirk.

"Which is a good thing."

"It's a very good thing," she agreed. "You have probably the most racially diverse staff in the entire county, boss."

"Sexual orientation as well," Shawnee made sure I knew.

"And so," Callie rushed out, wanting me back on point, "Gillian comes by yesterday—"

"Who?"

"The new director of personnel."

She and Kevin knew the hotel people; he was good with remembering all their names and titles and schmoozing with them, and Callie was good at trading food for service, so we always had people at the bell desk or with the concierge we could call on to help our guests. I was crappy at the things they both excelled at, and that was okay, as neither one of them knew the ins and outs of contracts or managing the facility or paying the bills.

"Go on," I directed her.

"So apparently they have a corporate visit next week and she wanted the HR people to come talk to us."

"Why?" I was confused.

"So they could pretend that we're actually part of the resort and they could use us, our team, to satisfy their diversity quota."

That made no sense. "That's the stupidest thing I ever heard. All they have to do is see that we're not affiliated with the hotel to know that's crap."

"She's hoping they don't look beyond the fact that we're on their property. And she did say that if the suit goes forward that they might cut us loose, as we're not part of the regular businesses that comprise the entire chain of resorts," Kevin explained.

"Mitch Powell owed Rand, and for that, we're in."

"But if it's bigger than him, if it's Mr. Powell's board voting to overrule him, we could be off the resort property and would need to find new digs for The Bronc."

It was odd, but neither he nor Callie or anyone else in the room looked particularly concerned over the news that we might have to move. It was disconcerting, to say the least.

"For crissakes, Kev, it's like pulling teeth."

He grinned at me. "But last night, after Bailey got off the phone with your doctor, she called Mr. Joss because she was told he was in here with you, and she wanted to know how you looked."

She was *very* thorough.

"And they got to talking, and she told him about the situation with the hotel since he's the one that worked out the original tenant agreement with Mr. Powell, and he told her that if the resort evicts us from the property, then they are contractually obligated to pay to relocate us, including building us a new Bronc if no suitable structure can be found."

"Really?"

"According to Mr. Joss, and you know, even though he's a college professor now, it doesn't mean he wasn't an acquisitions manager at one time. He still knows his stuff."

He did, yes.

"But he gave me the name of his attorney in Chicago, the lawyer for the Red Diamond, Knox Jenner, which I thought was one guy but is actually a whole firm and—"

"I will kill you, Kevin," I made known.

He cleared his throat. "So I talked to Mr. Richard Jenner this morning, and he told me that if they shut us down at our current site, then they do, in fact, have to pay to relocate us."

"Okay," I sighed. At least everything would work out.

"He said for you to get in contact with him first thing tomorrow."

"I can't believe he answered the phone for you on a Sunday."

"Well, it's like Mr. Joss said when I mentioned the same thing to him. I told him that no fancy Chicago lawyer would pick up his phone on the Lord's Day for a restaurant manager from a town in Texas that he's probably never heard of, but he pointed out that he'd sure as shit answer for the Red Diamond, no question."

There was that.

"I guess that ranch is kind of a big deal, ya reckon?"

"I suspect so."

"And Rand Holloway might be a good man to have on your side."

That was true. "Well, whatever, at least we know we're covered."

"Exactly," Kevin continued on, "and there's more."

"What?"

"Well, Mr. Joss wanted me to tell you that if we get booted, you should consider moving the restaurant out to the Red Diamond."

"Oh?"

"Yeah, he said that the restaurant could go halfway up the main drive and that they would build us a beautiful place and our parking could be tripled, and that way we could all work on the safety of the ranch."

It was terrifying that Stef knew Rand's mind so well, that he could speak to Rand's intentions at any given moment. The level of communication they must have had between them at all times was staggering. I knew, of course, that Rand wanted me on the ranch, but I'd had no idea that Stef did too.

"And for the record, I love the idea of that," Callie admitted. "Working on private land means that Rand Holloway could protect us and our personal property."

"You're still mad because someone stole your iPod out of your car."

"Hell yes," she said. "I mean, when we leave the restaurant at night, we have to walk together," she reminded me. "If we were on the ranch, then A, we wouldn't have to be open as late as we are now because we wouldn't have to conform to other restaurant hours at the resort, and B, we'd be safe and so would our stuff because who would screw with the guys on the Red Diamond? Everyone knows the scariest guys in the county work for Rand Holloway."

"So if we're booted off, you're all good relocating out to the ranch?"

"We all are," Kevin affirmed, smiling at me. "We took a vote."

Of course they had. They were proactive, my group. "Well, hopefully it won't come to that," I concurred. "But if it does, I could see us out there on the Red."

Silence.

"What?"

"Really?" Kevin asked me. "You would consider that? Really, really?"

"What're you, ten?"

"I'm just shocked, is all."

"Well, yeah, I would consider it."

"Ohmygod, that's awesome," Callie squeaked. "The only thing I was worried about in all of this was you not wanting to be on that ranch, but if you don't care, if it's fine, then I'm over the moon. I would never do anything to make you unhappy."

"I know."

She leaned over to hug me.

"Why're we doing this?"

"Just hug."

It was a brief clench where she kissed my cheek as she leaned back.

"I was so scared," she asserted. "So please don't ever put yourself in danger again."

"I'll do my best," I promised.

"Back to the situation at hand," Kevin told me, patting my leg. "Gillian's still going to try and get one over on her people, but just as long as we have a plan, we're good."

I nodded and watched Josie crook her elbow and rest her head on her fist as she regarded me. "So… boss."

God. "Yes?"

"So you have plans to be on the ranch?"

I did. "I dunno."

She coughed. "Mr. Joss said—"

"Say Stef, I'm sure he told you to."

"He did, but I wasn't sure it was appropriate."

"It is."

"Okay, so, Stef said that you might be seeing Mac Gentry."

I groaned and the whole room, at once, in sync, caught their breath.

"We're gonna see what's what when he gets back from the drive," I said diplomatically, not wanting to have my love life aired out for the room. Stef must have gotten back in touch with Rand at some point after he left me and the news was shared with him, and then he in turn told Josie. I would have to remember to smack him the next time I saw him.

"Which should be very soon," Josie announced. "Mr.—Stef—said that Mr. Holloway was home already. Apparently they rode through the night. And that they'd be here to see you today as soon as they all got cleaned up."

My stomach did a familiar roll over the possibility of laying eyes on Mac.

"So." Josie was back to grilling me. "Tomorrow when you get discharged, are you going home with Mac Gentry?"

"'Cause you'll already have a packed bag," Callie told me. "I mean, first we had to wash all your clothes because, damn, boss—disgusting."

"Which is what I said," Josie chimed in.

"You know what—" I began, glaring at her.

"But you're all packed and ready to—"

"Thank you," I said to Callie before turning to Josie.

"Oh, come on, I was kidding."

"Are you all right?" I asked Josie, ignoring Callie.

"Because I was orphaned the other day, you mean?"

"Yeah."

Her eyes warmed. "Yes, boss, because of you I'm okay."

"I was worried," I murmured.

"I know you were, and that's why I love you."

I looked at her.

"You know how I mean."

And I did. "Josie?"

Her gaze met mine.

"If I move, where will you live?"

"Mr. Joss said that there are many small one-room cabins on the ranch, and he would be willing to let me stay in one, under your supervision, in exchange for me watching his adorable little boy certain days of the week."

"Oh yeah?"

"Yeah. He said that he's teaching different classes next semester and Wyatt can't go with him every day anymore."

"And that's where you come in."

"Yes, but only as long as you're on the ranch too."

I was going to say something else, but the door opened and Rand was the first one through.

"You all should go," he announced, and even though they all worked for me and not him, the exodus was fast.

It could never be said that Holloway men couldn't clear a room.

CHAPTER 8

I WASN'T expecting Rand to stride over to the bed, lean over, and hug me even before the last person was out of the room.

"Is this us?" I teased, seeing Stef holding Wyatt right behind him.

"You saved my family, Glenn," he answered gruffly, and I could hear the shudder in his tone. "This is us from now on."

I chuckled into his shoulder as he held me close, hand on the back of my head for only a moment before he let go and straightened.

He was passed his son, who went from Stef to Rand eagerly, and then I had my arms full of the guy who might have given me my happily ever after because he made me start—though I didn't even finish—a cattle drive.

"It's okay," I told Stef as I patted his back and held him tight.

"I was so scared."

"I know."

"And if Wyatt hadn't been there—"

"I know that too," I assured him because people didn't know, but Stef was a brawler. He looked all sweet and pretty, but he knew how to defend himself. Just because he was small in comparison to Rand didn't mean Stef didn't know how to throw a punch that could put someone on the ground. But Wyatt had been there; dependent on Stef for his life, for his safety, and that had not allowed Stef the freedom of either fight *or* flight.

"If you hadn't been there… I don't even want to think what could have happened."

"Or what's going to happen on the Red." I snorted.

He tugged free and would have smacked me, but Rand warned him off.

"Just please don't lose your mind," Stef begged. "It's an isolated incident, Rand."

"People can tell you're a rich man," Zach—I hadn't heard him enter the room—pointed out as he slipped around Stef, bent over the bed, and hugged me.

"I'm fine," I told my brother. "I swear."

"I don't want us to fight no more."

"Agreed," I sighed, happy with the new place we were in, a place that could be better than any ever had been. We'd been raised together by Rayland Holloway, and because of that, because it had always been us against our father, having to bond together, especially after our mother died, we'd been close at one time. I wanted that back, and now, finally, we had a chance for a do-over and it seemed like we were both ready to try. I, for one, was willing and able to have my family back, starting with Zach.

"And I don't wanna be a dick to you, and I just want it to be like it was before I left home because I thought I needed to have a ranch just like Dad."

"Okay."

"Yeah?" he asked, pulling back to look at my face.

"Fuck yeah," I replied, grinning at him. "Life's too short, right?"

"It is," he agreed hoarsely before smiling at me. "You know, I went into the stable this morning and your horse bit me."

I grinned up at him. "She's got a thing for Holloway men."

He chuckled.

I turned back to Stef then. "Thank you again for making sure she was all right. That horse means the world to me."

He nodded. "Well, as I said before, I think she's where she should stay."

"I agree," Rand concurred. "We'll take care of both of you, or the Red Diamond will."

"Rand." I began. "You don't need to feel like—"

"I want her on my ranch and I want *you* on my ranch," Rand said flatly, so there could be no question.

"Yeah, but—"

"I don't expect you to cowboy anymore, be a rancher anymore," he said solemnly. "I know that ain't your dream. And if something happens with the resort, it would be Stef's and my honor and privilege to relocate The Bronc onto the ranch, but Glenn… more than all of that… I want you on the ranch just like I want Zach there."

"Why?"

"'Cause y'all are my family," he said like I was stupid, which was par for the course with Rand. "I want you with us."

I would never make him say it again. "I won't live in the house with you and Stef, Rand."

"That's right you won't," he agreed. "And I expect someone else might have something to say about where you'll be hanging your hat."

"I hope so," I said softly.

"Well, he was right behind us when we left the Red, but he stopped for something, though I expect he's parking his truck by now and then he'll be on up."

I nodded.

"I know he was eager to come check on you, and he already told me that tomorrow he plans to take you back to the ranch—back home with him so he can watch over you a bit."

My throat went dry just thinking about seeing Mac. "That sounds good."

"And so you know," Zach said brightly. "So you can tell the folks that work for you as well, the ranch is gonna be real secure from now on."

Stef flipped him off and I chuckled.

"We're getting us a closed-circuit television system put in; it'll be all state of the art."

"It's better than I thought," I teased Stef.

He groaned.

"Aww, c'mon," I told him. "It's not a small ranch, Stef, and you and Rand are not just everyday people living your lives. You have money, and as such, you have to take care. You can't fuss at Rand for wanting you and your son safe."

"No," he agreed, flicking his gaze to the man in question. "I can't."

When Rand lifted his arm for Stef to join him and their son, the door opened and in walked Mac, looking as beautiful and like home as the last time I saw him.

"We'll see you later," Rand said quickly, giving me a smile full of approval and happiness and everything else before he led the others out of the room, just as he'd led them in.

"Hey," I breathed out.

Mac's mouth was set in a hard line as he stood there fiddling with his hat. He was nervous, it was all over him, and I would have been worried, but I suspected that since I was the cause, I could be the fix as well. "I came to ask you if tomorrow, when you're discharged, if you would let me fetch you on home."

I sat up in the bed. "To *your* home, you mean."

"To our home," he corrected me. "*Our*. Ain't you gonna be livin' on the ranch too?"

"I have to be honest: you're the big draw for me on that ranch."

He crossed the room when I held out my arms. "I know it's fast as hell, but will you come see my house that I never brought anyone else home to ever?"

"I will," I said, drawing him close for a kiss, *the* kiss, the good kind, the claiming kind, and even better than the first.

"Thank God," he rasped when I let him breathe. "I had all kinds of things runnin' through my head on the way over here from the hardware store."

So that was where he'd stopped. "And what did you need from there first thing on Sunday morning, Maclain Gentry?"

After digging into the right pocket of his soft, faded jeans, he withdrew a key on a ring and passed it to me. "I needed to make sure I had this when I talked to ya so you'd know I was serious about you bein' with me."

"I already knew you were serious." I sighed, smiling up at him as he sat down beside me on the bed. "But I appreciate the key and the ring."

"That won't be the last ring you get from me," he rasped, his breath catching as he put his hat down on the tray table and pressed his hand down onto the pillow beside my head.

"Oh no?" I asked, barely able to speak, so overcome with Mac and his declarations.

"Not at all."

"Then I suspect I'll need to get you one as well."

"You do that," he said as he bent to kiss me again.

And I most certainly would.

MARY CALMES lives in Lexington, Kentucky, with her husband and two children and loves all the seasons except summer. She graduated from the University of the Pacific in Stockton, California, with a bachelor's degree in English literature. Due to the fact that it is English lit and not English grammar, do not ask her to point out a clause for you, as it will so not happen. She loves writing, becoming immersed in the process, and believes without question in happily-ever-afters, and writes those for each and every one of her characters.

TIMING

Mary Calmes

Timing: Book One

Stefan Joss just can't win. Not only does he have to go to Texas in the middle of summer to be the man of honor in his best friend Charlotte's wedding, but he's expected to negotiate a million-dollar business deal at the same time. Worst of all, he's thrown for a loop when he arrives to see the one man Charlotte promised wouldn't be there: her brother, Rand Holloway.

Stefan and Rand have been mortal enemies since the day they met, so Stefan is shocked when a temporary cease-fire sees the usual hostility replaced by instant chemistry. Though leery of the unexpected feelings, Stefan is swayed by a sincere revelation from Rand, and he decides to give Rand a chance.

But their budding romance is threatened when Stefan's business deal goes wrong: the owner of the last ranch he needs to secure for the company is murdered. Stefan's in for the surprise of his life as he finds himself in danger as well.

www.dreamspinnerpress.com

ALL KINDS OF TIED DOWN

Mary Calmes

Marshals: Book One

Deputy US Marshal Miro Jones has a reputation for being calm and collected under fire. These traits serve him well with his hotshot partner, Ian Doyle, the kind of guy who can start a fight in an empty room. In the past three years of their life-and-death job, they've gone from strangers to professional coworkers to devoted teammates and best friends. Miro's cultivated blind faith in the man who has his back… faith and something more.

As a marshal and a soldier, Ian's expected to lead. But the power and control that brings Ian success and fulfillment in the field isn't working anywhere else. Ian's always resisted all kinds of tied down, but having no home—and no one to come home to—is slowly eating him up inside. Over time, Ian has grudgingly accepted that going anywhere without his partner simply doesn't work. Now Miro just has to convince him that getting tangled up in heartstrings isn't being tied down at all.

www.dreamspinnerpress.com

FOR
MORE
OF THE
BEST
GAY
ROMANCE

DREAMSPINNER
PRESS
dreamspinnerpress.com